D0368972

POWER ON HER OWN

POWER ON
HER OWN

Judith Cutler

 St. Martin's Minotaur ✸ New York

www.minotaurbooks.com

Library of Congress Cataloging-in-Publication Data

Cutler, Judith.
    Power on her own / Judith Cutler.—1st St. Martin's Minotaur ed.
      p. cm.
    ISBN 0-312-31192-3
    1. Power, Kate (Fictitious character)—Fiction. 2. Police—England— Birmingham—Fiction. 3. Birmingham (England)—Fiction. 4. Policewomen— Fiction. I. Title.

PR6053.U864P69 2003
823'.92—dc21   2003046585

First published in 1998 by Hodder and Stoughton
A division of Hodder Headline PLC

First St. Martin's Minotaur Edition: July 2003

10　9　8　7　6　5　4　3　2　1

For Greg and for Tom

ACKNOWLEDGEMENTS

I would like to thank Keith Bassett, who told me to write this book; Sarah Bookey, who freely gave of her expertise; Maureen Carter, Frances Lally and Edwina Van Boolen, who have collectively and separately been towers of strength. I am also grateful to the following for their help: the Baptist Union; the Boys' Brigade; West Midlands Police.

PROLOGUE

'Listen, Kate. There's mistakes and mistakes. Some are little, spur-of-the-moment mistakes, like shooting traffic lights you could have stopped at. And there are the sort you think about and still make. And it seems to me you're specialising in those at the moment.' Tom dropped his voice, big and booming after all those years of yelling at young constables, and glanced at the other mourners in the church. 'For a start, why on earth did you come here today? I mean, I know you were both in the squad, but there's his wife and all his family, for goodness' sake.'

Kate turned her face away. He was right. She and Robin had been live-in lovers but he was still very much married. Spent three or four evenings with his kids. Did all the right fatherly things: parents' evenings and swimming lessons. She'd never asked otherwise. It had been part of their relationship. Like her forays up to Birmingham to keep an eye on Cassie, her father's aunt. Family ties. You had them and there was no point in making a song and dance about it.

But there was no denying that she wasn't wanted here. Oh, her mates from the Met, they were solid beside her, like Tom and Mike, silently reading the order of service. But his family had preferred to ignore her. Not just his wife and kids – and who could blame them? – but his parents, who'd seemed so fond of her. She should have said her last goodbyes in the chapel of rest and left the ritual of mourning to those who were entitled to it.

Tom gave her shoulders a quick squeeze. She turned back to him, managing a smile.

'And then there's all this business of going to fucking Birmingham,' he began.

She touched her lips; they were in a church, for goodness' sake. The elderly couple in the pew in front of them had obviously heard: you could see their necks stiffening.

'Sorry. But why the – why on earth leave the Met? And London?'

'It's – Oh, God!'

Everyone was standing. They were carrying in his body. Cramming her knuckles against her mouth, she stood too. The coffin. Six policemen, shoulder to shoulder, carrying it. A symbolic helmet – Robin had always been a man for a flat-topped cap – stood proudly on top.

There were so many in the church that the hymns, familiar tunes with familiar words of faith and comfort, sounded convincing. Just at this moment she wasn't so sure she could ever believe in anything again. All these monuments: other people had kept going in the face of death and loss. She stared at the memorial tablet nearest her. Anno Domini 1783. Henry and Charlotte Cavendish and their seven children, none of them older than four. How had they dealt with all that grief?

No, there were no answers in the stained-glass window behind the altar, although the summer light made it blaze with reds and blues. And she was afraid the clergyman wouldn't have any answers either. They sat down to listen to him.

He'd done his homework, tried to make it sound as if he'd known Robin all his life, whereas he'd really only known Kathleen's parents, bastions of his comfortable suburban parish. He spoke of the devoted family man, the honourable police officer, the keen sportsman. Everything except Kate, come to think of it. The widow – Kathleen, never abbreviated – sobbed audibly. The children wailed.

Kate took Tom's hand and held it tightly. Fellow officers were entitled to look grim. And she was here as a fellow officer. Full stop. If she forgot that she'd howl. She forced herself to listen to the rest of the eulogy.

'. . . Called on to make the Ultimate Sacrifice . . . Dying in the name of Law and Order . . .'

He sounded as plummy as a Home Secretary.

Tom's mouth breathed warm against her ear. 'Not so much a sacrifice, more a cock-up, I'd say.'

Robin had been hit by a police car, smashed into a wall when someone had shot out the driver's windscreen and he'd lost control.

And then they all stood to pray.

Robin had wanted to donate his organs and to be cremated. He'd always said so: been one of the first on the squad to wave a donor card around and press others to sign up. Kathleen had refused to give consent until it was too late, and she was having him buried. Even from where she stood, at the back of the little knot by the open grave, she could hear the thud of the earth as Kathleen threw her handful on to the coffin.

'Ashes to ashes, dust to dust . . .'

She heard no more. All she could think of was the worms that would consume his dear body. No. She wouldn't disgrace him by being sick. Swallow hard and breathe through your open mouth. That's what they told you. She looked at the flowers on other graves; that was a mistake: they were dying fast on the sun-bleached grass. In fact the greenest thing in the churchyard was the artificial turf around the new grave. Even the birds had stopped singing in the heat of the late morning. Maybe they felt they couldn't compete with the constant roar of traffic and now – God help her! – an ice-cream van chiming 'The Happy Wanderer.' All she could do was hang on.

'You never told me: why Birmingham?' Tom turned to face her, his bulk between her and the family. One by one, they were leaving the grave to go back for ham sandwiches and tea at the family home. A couple of senior officers would put in a token appearance there. The rest of them would hold their own wake: the landlord had been warned.

'Aunt Cassie,' she said, 'for one thing. I'm the only family she's got.'

'Even so – hell, Katie, when you were with Robin you managed to go and see her at weekends: why not do that now?'

'It's not as if I don't know the place. Two years on that undercover stuff.'

'Even so – No, you don't want to leave all your mates.'

'My mates aren't going to be in London anyway.' She stretched her fingers, counting. 'You're off to the Sierra Leone police; Mike's being invalided out; Moira and Ted are so wrapped up in each other they won't want an old misery like me around.'

'Old? Misery you may be, but you're only a kid!'

'Twenty-nine.'

'Well, then. Anyway, there's the others. Andy. Griff.' Tom unclipped his black tie, and, stuffing it into his pocket, turned away from the grave. 'What's up?'

No one would notice now, and she didn't care if they did. Like Kathleen, she stooped to pick up a handful of warm, dry earth, and scattered it on his coffin. It made the same hollow rattle. Nothing to say goodbye to.

And then Tom was at her side, arm round her shoulders, turning her towards the waiting car. 'Come on, sweetheart. We'll all be there for you. Time to get pissed.'

Chapter One

———⟫•◇•⟪———

Kate strode down the endless corridors. OK, they'd scored a hit. They'd sent her to the back of beyond to collect a set of files. She'd bet no such files had ever existed. Everyone must have been in on it – whoever she spoke to referred her to someone else on a far distant floor. She grinned even as she cursed herself for falling for the trick: the sort of thing you'd do to anyone new to the squad, just to test them.

So why was no one in the office when she went back in? The phone started to ring. Who the hell had been stupid enough to put it right at the back of the desk? She bent to reach it – and was pushed hard forward, arms pinioned. A hand clamped her mouth, the thumb rough against her nose. She tried for a bite: it pressed harder. She struggled, elbowed – used all the tricks in the book and then some – but he was bigger, heavier. Her chest was parallel to the desk top. Now something was pressing hard against her skirt, against her buttocks. Into the cleft between her buttocks. Thrusting, again and again.

If she let go, if she made her knees bend so he fell forwards . . . But he pulled her back. She twisted her foot: with a bit of luck she could land a kick.

And then she didn't need to. There was a rush of footsteps into the room. Someone tore the man's hands off her and sent him flying across the room. 'Stupid fucking bastard. Get the hell out of here!'

She fell forwards on to the desk top, scattering papers, and lay there panting. Another hand touched her, gripping her upper arm to lift her up.

'Kate? Are you OK?' the same Brummie voice asked kindly.

Swallowing tears and spittle, she bit her lips to stop them quivering. She waited for her chest to stop heaving, her pulse to slow, before she spoke. Why was she overreacting like this? 'Fine!' she said at last. But her voice cracked.

Who on earth had rescued her? That guy – the young constable – at the back of the room who'd just smiled and nodded when all the other lads in the squad had yelled and catcalled. What was his name? He pulled a chair up. Sally, the Welsh airhead, was talking about getting her a drink. 'Water, that's what you need.'

Kate needed water like a hole in the head. Whisky: that might just help. Mustn't think of whisky, Kate, not till six, no, better make it seven tonight.

'Sit down a bit,' the young man said. Colin, that was it. Colin Roper. Sally's partner.

'No. I'm fine. Honestly.' Her knuckles were white on the back of the chair. 'Not hurt. Just bloody annoyed. Falling for an old trick like that. The second in ten minutes, too.'

'Here you are – best if you sit down.' Sally inched the styrofoam cup towards her.

Out of the corner of her eye she saw a couple of figures in the doorway. DI Cope, that was the beer-belly and her immediate boss; the other was the DCI, his boss, Graham Harvey. Four inches shorter than Cope, and four stones lighter, he managed to bring stillness into the room. He looked around him, for all the world like a school teacher bringing the class to order. He had the slight stoop of a teacher, too, and a weariness about the eyes.

'DS Power?'

He even sounded like a teacher. They'd all pulled themselves to attention: she wondered if he'd notice if she tried to smooth the back of her skirt.

'Sir?'

'My room, please. Now. You two – where's Selby?'

They were at attention too, shaking their heads. If suspects stood like that, they might as well plead guilty straightaway. 'If you have to lie, lie good,' Robin used to say. Mustn't think about Robin now.

'Canteen, Sir,' Sally said.

It was a pity Colin Roper opened his mouth at the same time: 'Having a slash, Sir.'

'I'll talk to you two later. Remind your colleagues that we're supposed to be fighting crime, will you, not arsing around. There's a small matter of a missing child, in case it had escaped your memories. Power?' He gestured with his head.

He was holding the door for her. Old-fashioned courtesy, of course. And it meant he could look at her more closely as she passed. He wouldn't miss the finger-shaped pressure marks across her face.

She waited in the corridor for him, so they could walk side by side. But he didn't speak, not until he'd opened his office door, again standing on one side for her to go through first. She stopped in front of his desk, like a school kid in front of the head's desk, turning to watch him as he closed the door behind him. Although the room was standard issue, he'd got geranium cuttings on the windowsill, and some posters for art exhibitions on the walls. On his bookshelf stood a kettle and a plastic bottle of water.

'Sit down, please.' His voice was angry, exasperated, and, somewhere, kind.

'Sir.' Which chair? Not one of the armchairs. A hard one. She sat, knees together, upright, not letting her back sag. In spite of themselves, her fingers clasped and unclasped. Eventually she gave up the fight, gripping both sets of fingers in towards the palms. At least while he could see the white of her knuckles he couldn't see the bitten nails.

'You look as if you could use a cup of tea.' He busied himself with the kettle. When they chinked against each other, the mugs had the ring of china. No green fur, not like her last nick where there was a proper penicillin factory.

7

'I'm fine, Sir.' What was a DCI doing, fussing round making tea? It was usually a brusque yell to whoever was passing to bring coffee.

He turned to her, tea bag in one hand, mug in the other. 'Who are you trying to kid? Selby been his usual charming self?'

'There was some horseplay, Sir. I couldn't say who was involved.'

'Little DS Arctic, eh? Look, Kate, you've had a rotten time this last year, and anyone on my squad who makes it worse will feel my boot up his arse.' He looked at her closely. 'What have I said?'

'Nothing, Sir.'

'Young lady, you're not telling me the truth. Something happened in there to upset you. I've a shrewd idea what it was. If you don't make a complaint, I can't fix it.'

'If I make a complaint, Sir, I've blown my job here. There's these things wherever you go, aren't there. And I've got to work with – with everyone on the squad. Last thing I need's the reputation for being a grass.'

'I don't agree.' He stared at her for a moment, lips tight. She didn't let her eyes drop. 'OK. I won't press you at the moment. Let me know if you change your mind. And remember, there are others involved. You can't think just of yourself. What about other women recruits who may face the same unpleasantness? Think about that, Kate.' He poured water in the mugs. A strange smell, like grass cuttings, pervaded the room. The DCI was only giving her herbal tea, when every nerve yelled for caffeine.

The taste – suddenly she saw worms, little pink worms in a compost heap, the sort of worms which were eating Robin's flesh.

She made it out of his room to the nearest loo. Heaved until there was nothing left but bile, and heaved again. It had gone straight to her stomach, all that business. Shock, the doctor said.

She soaked wads of loo paper in cold water and pressed

them to her eyes. Then all over her face. The door opened; she swung away, so no one could see her like this.

'Only me,' said Sally. 'Hang on!'

She was out of the door and back again before Kate had done much more.

'Here: take this.' She offered a bulging make-up bag. 'All that mascara running – look a bit like a panda, you do.'

Kate peered at herself. Panda was the right word. She smiled and opened the bag. Sally went in for bright lipsticks.

'Thanks. That's really kind of you. There: that's better. Just what I needed. And – about earlier – thanks.'

'No problem. Maybe you've got too much blusher there. Wipe a bit off, eh? Time to move, d'you think? Harvey sent me to find you. Well, to see if you were all right, really. Funny bloke, bit of a pussy cat. Sometimes. Best not to keep him waiting, though, eh?'

Back down the corridor. Though she couldn't see them, she knew that eyes watched her through cracks between doors and frames. She could feel the silence fall, deepen. Suddenly Roper put his head round the door of the gents: he grinned and winked, making a silent thumbs up. She smiled back.

Bracing her shoulders, she tapped on Harvey's door. The concern on his face as he let her in panicked her: what if she started to cry again?

'Sit down, Kate. My God, I didn't know my tea could do that to anyone. It's supposed to be healthy, this herbal stuff. No, have the arm-chair, girl.' Watching where the sun would fall on her face, he fiddled with the blinds.

'It –' She couldn't go into all the explanations he might want. But there was something about his face that made her want to tell him the truth, if not the whole of it. 'It reminded me of something, Sir.'

'Something?'

'Worms.' The word came out baldly.

He nodded. Perhaps he understood. 'I hope this won't.' He

smiled very kindly. It was drinking chocolate this time. Not the packet sort, either. More like the expensive stuff she'd always sent Aunt Cassie for Christmas. And that was another problem, of course.

'I've been thinking about what you said,' Harvey said, pulling his chair round to her side of the desk. 'I'll let it be known that you've taken it in the spirit they'll say it was intended. You'll be taking hammer, anyway, coming up from the Smoke. An outsider. I don't want to make it worse. But I tell you this, Kate — ' his voice hardened again '— if there's ever even a whisper of any other woman enduring — what did you call it? Horseplay? — I'll whip the perpetrator through every disciplinary procedure there is and have you as a witness. Clear?'

'Clear, Sir. They'll have other goes at me, Sir, just to make sure I'm sound. They did earlier, as a matter of fact. I went through it in the Met. I can handle it.'

'I've no doubt you *could*. That was before all that business with — your colleague.' He leaned over to his desk and patted what must be her file. 'Things like that mean you lose your — resilience. Heavens, woman: all those stress factors.' He ticked each item off on his fingers. 'The bereavement. Your own injury. Changing jobs. Moving house. No need to be quixotic.'

Quixotic? Perhaps she'd been quixotic about the house. But she thought about that enough out of working hours not to want to think about it now.

'Remember, now, if you should want support but don't want to drag me in, a Skilled Helper's just at the end of the phone. Right?'

What had Sally called him? A pussy cat. She found herself nodding and smiling a little. Harvey smiled back.

'Now, Kate,' he continued, in a slightly different voice, as if he were reading from a checklist. Perhaps this was what he'd been meaning to say all along, but had had to defer. 'There'll be plenty of people to say you were wrong to leave the Met, but you'll find the West Midlands Police pretty much on the ball. We'll be able to give you all the experience you need for that accelerated promotion scheme you're on.'

Kate responded in kind – alert, professional. 'Sir.'

'Oh, for goodness' sake call me Graham. Everyone else does. You'll know – even that lot know – when it should be Sir. You'll find they call me the Gaffer: that's Brummie for Guv'nor.' His sudden grin took ten years off his age. Not that he was that old. Forty, perhaps a couple of years more. Funny how having their hair go grey at the temples made men look attractive. Then he looked at her sternly: 'Some of you folk from the Met have been known to take the piss out of us Midlanders on account of the accent. But you want to remember that we don't wear woad and some of us can even do joined-up writing.'

'Even Selby, Sir?' It was out before she could stop it, or she could stop her dimples.

He grinned again: 'I wouldn't guarantee that! But maybe you don't need reminding about all this – you've worked up here before, haven't you? Undercover at that old people's home? Where the matron had Munchausen's by Proxy Syndrome?'

'Then she had that heart attack before we could get her to court. Funny, I was quite relieved. In many ways she was quite kind – paid the staff decent wages for a start!'

'And killed the residents. OK, Kate. So at least you know your way around the city. You'll find there have been a few changes.' Then he returned to that agenda of his. 'Have you found anywhere to live yet?'

Found! Had it wished on her, more like! 'I've got an aunt up here. She's had to go into a home, so I've got her house.'

'Very nice!'

Except it wasn't, of course. It was a house from hell, with garden to match.

'Good area?'

'Kings Heath.' Solid traffic from the front door into the city centre, as far as she could see. Next task, find a rat-run.

'Excellent. A pleasant residential area. But they have the odd spot of bother on the High Street at weekends. Kids: too much money and too much booze. Bit of a dust-up there last Saturday. Parking's dreadful.'

She nodded. 'Even after London. And no tube, either.' And Birmingham couldn't be London, no matter how hard it tried. And no matter how hard she tried to ignore that whining accent.

Harvey smiled formally, as if he'd concluded the items on his agenda. But then his face softened properly. 'Tell you what, Kate. After this morning I'm inclined to believe what the medics say. I think this business has knocked you around more than you admit. Even to yourself. And I think they're right – you should be on light duties for a bit. Now, in this squad we don't have passengers –'

'Sir! You're not going to transfer me!'

'Who said anything about transferring? No, all I was going to propose is that for a couple of weeks, rather than legging it round Birmingham and getting yourself –'

'Sir, I'm running again. And swimming. The knee's fine – it was only a dislocation!' But she had gone too far.

'Hang on, young lady, hang on.' He was back into schoolmaster mode.

'Sorry, Sir.'

'OK. Here's what I was going to say. There's more than one way of skinning a cat. You can take to the streets or you can sit here and get stuff off the computers. Some of the lads have the keyboard skills of the average gorilla. And it's here in the records – you've been on a couple of computer courses, haven't you? Quick accurate retrieval and cross-referencing of material would be invaluable. You'd also establish yourself as a member of the team. Give yourself time to make friends. Then we can work out who to pair you up with. OK.' It wasn't a question; it was an order.

She smiled politely. Yes, she'd have to make the best of it: the man was only doing what he thought was right. If she didn't like benevolent paternalism, she'd have to lump it – and with good grace.

'Now, you'll be meeting the other senior officers in due

course. Superintendent Gordon. He's as decent a man as you'd wish to meet. Career officer, very dedicated. The only trouble is, he tends to keep his door shut, if you see what I mean. But then he's out all weekends working for the Scouts so –'

The phone: he snatched it.

'Harvey.' He listened in silence, interjecting an occasional, 'Ah. Thank God!' At last he covered the mouthpiece, mouthing, 'They've found the child!' Aloud he asked, 'Which hospital? You'll let me know if there's anything I should know.' He replaced the handset. 'Happy ending. They've found young Darren Goss in the Bull Ring Centre. They know it's Darren because of the name tag on his scarf but he's not saying anything. Anything at all. And I'll tell you, Kate, I've got a nasty gut feeling about that kid.'

'Any reason, Sir?'

'Something to do with his not speaking. And this twitching in my thumbs.' He smiled before looking her straight in the eye. 'Kate: I know you'd rather be up and doing, but you're going to be searching through every file on the bloody system.'

There was no sign of Sally or Colin Roper when Kate emerged from Harvey's office. Since it was just after midday, she might find them in the canteen. She might find other people, too.

This wasn't going to be easy. Perhaps a visit to the loo might give her thinking time. She could get some of Sally's make-up off, too: no need to look like a refugee from a teen magazine. And yet, why not? A bit of camouflage never came amiss. Shoulders straight, she strode in, grabbing a tray and checking the menu as if food was the only thing on her mind. But she listened: if it went quiet everywhere she was in trouble. No: the hubbub was normal. She had allies. And there were Sally and Colin, over the far side, with a bunch of the others. She waved and pushed her way over.

'God, she's one of the lettuce leaf brigade,' Selby announced to anyone who wanted to hear. 'Give me a woman with a bit of meat on her.' He made squeezing movements with his fingers.

'You're right an' all!' Another bloke gestured, holding his elbow and pumping his forearm upwards. 'Here, they was saying you had a spot of bother this morning, me love. Come and tell me all about it and I'll sort him out for you.'

Despite the laughter, Kate knew she was being set another test.

'Trouble? No. I'm not worried by a little prick like that.' Yes, that was better. It was nice to have the laughter on her side.

Chapter Two

There was nothing to keep Kate in the house: everything to drive her out for a long run. For all she'd insisted to Graham Harvey that she was fit, she hadn't run much recently, and would have to take it gently tonight. And that meant taking her stretches seriously.

Her route would take her from where she lived to the far side of the High Street, so she could check out the parks that lay there, and would return her along the High Street for some comfort food from one of the chip shops. In fact it was the thought of the food that kept her going when drizzle brought the night closing in.

Choosing a chippie at random she found something she hadn't expected: chicken tikka in a naan bread. She'd have a double. And then wondered if she'd been right, as the Asian lad piled the naan high with salad.

'Chilli-sauce-mint-sauce-lemon-juice?'

'Please. But go easy on the chilli, eh?'

'Sure, Miss.' He tipped a succession of vivid liquids on to the salad. 'There you go. You new up here?'

'Just moved.'

'Thought so. Don't talk like you come from round here. London, is it?' He wrapped the naan, laying it on the counter while he took her money.

'London.'

'Me cousin's got a place down there. Hither Green. D'you know it?'

She shook her head. 'London's a big place.'

'Let me know if you go back: I'll give you me cousin's address.'

Funny to hear Asians with a Brummie accent. No funnier than with a Sheffield or with a London one, she supposed.

'Thanks. Goodnight!' She gathered the parcel, warm against her stomach.

'See you later!'

Which must mean goodbye.

She jogged for home. Safeways. Dixons. Familiar but in the wrong place. And then a scream. Cut off short but still a scream. Kids messing around, she told herself. Just kids. She had her supper to eat.

But when it came to it, there was no contest. A scream took precedence over a tikka, and it would only take a minute, just to check.

There was a carpark behind Dixons and the other shops. Someone had warned they'd clamp illegally parked vehicals. A lot of commercial waste bins. A skip at the far end. A couple of cars lit up by the security lights. Come on, cursory looks are no good. Have a good nose round. And –

Yes!

The boy had the girl – an Asian kid, not much more than sixteen – upright against the wall hidden by the skip. One forearm pressed across her throat, the other hand digging into her buttock. Stupid bastard, couldn't he tell the reason she wasn't screaming was that he was choking her? Throwing down the naan, Kate hurled herself, grabbing the youth by the hair, yanking till she could arm-lock him. And then she was tugged off and thrown to the ground.

They fled, two dark figures. With those hooded jackets they could be any race. Give chase or see to the girl? The question answered itself: the girl crumpled, falling on to the wet tarmac. Pulse? Breathing? Better put her in recovery position just in case. And then find a phone. Fast.

The local uniformed lads didn't take long to arrive. By then the girl was crying and moaning: they might need an ambulance.

★

'Good job you were there,' Guljar, the night sergeant said, getting back into his car. 'Hey, want a lift home?'

'I'm only a couple of roads away.'

'Hop in anyway. We'll talk ID tomorrow, OK?'

'You can talk all you like. I only saw the rear view.'

'ID a bum, if you like.'

'Spare me!' She fastened her seat belt.

'Well, was it a brown or a white bum? I know things look different under these lights, but you must have some idea. Kate?' he prompted.

She shook her head. 'You'd think all these years of training – Guljar, I'd reckon it was light brown. But I don't want to think stereotypes –'

'And there are some pretty evil white bums around too. Poor kid. This won't go down well with her family.'

'Eh? She was raped, for Christ's sake!'

'Don't tell me, Kate. I know. But you saw her clothes: all that black gear. Locals call them ninjas. Can't say I blame them. I mean, shoving your religion down people's throats. I mean, I'm a Sikh, and proud of it, but I've cut my hair. Doesn't mean I'm any the less devout. Bring my kids up in the family tradition. All this black gear rubs people's noses in the fact you're different.'

Kate didn't feel up to a discussion on religion and social conformity, not at this hour.

'But even if the family's far right fundamentalist, they couldn't blame her for –'

'Kate: last year on my patch – when I was still in uniform – there was this shooting. Mum, daughter, kid brother; then the dad turned the gun on himself. For why? Cause some kind auntie had seen the girl kissing an African-Caribbean kid down the park, that's why.'

'So she won't just need support from the Rape Unit – she might need protection from her own people! My God!'

'Thank God for safe houses.' Putting the car into gear, he reversed smartly.

'Hey, I just realised my dinner's somewhere here. Tikka in a naan.'

'Into local delicacies, are you?' Guljar stopped, getting out and peering round. It was he who found the little parcel, flat under his back tyre.

He took her back to the chippie, of course.

The lad behind the counter looked at her with obvious respect when she asked for a repeat. 'You sure you can manage another, Miss?'

'Two, I should think.' One of them for Guljar, waiting in the car.

'Bloody hell. What you Londoners got? Hollow legs?'

She was trying to jiggle the Yale key into the front door when a figure came up the shared front path.

It was a woman. What had Aunt Cassie said about her neighbours? Immigrants. Jamaicans, Aunt Cassie had called them, in a slightly lowered voice.

Kate smiled, and held out her hand. 'I'm Kate Power. Cassie's niece. You must be Mrs Mackenzie?'

'That's right.' Her accent was more Barbados than Jamaica but mostly Brum. So much for Cassie's judgement – Kate wondered how many years she'd been over here. 'Now, what you been doin' to yourself? All that blood?'

Kate looked down. Now she came to think of it, her thigh was throbbing.

'I fell over. Thought I'd just bruised it. Must have landed on some broken glass.'

'You just step inside, Kate girl. Come your ways in. Here.' Kate followed.

After the gloom of her aunt's house, this was a revelation. To be sure, not all the furniture would have been Kate's choice, but the rooms looked twice as large as those next door. Amazing what a coat of light paint could do. New, by the smell of it.

'It's the radiators. First time I've had the central heating on since they were painted. Into the kitchen and take down those pants. Royston, we have a visitor. Now, Miss Kate's hurt herself and I'm going to patch her up, so don't you come back in here without you knock first.'

The lad – about sixteen, Kate supposed – slipped something into a drawer and put his hands behind his back.

'Hi, Royston.' Kate held out her hand.

He stared as if she were offering him a bad fish and went out.

'Royston! What I tell you about manners? Come back here!'

Royston returned. 'Hi.'

'Hi! Nice to meet you.' She spoke to his departing back. Why did it look so guilty?

Mrs Mackenzie shrugged, and busied herself with an impressive first aid box. 'Let's see. No, not so bad as it could be.' She put on gloves and swabbed gently.

Kate peered. She had a neat cut in her thigh. She decided to look at Mrs Mackenzie instead: in the bright light of the kitchen she looked younger than she had outside – forty-five, perhaps. She'd had her hair relaxed, and wore it pulled back into a neat knot.

'Anti-tet?' she asked, looking up.

'Last year. It doesn't need a stitch, does it?' It wasn't the stitching she dreaded, but the three or four hours in casualty. The jog had made her sleepy and hungry, she couldn't tell in which order.

For answer, Mrs Mackenzie produced butterflies. 'That should do you. Though your trousers may never be the same again.'

'I don't think they owe me anything. I'm so grateful, Mrs Mackenzie. Thank you.'

'My job, Kate, girl. What's an extra five minutes on top of two hours' unpaid overtime, eh? How's the old lady?' She stripped off her gloves, dropping them inside out into the pedal bin, and turned on the taps.

'Good as she'll ever be. She's going to stay in the home, though. She might have every last marble but her body's – well, you know what arthritis can do.'

'Very cruel it can be, Lord knows. What's that you got?' Drying her hands, she pointed at Kate's supper. 'Can't cook in that kitchen of hers, eh?'

'Not much of a kitchen. Not like this.' Kate looked around her.

'This my husband's redundancy. Twenty-five years a teacher and – she drew a finger across her throat. 'But then he walks straight into another job, and hey presto! Like it?'

'Lovely. Gives me ideas for mine. Aunt Cassie's been really kind – she's given me the house, you see.'

Mrs Mackenzie looked at her sideways. 'Well, there's gifts and there's gifts,' she said. 'When I was a girl in school, they made us learn these poems. There was this one about an albatross.'

The tired, damp smell hit her as soon as she opened the front door. Neglected house plus old person smell. She'd met it in countless houses; she'd never thought she'd live in one smelling like it. At least it wouldn't smell like that when she'd finished with it. The trouble was, knowing where to start.

The kitchen. She couldn't live without a proper kitchen. Aunt Cassie had survived with a minute kitchen and a scullery. Knocking out the wall between them would make a lovely long light room. She could picture it now: a working surface there, the sink where it would catch the sun. And a nice round table in that corner by the radiator. Pale green and a warm coloured wood. And some pretty tiles. All she had at the moment was an old brown porcelain sink in the scullery, complete with a splash-back that looked like Challenger coming in to land, minus a few tiles. Kate supposed she could risk the stove, but was reluctant, on grounds of hygiene, for one thing. Arthritic joints don't take kindly to wielding a Brillo pad. No such thing as a microwave, of course: she'd have to eat the tikka cold. At least what it lacked in thermal power, it made up in spice. She'd go to that chippie again.

And then to bed. She was making do with an inflatable

mattress and sleeping bag on the living-room floor until the builders had sorted out the plaster in the upstairs rooms: during the hurricane Cassie had lost a chunk of roof, which she'd had to have repaired. But apart from having the plaster directly underneath patched, she'd never wanted the mess of having the rest of the ceilings skimmed. That was Kate's priority: to get the upstairs into a state where it could be decorated. And the problem was the money it would take. The house she and Robin had shared in Croydon had been in her name, while he'd paid his way with household expenses. Until she'd sold it, she couldn't afford the £10,000 or so it would take to knock this house into shape. Or at least until she'd got a regular tenant.

The more she tried to sleep, the faster the problems marched across her eyes: the guttering, the garden, the bathroom, the front wall. And the wiring. That was her first priority. Aunt Cassie had admitted that when you turned some switches on, there was a smell of hot rubber. And then there was the matter of that boiler . . .

At least there was still some whisky left. Tomorrow she'd check out Sainsbury's own brand. Except it was well into tomorrow already, and still sleep was no nearer.

And then she slammed the whisky glass down and peered at the cut on her leg. Glass? She'd have noticed broken glass when she'd laid the girl on the ground. Wouldn't she? Pulling her clothes on, bloody trousers and all, she knew she had to go. And knew, just as well as she knew there was no pot of gold at the end of the rainbow, she'd find no glass.

One of those lads had used a knife on her, hadn't he?

Chapter Three

'So the good news is the kid'll live,' Harvey announced. 'The bad news is he's deeply traumatised. Still not speaking. Crying. Sucking his thumb. Wetting the bed, dirtying himself.'

Anger sizzled round the room.

'Is there – sexual interference, Sir?' Kate asked the question first.

'No doubt about it,' Harvey replied. 'Abnormally bad damage to the poor little bastard's anus and rectum.' Looking round the team, he added, 'There isn't one of us wouldn't want to crucify the bugger that did it. Now, I reckon paedophiles don't hunt alone.'

'Isn't that down to Vice, Gaffer?'

'Darren Goss lives in Newtown, Selby. Newtown's our patch. We'll be liaising with Vice, of course. But we'll be working our arses off here to sort it. Right?'

'All of us, Sir? They did say that Miss Power wouldn't be out on the streets with the rest of us.'

'*Detective Sergeant* Power will be working back here, Selby.'

'All the time, Sir? Coming in at eight, like the rest of us?'

'Most of you aren't trying to ID a rapist, Selby. That incident in Kings Heath: Power was the officer on the spot. Well done, by the way, Kate.'

'Right place, right time, Sir,' Kate mumbled. It was nice to be praised, provided it didn't set any of these sensitive backs up. And, for goodness' sake, it was what she'd joined the Force for, helping people.

Harvey was speaking again. 'Most of us have hands with ten thumbs. Kate's been on a couple of courses: her fingers should be speedier than ours. She'll be far more use here than on streets she doesn't know yet.'

'But —'

Couldn't the stupid bastard sense he'd gone too far? She wouldn't have wanted Harvey to turn on her like that.

'When I want your advice, Selby, on how to organise my team, rest assured I'll ask for it. Now, this is how I propose to rota you all —'

Routine. She'd never liked it. You join the police because you want something better. And there you are, stuck at a computer all day. Two computers: she was jotting information she'd picked up from one directly on to another to pull together later.

The trouble was that Harvey had been right. Her typing speed plus her trained eyes should make connections. *Would,* when her hands found their rhythm at the keyboard.

'Here: what do you make of this?' Colin Roper said, perching on the corner of her desk and smiling down at her. He was about her age, she supposed, blond and fine-featured. 'The report from the hospital says the kid still isn't talking.'

'They've tried all the stuff with sexually explicit dolls, have they?'

'All he wants is his teddy, poor little kid.'

Like Robin's kid — she stopped herself short. No matter how hard the job made you, there were some things you couldn't take. Blinking back tears, she stared at the sheet of paper Roper had given her: 'What's this about a duck?'

'It's what he's muttered in his sleep a couple of times.'

'Has he got a duck? Did he ever have one?'

'You mean real or a toy?'

'Either. What's the mother say?'

'Sally and I are just off to talk to her again, go through his toy cupboard and any photos they might have.'

'We could have a whip round. Get him a new one.'

'Nice idea, Kate,' said a new voice.

She jumped: she hadn't realised Harvey was in the room. 'Get an envelope going. Start it off with this.' He dug in his wallet and flicked a tenner at her. 'Don't forget to write my name down and tick it, will you?'

'Afraid of getting asked twice, are you, Gaffer?' Colin asked. 'Look, there's a moth flown out!'

'That's me. Scrooge is my middle name.' He made a show of closing his wallet and stuffing it away. 'What are you on now, Kate? Anything on MDisk?'

'Nope. I've checked all the tagged addresses: there's no one in the neighbourhood, no family member or friend with a history of domestic violence or child abuse.'

'NCIS?'

'Same again. No one on the sexual offenders database with paedophile habits like this bloke. I'm just about to start on STATUS.'

'No, you're not. You're going to get that envelope round –'

But Kate had a shrewd suspicion that Harvey had an ulterior motive: he wanted her established as one of the team as quickly as possible. Whatever the reason, the envelope was impressively heavy when she handed it to Sally who'd offered to pick up the toy on her way home.

Her back and shoulders were so stiff she thought she'd never stand straight again. But she mustn't stretch too obviously: that would be to invite Selby to offer a massage. There'd been enough stress for one day. Not that it was over yet. There was still Aunt Cassie to deal with.

No, that was unfair. She'd got to go and visit her, that was all – to take her some fruit and the evening paper. And it spared her going home to that house without Robin. And Aunt Cassie was good company – as she frequently observed, her brain was still functioning: it was just the rest of her that incommoded her. It had been Aunt Cassie's decision to go into a swish retirement home, and Aunt Cassie's decision that

Kate would have her house. Looking at it, no one would ever have dreamed that Cassie had money in the bank. Not just the bank, but a number of building societies, a great deal of shares and several very lovely diamond rings. A choker and several sets of earrings had been discreetly disposed of.

'There's no point,' she'd said, fidgeting with two of the rings, loose on the flesh between her swollen joints, 'in being the mistress of a man in the jewellery trade unless you show it.'

Perhaps leaving a house with dodgy wiring and a central heating boiler leaking gas – the heating had been installed twenty-odd years ago when one of Cassie's premium bonds had come up – you managed to accumulate enough money to keep you in a private home, which was where, a couple of weeks ago, Kate had been summoned to meet her aunt's solicitor. The dapper little man had sat easily in one of the Parker Knoll visitors' chairs: presumably he was more used to relieving old ladies of part of their fortunes than Kate was to accepting gifts like this. Aunt Cassie reclined on a day bed, and gestured. Although every joint was hugely swollen, the index finger and thumb driven to wild angles, the gesture was still an autocratic waft.

'There, Kate dear, all you have to do is sign. Yes, it's all legal. Mr Robson has seen to that. All I have to do is live long enough for you to enjoy the tax benefits – isn't that correct, Mr Robson? Seven years! Well, I'll do what I can.'

No one – least of all her aunt – had ever asked Kate if she wanted to be saddled with the house, or indeed, its overgrown garden.

'Now you needn't worry about that house of yours – she's got a place in Croydon or somewhere.' The old lady made it sound like Outer Mongolia. 'Have a skip for all my old furniture. I can't believe even one of the charity shops will want it. And burn the carpets – they're no better worth. Just there – is that right, Mr Robson?'

★

This time Aunt Cassie was in bed by the time Kate reached the home: 'And is there any hint of pee when you come in? Because that's how you can tell a good home from a bad one. The bad ones all smell of pee. The good ones don't. So I shall rely on you: as soon as you detect the slightest whiff as you come in the entrance hall, you tell me. I shall see something's done about it. Or I shall move. Mr Robson tells me I've enough money. What about you? Got a tenant for that house of yours yet?'

She realised Aunt Cassie was waiting for an answer. 'Not yet. But –'

'I thought not. Here.' She pushed a fat envelope across her bedside cabinet. 'Go on, take it. Mr Robson tells me I can afford it. You can pay me a nominal interest – purely nominal – if it makes you feel better. And you can pay me back when the money comes through. No, don't open it now. Talk to me a little more.'

'But –' Cassie's eyebrows stopped her. 'Thank you – if you're really sure.' Kate took the envelope. There were so many age blotches on her aunt's hand you couldn't tell where one started and another finished. Tonight the joints looked red hot with pain. But she still managed to do the *Telegraph* crossword, using ball-points in a fat holder it had taken Kate only a few minutes to run down, thanks to the disability shop just down the road. Aunt Cassie had sniffed with disdain; she liked to be the one to give presents, apparently. But she'd used it ever since.

'Of course I'm sure. Now, tell me. What is happening to the house? Chapter and verse, please.' Aunt Cassie laid those tortured hands carefully on the counterpane, closed her eyes and tipped back her head.

Kate spoke as if she was telling her great aunt an adult bedtime story. She could always let her voice tail off if the old lady drifted off to sleep. 'The first thing is the garden. I've had to have those sycamores cut down, I'm afraid.'

'Quite right. The roots would be getting under the foundations. What about the ash tree?'

'Now the sycamores have gone, you can see they were pushing it to one side. I think I may have to have a tree surgeon in.'

'All these fancy names. Tell me, do they wear green gowns

and ask for scalpels? I think not. A chain saw and wellies, in all probability. What did you do with the wood from the sycamores? You should have got a good price for the logs. All these people with their Agas.' She opened her eyes wide. 'You didn't, did you? What – a bonfire or a skip?'

'A skip. Two, actually.'

'You young people call yourself green and save paper bags, but you can't manage the real thing, can you, real recycling?' Her aunt tutted sharply, and it was some time before her face fell into repose. 'Which bedroom do you occupy?'

Kate jumped. 'I'm still in the living room at the moment.' Better a single air-bed than a half-empty double bed. Would there come a night when she slept through, not waking to snuggle up to his back?

'Hmm. You've got to make it your own, Kate. But I suppose if you've got to have workmen traipsing round upstairs, you might as well stay put for a bit. By the way, there's enough money there for the bathroom. Comfortless place. You won't be able to do much with it, of course, it's too small. But I'd appreciate a few of those instant photographs – what do they call them? Polaroids? Just to see how you're getting on.'

That meant getting a camera. She and Robin had had a succession of cheap ones – a waste of money, of course, and the results were never very good. That's why she had no decent photos of Robin. It wasn't the money she begrudged, not with this fat envelope in her hands, but the time. Police work wasn't something the corners of which could be cut. Overtime was the norm. Her days would stretch into evenings, into nights when a major case occurred. She felt the envelope again. The least she could do, wasn't it, buy a camera?

Her aunt drifted into a doze, and the *Evening Mail* slipped towards the edge of the bed. Kate fielded it. Glancing at her watch, she thought she'd stay just ten more minutes in case Aunt Cassie woke up. She scanned the headlines and turned to the letters.

'I was talking to Mr Elford today.' Aunt Cassie spoke as if she'd never paused. 'The minister. Brayfield Road Baptist

Church. He came to do his duty, I suppose. Sat where you're sitting and talked my head off. As if I'd been to chapel in years. Anyway, he said their organist's been taken ill. Did I know anyone. I told him he must be crazy, expecting me to be up-to-date in things like that. I suppose he only said it to make conversation, which was dragging. But then I remembered: so I told him you'd help out for a couple of weeks, just until they found someone permanent, of course. So he'll be phoning you later. What time is it? Nine? You'd better dash off, my dear.' She proffered her cheek for a kiss.

Kate laid her hand briefly on her forearm, and kissed her. It wasn't until she was in the thickly carpeted corridor that she let herself lean back against the wall, eyes closed. What a pity Cassie was one of that lost generation of women whose careers never matched their abilities. The old woman would have made a wonderful general.

Almost as soon as she'd let herself in, there was a knock at her door.

'Mrs Mackenzie! Come on in!'

'No, girl, I haven't come to take your time. I thought you could maybe fancy some of this.' She pushed forward a covered casserole. 'Peas and rice. Since you can't be cooking.'

'That is kind of you – are you sure you won't step in?'

'Just out of the rain. Lord, Kate: the smell!'

'Old ladies and wet plaster. And the dust of ages.'

'You sure got that, all right.' She hovered. Something was worrying her.

To fill the silence, Kate said, 'I shall have to get a skip for most of the stuff. Charity shop wouldn't look at it.'

'No, but an antiques dealer might. You talk to my Joseph. He know these things. Hmm.' She peered at the over-mantel.

Better say something else. 'The leg's going on fine, thanks to you.'

'Oh, that's nothing. That business up Heathfield Road:

that where it happened? That girl? It was on TV.' Her voice was sharp.

'I was just on my way from the chippie. Heard a scream. Thought I'd better do something.'

'And they pushed you down? On to some glass?'

What was she trying to find out? 'By the skip,' Kate said, non-committal. 'But it's all in the hands of local CID, now. Hope they get them.'

'Did you see them? I mean, you were close, weren't you?'

The woman was worried, wasn't she? Worried enough to ask risky questions. Surely she couldn't suspect her own son? Honesty might be the best response. It usually was. 'Only the back view. I was on the ground. Not much to go on. I hope the poor girl will be more use than I am.'

Mrs Mackenzie nodded. 'She all right?'

'She was sixteen. She was raped. How all right can you be after that?'

It was terribly hard to yell at anyone who began a phone conversation with the words: 'I'm sure you wish me at the devil, Miss Power, but I promise you it wasn't my idea.'

'I believe you.'

'I was only trying to fill up a silence.'

'I believe you.'

'And I have got the feelers out for anyone who could – I suppose, just until I find someone, you couldn't consider it, just for a couple of weeks?'

'I'm not really what you'd call a Christian.' Not on speaking terms with God. Not now.

'I don't ask you to pray, just to play. You'd be a god-send. Please.'

'I couldn't do both services.'

'You could choose.'

She liked his voice. Admired his cheek. And fingered the wad of fifty-pound notes that her aunt had given her and meekly agreed to play for the morning service.

Chapter Four

Whenever their shifts had let them, Kate and Robin had luxuriated in Sunday mornings. Often – if the kids hadn't been round – they'd enjoyed nice relaxed sex, and then the papers over coffee. Then brunch, with the whole cholesterol works: bacon, egg, sausage, though no fried bread latterly. As if looking after his health had helped Robin.

Kate pushed away her plate. Suddenly she didn't want even the modest bacon sandwich, though she'd tried to work up an appetite with an early morning run round Kings Heath Park. A jog to warm up and cool down, but a good brisk run for a mile. The knee had stood it remarkably well. It was good to be getting control over her body again. Except for the matter of Graham Harvey's herbal tea, of course. He still looked at her with disconcerting kindness each time he came across her in the office or along the corridors, as if wanting to ask if she was settling in, but being too tactful to do so. When she'd asked if he could spare her so she could play the organ this morning, he'd insisted that she should take the whole day off.

'All day on computers,' he'd said, smiling, 'your eyes and shoulders'll need a break. Not to mention your brain!'

With the young men, he was more often in schoolteacher mode.

'Thing is,' Sally said, 'he's straight. Straight as a die.'

Or was it straight as a Dai?

She liked Sally and was getting on well with Colin. Only

Selby still seemed to think that honours had to be evened. Best not to think of him on a Sunday before chapel.

Pecking at dry bread she looked at her watch. Ten. Time to get dressed, and in something appropriate, too. With most of her clothes still in Croydon or in suitcases, to avoid all the mess, her choice was limited. The suit she wore to court might be the best thing, except it wasn't, now she came to hold it up, wide enough in the skirt for working the organ pedals. She grabbed the next best, a bottle-green pleated affair in which she always looked hung over.

It would have been nice to get the feel of things first, of course, but there'd really been no time. So it would be in at the deep end with a strange organ, a strange choir and a strange acoustic.

She'd cut it slightly fine and had to go into the chapel as if she were simply one of the congregation. She was intercepted at the door by a stringy woman aged anything between fifty-five and sixty-five – a deaconess whose job it was to welcome the congregation and pass them hymn books. Kate smiled. Maybe the woman smiled back: it was hard to tell. Her handshake was perfunctory, to say the least.

Kate tried again: 'Hello. I'm Kate Power. I believe Mr Elford is expecting me. I'm your temporary organist.'

The woman's nose thinned. 'You'll find him in the vestry.'

'Which is where?'

She was treated to a curt sideways jerk of the head. My God, not another case of the deaconess being in love with the minister? Such relationships, if that was what they ever were, had enlivened her Sunday-school classes and later her time in the chapel choir. Smiling the neat, undimpled professional smile she'd learned, she pushed open the door to the chapel. And stopped short. She'd never seen anything like this. Not your usual plain wood-panelled building, with a big central block of pews and a smaller one each side. No. This was – heavens, it was like a mini Sacré Coeur! All stained glass and polished tiles. There was a central aisle, like in the church where they'd buried Robin. A few deep breaths.

'Is there a problem, Miss – er –?'

Kate spun round. It was the deaconess. 'Power. Kate,' she repeated. 'No, I was just – taken aback – by this.' She gestured. 'You'll find the Minister through there.'

'Thanks. I don't know any of your names yet. You're –?'

'Mrs Walters.' There was a certain emphasis on the title.

Kate knocked on the vestry door, waited a moment, and went in. All she could see was the back of an academic gown, as someone struggled into it. She gave it a firm hitch, and waited for the owner to turn.

He was too busy shifting the gown's weight more firmly on to his shoulders to take in who had rescued him.

'Hello. I'm Kate Power.'

When he finally looked up and round, she could see nothing but puzzlement on his face. But when it cleared, it was transformed: no wonder Mrs Walters wanted to defend Mr Elford from all comers. Half the women in the congregation must be in love with him. He was classically handsome, with the sort of bones that would go on looking elegant until he died. Since he couldn't have been much more than forty, this might well be a long time in the future.

Mr Elford's smile faded. 'You can sight read, can't you?'

Kate had probably expected, if she'd thought about it, effusive thanks and apologies, which she would have laughed aside. As it was, she felt put out. It was like being interviewed belatedly for a job she didn't even want.

'Yes.' Perhaps her irritation showed. Perhaps she didn't at this moment mind if it did. 'As long as you stick to the old Baptist Hymnal and don't want anything trendier – syncopation's never been my strong suit – we might just get through. Prayer seems entirely appropriate, all things considered.' She found herself laughing away her bad temper.

He joined in. 'We'd better have a word with Him then: the lady who organises the choir – Mrs Griffiths, that is – tends to rewrite the hymns somewhat.'

It was possible after all that she might like Mr Elford. 'How much rewriting?'

'Just enough to get them into the choir's range, I believe. It's a very small choir.'

'Reedy tenors, one bass and loads of sopranos?'

'They all work very hard.' He lifted his voice so it would carry. 'Ah, Mrs Griffiths. Margaret. This is Kate Power, who's so kindly agreed to play for us for a few weeks.'

A few!

Mrs Griffiths was a top-heavy woman, to whom middle age was not being kind. While her body had thickened, her hair had not, and although a talented hairdresser might have done something, Mrs Griffiths was currently displaying an area at the front almost bald. The bags under her eyes suggested chronic sinusitis. When she had swept Kate from head to toe she nodded briefly. Another one in love with Elford, presumably. Kate caught herself wishing that Elford was gay, just to confound the predatory women.

'Of course,' Mrs Griffiths began, 'our last organist was BMus, Durham.'

'I'm B Soc Sci, Manchester. With an MA in Criminal Psychology.' So why was she stung into such a silly boast? Normally she never spoke of her qualifications. It wasn't what you had on paper that counted: it was how good you were at your job. Clearly she had gone too far: Mrs Griffiths' nose, with its rather long tip, reddened.

Not an auspicious start, then. The service was long and enthusiastic, but the choir, for all Mrs Griffiths' training, dawdled badly, dragging the lovely tunes into dirges. And they sharpened and flattened at will. Despite the nice Mr Elford, she'd made a bad mistake — or rather, Aunt Cassie had made one for her. She was too irritated to be uplifted, and the thought that she could have stripped a whole roomful of wallpaper during the sermon alone made her irritation worse.

She was slipping out of the chapel when Elford intercepted her. 'Are you in a terrible hurry, Kate? Because I was hoping you'd join us for a pre-lunch sherry. I'd like you to meet the deacons — see the sort of community we are.'

Her first impulse was to refuse: but she straightened her

shoulders and accepted. If it provided nothing more, it might afford a few moments' grim comedy.

The manse was a modern house, clean and cheerfully decorated. There was a clutter of toys in the hall, and the sweet smell of roasting lamb.

'Let me have your coat,' Elford said, reaching for it. 'Maz! Maz, love.'

If Kate had been one of Elford's fan club, she'd have given up. Maz, taking off her apron and stashing it behind an out-of-control Swiss cheese plant, was a couple of inches taller than her husband, slender and blonde. No wonder she hadn't gone to the service: the elderly women who dominated the front pews would have spent their time praying for her instant death.

'Maz, this is Kate. Our temporary organist.'

'It's good to meet you. Come along in! Giles: get in there! They're all waiting for you. Hang on, Kate – you'll need a glass. I only put out the usual number.' She grinned as if they were accomplices in something.

And then there was a yowl from the kitchen. Maz turned tail, and Kate followed, running. Two or three children were doing something with apples. One of the girls – she must have been about six – was screaming as blood oozed from her clenched fist.

'My God! Let Mummy look, love.'

'Here, let me. Get me a clean tea towel, will you?' Kate uncurled the fist. There was a long slice across the thumb. 'No, it's not deep. There's a large flap of skin there. Have you some sharp, clean scissors?' She snipped before the little girl knew what she was doing, and squeezed the tea towel. 'Just hold that, tight as you can. Tighter! What's her name? Jenny? Good girl, Jenny. Got a first-aid box? We could do with those adhesive strips – butterflies. Excellent. Come on, sweetheart, we're just going to put these strips across here – there, you can see it's bleeding less already. Another one just there. Good girl. Now, we'll just clean you up a bit and you'll be as good as new.' She swabbed and dabbed till the thumb was clean, and then rooted through the first-aid box. 'Non-stick dressing, that's what we could do with. Yes, we could cut a bit off there. And some adhesive. And then it's just a matter of getting the rest of the blood up and Bob's your uncle.'

'Or even, in these enlightened days,' said Maz, 'your aunt. Golly, Kate, that was all very brisk and efficient.'

'First-aid, training. And not being involved.' Then she thought of Mrs Mackenzie's work on her leg: 'Hey, has she had anti-tet?'

'Last month.'

'Come on, sit down. Head between your knees. You look as if you could do with a drink.' Not as much as Kate herself could do with a drink. She'd meant to turn down even sherry – no true Baptist would be surprised to find a tee-totaller in their midst. But she'd have killed for a drink. As it was, she hunted for the kettle. 'Stay there. Tea or coffee?'

'Gin,' Maz said. 'It's in the fridge. Unless you're –?'

'Gin sounds great. But mostly tonic: I'm driving.' And I'm halfway down the road to being a lush. She turned to the children, so no one could see how much she wanted that drink.

'But you must stay to lunch. Apple pie if I can find enough apples without blood. What did you cut yourself on, Jenny? I said no knives.'

'I was trying to take the core out.' Jenny held up an old-fashioned potato peeler.

'Ah! What you have to do is pull the blade off here, turn it round and use this round end. Pour that gin, Kate, there's a dear. See, that's how you do it.'

Kate busied herself with the fridge, finding ice cubes and a tired lemon. 'Tonic?' she prompted.

'Cupboard under the stairs. On your right, as you go in. Mind how you fall over the empties. Haven't been to the bottle bank for a few weeks.'

That was quite obvious. Clearly these Baptists weren't total abstainers, nor did Maz seem to feel guilty about drinking. At last she managed to unearth a couple of new bottles of tonic, so she rescued one and carried it back in triumph to the kitchen.

'Now you see how I keep the place tidy. Shove everything into cupboards and slam the doors tight. Only problem comes when you open the doors and there's this avalanche,' Maz said, rolling out pastry she'd conjured from somewhere. She'd found another apron, this one with teddy bears all over it. 'Cheers.' She grabbed the glass with a floury hand and drank extravagantly. 'Hell, you're not supposed to be here! Thank God gin doesn't smell too much on the breath. Sherry's OK. It's genteel, you see. Off you go: second on the right. Here, swig that down and put some orange juice in your glass. What the eye doesn't see . . .'

'Right! Over the top!'

'Good luck. But I said lunch and I meant it. See you in a bit.'

The room must have been light, airy and welcoming, but someone had arranged dining chairs around the edge of the room, punctuated by stools or easy chairs. It had the air of a dentist's waiting room. Silence snapped into place as soon as Kate entered. She had a choice between a stool and a big leather wing chair, old enough to be an heirloom. She made brazenly for the wing chair.

Before she could sit, Mrs Walters coughed. 'That's Mr Pugh's chair.'

There was no sign of him. Kate looked at the door – had he gone to the lavatory?

Elford shifted in his seat with embarrassment.

'I'll remember for next time,' Kate said at last, sitting down.

Mrs Walters' mouth shrank. Robin would have said it looked like a hen's backside.

The silence became embarrassing.

Elford coughed and smiled: 'We were just agreeing how well it went this morning, weren't we? Mrs Pritchett was saying how the choir appreciated a good lead.'

Kate and Mrs Griffiths smiled at each other. They both knew Mr Elford was lying: so for that matter did everyone else in the room. What Mrs Griffiths' smile said was that the organ had forced the choir out of its habitual funereal pace. The congregation had had to struggle to keep up.

Mrs Walters and Mrs Griffiths rose to their feet like a

double act. No time for Elford to introduce anyone else. Two tall, well-dressed men – middle-aged father and son – came sharply to heel. Walters or Griffiths? And once they were moving, the two or three others had to abandon ship too. A sweet-faced old woman smiled and said something, but her Birmingham – no, not Birmingham – accent was so strong Kate couldn't understand. Two elderly men, one as straight as the other was bowed, shook her briefly by the hand. Lastly, a strong-shouldered young man grinned and said, 'Paul Taylor.'

That gin seemed a long time ago.

She followed them all out into the hall, wondering how to tell Elford that she wasn't leaving with the others without offending them. In the event – so promptly she might have been listening for the right moment – Maz appeared.

'Kate, could you have just one more look at your patient? And Paul, if you go off without seeing the kids, there'll be hell to pay.' She smiled equally at the others. 'Sorry I couldn't join you earlier. There was a bit of domestic crisis. Lots of blood. Kate saved yet another visit to casualty. I think we should take up residence there, don't you? Tim last week, Lynn the week before that.'

Probably before they knew it, the others were smiled outside.

Paul turned to Kate: 'What's been going on?'

'Just an incident with an vegetable peeler. Nothing major.'

'Major enough,' Maz said, coming back into the hall and dithering. 'Rain any moment. Won't be too many at the evening service, I should think. And my poor Giles has prepared a knock-out sermon.'

'He can always recycle it,' Paul said. 'How major? They're my flesh and blood, Maz!'

'Let's just say that there's still the same amount of flesh but rather less blood, in Jenny at least,' Kate said.

'What –?' He frowned, apparently more stressed than Maz had been.

Maz laughed. 'Kate flew in like Superwoman. Giles, come

and kiss Jenny better. And – both of you – remember that a bandage is a fashion item.'

Giles' shirt was spattered with rain. 'Why do people always find it necessary to talk when they get outside?'

'Because they've got coats on. Come on, all of you. The table's laid, the soup's bubbling and I'm afraid the lamb will dry out.'

Kate discovered over the soup – carrot, but with something extra – that Paul was Maz's brother. They were a striking looking pair, though neither had the classic good looks of Giles. The children were seraphic-looking: Kate hoped they wouldn't behave like little Lord Fauntleroys. Lynn was the oldest: she'd just taken her eleven plus.

'I'd no idea such an exam still existed!'

'It's alive and kicking in Birmingham, all right. All the bright kids are creamed off so what they call comprehensives are really –'

'OK, Paul. It's my day for sermons, not yours,' Giles said. 'Any more meat anyone? No? Does this mean we shall have one of your cold lamb curries, love?'

'Are you a teacher, Paul?' Kate asked. She liked people with passions.

'I'm in FE. Further education. So we see the effect on the kids of this so-called comprehensive education. It's no more comprehensive than – OK, Giles. What about you, Kate? How do you earn a crust?'

How would his expression change when she told him about her job? Sometimes she would pussy-foot: 'I work for the police.' Or she could aim to shock: 'I'm a detective.' But whatever she said, a glimmer of fear? suspicion? challenge, even? flashed momentarily in the questioner's eyes. This time she went for the middle ground: 'I'm in the CID. Based in the city centre.' And she could have sworn she saw fear in Paul's eyes. Just for an instant. Less. Within a second they were interested, amused, even. And she knew he'd come out with the line about not expecting to see good-looking women like her in uniform.

He did.

'I'm not in uniform. Plain clothes.' As she was sure he knew. 'Come on,' she laughed, 'you must have seen *The Bill* often enough.'

Maz, laughing with her, shook her head. 'To be honest, Kate, I doubt if he ever watches TV. He's doing something every night of the week.'

Giles nodded. 'He's a bastion of the Boys' Brigade apart from anything else.'

'Boys' Brigade? You're a bit grown up for that, surely.' He'd deserved that after his silly quip.

'People often find themselves making a lifetime commitment,' Giles said gently. 'You join when you're a kid for the uniform. It gives you somewhere to go and people to meet when you're in your teens. Many people want to repay what others have done for them.'

'I was unclubbable,' Kate said.

'It's odd you've joined the Fuzz then,' Paul said. 'I'd have thought that thrived on comradeship. Or is it throve? All mates together.'

'True. But we don't have to work for badges! And I thought I was too musical in those days – a bit too snobby for the Girls' Brigade Band. Maybe I'd have enjoyed it.'

'Funny,' Maz said. 'I hated it too. But Paul lived for it. Even stayed in when he was at university. And Tim won't join, but Jenny can't wait till she's eight and old enough, can you, love?'

'Boring kids' stuff,' Tim muttered. 'Can we get down, now, Mummy? I want to do some more work on my train set.'

'If you'll say grace first.' Giles folded his hands, and lowered his eyes.

Tim stood. 'Thank you, God, for the really bad food and Mummy's wicked cooking. Amen.'

★

So why had she told Maz she was driving? She'd walked, hadn't she? Why hadn't she simply said she didn't like to drink too much at midday? Other people said that, made cryptic references to the yard arm. Why had she lied?

'Can I give you a lift?' Paul asked, after their third coffee.

'She's got her own car, love. Where have you parked?'

Deep breath time. Truth time.

'You get so used to people offering you booze,' she began, 'you have to say something. Automatic. At least I didn't say not while I was on duty!'

'That's my usual line,' Giles said. 'But I usually get offered cups of tea. Stewed tea.'

'You're lucky. I get to make endless cups of tea while people wait for you. A minister's wife could get GNVQ'd in tea making.'

'To return to my original question,' said Paul, 'can I offer you a lift?'

'I'm six hundred yards down the road, but if you're going that way, yes please.'

They said very little – hardly had time, to be honest – but as he parked, Paul said, 'I know this is a bit of cheek – I mean, I hardly know you – but I wonder if you're busy in the evenings?'

Kate could feel herself blushing: this was turning into a cliché. Hell! Had Maz set this up? She said coolly, 'It depends how busy the squad is. It's frantic at the moment.' That sounded too equivocal. But she could hardly tell him she'd lost her man and didn't want to be cheered up the way every red-blooded man would want to cheer her up.

'Well, it might not be too many evenings. It's just that my lads need to study the community for their badges, and it'd be good to get someone from the police to talk.'

'OK. Give me some dates and I'll see if I can fix it. Just me or a number of officers?' Thank goodness she hadn't snubbed him.

'Just you, I should think. For a start, at least.'

They consulted diaries, found some spare evenings, closed the deal. And then there was a polite goodbye.

At least she'd have something to tell Aunt Cassie.

Chapter Five

Bloody car! It sat there on the road outside her house declaring as clearly as if it could speak that this was a nasty, damp Monday morning and it was damned if it was going into work. Kate had tried everything she knew to make it start. And now there wasn't even time to call the RAC.

Changing her jacket – already soaked through by the thin, vicious drizzle – for a raincoat, no time even to button it, she ran down to the High Street and the buses. Seven-forty-five! The traffic heading for town was solid as far as she could see. Ignoring the pedestrian lights, she dodged between cars and hurtled to the stop with the shortest queue. Two buses went past full. A third, its windows streaming inside and out, crept at last to the stop and took aboard more than it should; but in weather like this no one was going to moan about overcrowding, especially when the driver, already pulling out, stopped to let on a man with a heavy limp. Most people flashed passes; she had to fumble for her fare. She'd forgotten about paying on entry, assumed that she'd be given change, then remembered that Birmingham's one-man buses didn't rise to such sophistication. At least she'd only lost a few pence.

Better find a rail to hang on.

A sudden jerk flung her staggering along the aisle. The bus was moving forwards, was it? She grabbed the back of a seat more firmly. The conversation from its occupants – two teenage lads who should be offering the man with a stick a seat – was about how they'd scored with their women last night. She tapped the nearer one on the shoulder and pointed to the lame man. She half expected to be sworn at; but the lad got up promptly. The man nodded his thanks. She shifted her grip. Not so bad, after all, these Brummies.

'. . . did think about calling the police, but then, what could you say?'

Kate's ears pricked. She leant forward to hear better.

'I mean, it's not against the law, is it, to buy a house and not live there? I mean, they keep it nice enough, no doubt about that, at least since we complained.'

'How did you complain if there's no one living there?'

Two middle-aged women, both smartly dressed. Gloves and handbags were leather.

'Put a note through the door, of course. Saying cut your grass or we'll report you to the council. That soon worked. There's this couple – oh, quite old – come along every week and mow the lawn. They've planted a little hedge, and made a flowerbed. They seem to be doing something at the back, only the angle of the garden means I can't see.'

'So what's the problem?'

'It's just – well, you do hear cars at night. Late at night. And sometimes there's a car drives away just as I'm coming home.'

'What do the other residents think? I mean, it's a cul-de-sac.' This woman sounded as intrigued as Kate herself.

'Well, no one else knows anything, do they? We've all got jobs. And the houses don't overlook each other. The front doors are at the side, if you see what I mean. And they've all got trellises. I mean, you expect your privacy if you pay that sort of price.'

'Quite. But it's lovely being just a little bit nosy. Have you ever been to the door or anything? Just for a little look?'

Say yes! Please say yes!

'Well, I did do the Christian Aid envelopes. You know, it's a funny thing, but people don't give much, do they? All those nice big cars and most people only gave a pound coin.'

You're telling me! You try tin-rattling outside Sainsbury's on a wet Saturday.

'Perhaps they give with standing orders or something. You know if you promise to pay for a certain number of years, they get some sort of tax benefit? That's what we did for Oxfam. Covenant, that's what it's called.'

Come on! Get on with it! I want to hear what happened when you went to the door. Please!

The bus was now moving quite briskly. Any moment now, of course, they might get off. She'd get off with them, if necessary.

'And there's this advert on Classic FM about a charity card. That man with the nice voice – you know.'

Don't let her drift from the point. Please!

'I know. Got such a worried face. Though maybe that's the parts he plays. Fox, is it? Edward Fox?'

'That's right. Now what was he in?'

'Wasn't it something historical? Goodness me, it's nearly my stop! Pam: you've still not told me – what happened when you went to that house? Did an ogre open the door?'

'No one opened the door. No one. I was sure someone was in. I could hear this funny whirring noise. Only very faint. But when I pressed the bell again, it stopped. And there was a tiny noise as if someone was going to speak and changed his mind. Do you know, I nearly – well, to be honest, I did. I leaned down to the letter box. If anyone had seen me they'd have thought I was calling in. But I was trying to have a look.'

'Really? Quickly!' The woman was gathering herself up to move. 'What did you see?'

The first woman waited a dramatic moment. 'Nothing! Nothing at all. Someone had pinned heavy felt across. There!'

'Here I am. See you tomorrow, Pam. Go and ring that bell again!' The woman edged down the bus, pressing the Stop button as she went.

Pam. Right, Kate would have to press Pam for further details. She shifted her grip to slide into the vacant seat. And was hurled forwards, staggering to a halt right by the driver.

'What the hell –?' And then she saw. The car in front had hit a pedestrian. 'Better let me off,' she said. 'I'm a police officer.'

★

It hadn't taken long for a Panda to turn up, in response to the call from her mobile phone. The ambulance was somewhat slower. Eight-thirty! The bus passengers had poured off. Kate should have intercepted that woman Pam. She knew she should. But she was too busy giving the injured pedestrian first aid. He'd been hit by one of those wretched bull-bars – were there really wild cattle in the Bull Ring to confront innocent motorists? – so there might well be internal damage. Bloody things. Why didn't someone have the guts to ban them?

At last, leaving everything to the experts, she looked for another bus herself. She was going to be late. Very late. She phoned in. She didn't recognise the voice at the other end but he promised to explain to Cope. There was no way she would risk irritating – what was it they called the Governor up here? – that was it, the Gaffer.

She'd been busy on the computer for fifteen minutes when the room went quiet around her. She looked up: no, it wasn't Selby creeping up behind her. He was safe behind a pile of files, fingering an angry blackhead on his forehead.

'Good heavens, if it isn't little Miss Power, deigning to make an appearance.' It was Cope, his voice awash with sarcasm. 'Well, I'm blessed. And to what do we owe the honour? The Smoke getting too boring for you, is it? Thought you might pop in on your little provincial friends for half an hour before you go and powder your nose in time for luncheon?'

'Sir –'

'Stand up when you're talking to me, Power. That's better.'

She stood fiercely to attention.

He walked behind her. 'What do you call that?'

Something scraped the back of her neck.

'Sir?'

'No, you wouldn't know, would you. It's a neck, Power. A

neck. And in my day women police officers wore their hair in some approximation of neatness. I suppose you la-di-da folk from the Met think you're above such considerations. But we don't here, Power. Oh, I know we're CID, and posh with it, but a neck is still a neck, Power. And it isn't supposed to be covered with hair. Understand?'

'Sir.'

Cope stalked round to face her. She focused two inches above his head.

'And what has her ladyship been doing since she graced us with her presence?'

'Collecting data from STATUS, Sir. And preparing a report.'

'Goodness me. On this pretty little computer? Lap-top, d'you call it? Is it your own, Power?'

'Sir.' It was quicker to type straight on to computer than prepare a hand-written document no one else could read. And all the main frame ones were occupied.

'Dearie me, how very generous of you to bring your own equipment in. And what happens if I pull this plug out, DS Power? What's the word when one of these things packs up?'

'Crashes, Sir?'

'The computer crashes, does it. Dearie me. And crashing would wipe the morning's work, Power?'

'Sir.'

He yanked. Turning to his audience, he concluded, 'Dearie me, how very careless of me. Well, I'm sure you'll be able to do it all again. Well, what the hell are you lot gawping at? Haven't you all got work to do? Or has crime suddenly disappeared from the streets of our city?'

So what bastard hadn't passed on her message? She looked round at her colleagues, thawing after their rigid silence. She'd spoken to a man, which, come to think of it, didn't rule out too many people. A man with a Brummie accent. Half the squad were Brummies.

There was no reading anyone's mind, however, and

she plugged in the computer again and carried on with her work.

'You must wish me in hell.'

She jumped. 'Colin?'

'You asked me to tell Cope you'd be late.'

'I didn't realise it was you: I'd have been friendlier.'

He shrugged. 'Well, it was. And I wrote it down to give it to Cope. Left the note on his desk as a matter of fact.'

'You're saying all that song and dance was a put-up job?'

'Maybe. Or maybe he didn't get the message.'

'Come on, Colin.' It was Selby, yelling across the room. 'We've got work to do, mate. When you've finished peering down Power's tits, that is.'

Colin grinned briefly and was off.

Kate typed hard for another fifteen minutes. Darren still wasn't speaking. When the team questioning him had shown him pictures of ducks they'd met blank amazement. The toy duck they'd bought with the collection money – just the right size for a sad child's arms – had been so inappropriate they'd brought it away and given it to the Children in Need appeal. Kate scribbled a note to herself: *Look up ducks and synonyms for ducks.* She sat and stared at it: it must mean something if the child still shouted it in his sleep. At last she shook her head. It must be safe to get some coffee by now. It must be safe to go a circuitous route to the machine, via Selby's end of the room. Specifically, via his waste bin. She dropped her handkerchief. Yes, there it was, nestling between an empty condom packet and a final demand, a screwed up note with her name just visible. She scooped it up, crumpling it in the tissue. Might as well wait until she'd got safely to the ladies', but she'd take bets on what it was. Colin's note to Cope.

This time when Harvey met her in the corridor, he did not look inquiringly at her, but gestured her with a curt jerk of his head into his office. This time there was no question of an armchair and tea. She stood in front of his desk.

He withdrew to the other side. 'One way to lose the approval of your colleagues is to grass them up. Another is to slack. That loses the sympathy of management. Today you were well over an hour late, and since your colleagues are working many hours of unpaid overtime, for you to come swanning in without a word of apology to DI Cope or myself is going to endear you to no one. Well?'

'Do you want an explanation or an excuse, Sir?'

'I certainly don't want excuses.'

'I won't tell you my car wouldn't start, then, and the traffic was solid from Sainsbury's to the traffic lights in Moseley.'

He grimaced. 'You'd have been stuck in that in your car.'

'Rat run, Sir.'

'And your explanation?' He sat down and motioned her to a chair. She chose the hard upright one.

'An RTA. The vehicle in front of the bus hit a young male pedestrian. I called for assistance and gave first aid until a mobile arrived. I phoned in, Sir, as soon as I realised how late I was going to be – obviously the accident caused even more of a hold-up and there weren't any buses. And taxis don't seem to cruise round the suburbs – they wait for you to find them.'

'You phoned in? DI Cope had no note, neither did I.'

'I think the note may have got mislaid, Sir. Or mistaken for rubbish.' She dug in her pocket for the note. She smoothed it out but didn't pass it him until he held out his hand.

'Thanks. That's Colin's writing. He's usually reliable.'

'Sir.'

'Shit!' Harvey balled it, hurled it hard at his litter bin. 'Another merry jape from someone. Well?'

She smiled her official smile. 'No comment, Sir.'

'OK. So what's this about your slacking over the computer work? I hear you took half an hour to do what one of the pros. would have done in ten minutes.' He wanted to believe her: she could tell by the softening of his voice.

She took a risk. 'Well, I'm not a pro. If I were, I'd be making a fuss about the height of the desk, the height of the chair, the glare from the screen and the fact you haven't offered to pay for an annual eye test, which it is your legal obligation to do under European law. I'm not sure I'm having adequate breaks, either.' She allowed herself to relax against the hard back of the chair.

There was no doubt, he was suppressing a smile. Then his mouth hardened again. 'Just because a senior officer rebukes you there's no excuse for going slow.'

'Sir —' She bit her lip and stopped.

'Yes?'

'Where did you get the idea that I hadn't done much this morning?'

'You can't expect me to tell you that.'

'There could have been a little glitch, Sir, around the time DI Cope was speaking to me. Someone accidentally pulled the cable on the computer.'

'Ah. So you had to retype stuff you'd had wiped. That's interesting.'

'As a matter of fact, Sir, I didn't touch the stuff I'd done earlier. I just carried on.'

By now his eyes were twinkling in response to what she knew was a gleam in her own. She wasn't about to admit to sulking, to refusing to re-do something some idiot had wiped.

Harvey leaned forward, resting his arms on the table. 'You're going to make this all clear, aren't you, Kate?' But his smile broke out.

She smiled back, and couldn't prevent her dimples joining in. 'Sir, it works on rechargeable batteries, so nothing happens when you pull out the mains. In any case, there's an element in the program to cater for exactly the sort of circumstance we might have had this morning. It saves every thirty seconds automatically, and prepares automatic back-up files. I keep a back-up disk, too, as it happens, safe in my desk.'

'I'm not sure that the word "safe" is appropriate with all these little accidents happening. I'd like to suggest you keep back-up disks here. In my room. In fact, here in my desk drawer.'

'Thank you, Sir. Shall I continue to keep copies in my drawer?'

He looked at her very hard. 'Are we talking bait, here?'

Kate took a deep breath. 'There's a very fine line, isn't there, between horseplay and bullying. As you said yourself, Sir, one day there may be other people involved.' She realised how angry she was: 'Do you know what really makes me mad, Sir? That something *could* have been wiped, this morning, something really valuable. When there's a bastard out there doing that to innocent kids, and some pillock's too interested in playing Hitler to worry about holding up our work!'

He nodded. 'Exactly. I wondered how long it'd take you to work that out. OK. Keep a record. Not in your desk.' For a moment, as if he, too, were contemplating the possible consequences of what they were doing, he sat silent, grim. At last he stood up, smiling: 'Tea or coffee, Kate?'

'Tea would be lovely, Graham, so long as it isn't that liquid compost heap.'

Chapter Six

'Come on, our kid, a bit of a walk'll do you good,' Colin said, gathering up Kate's raincoat and throwing it at her.

'But I was so late in —'

'And have worked bloody hard since. Plus having a couple of bollockings. Come on. Won't take no for an answer.'

Only one bollocking: but she wouldn't admit that to anyone, no even Colin. 'So long as we can take in Halford's — maybe it's my spark-plugs, the battery's new — and find somewhere to buy a Polaroid camera. My great aunt wants photos of work in progress.'

'You won't find a Halford's. Not in the centre. But there's one by your bus-stop, virtually, in Kings Heath. Spitting distance from where you interrupted the rape. Any news on that yet?'

'Not a dickie bird. Hey, the sun's shining!'

They set off, ducking through underpasses.

'They're planning to turn all this lot round,' Colin said apologetically. 'Ruined Brum, they did, back in the sixties. Worshipped the great god Car. Cars whiz round up there, while we're sent Down Below. And low-life like that pester you.' He stopped long enough to stare hard at a beggar. 'Come on, mate. On your way, now! Silly bastard,' he added, as the young man scrabbled to his feet, 'he must know half West Midlands Police use this route to the shops. Not all as soft-hearted as me.'

'So much for care in the community. I mean,' she added, as if she needed to justify herself, 'no one in his right mind would want to huddle up in this wind tunnel with nothing but an empty styrofoam cup for company.'

'Nasty cough he'd got, too. Tell you what, I know this guy in the Sally Army: I'll get on the blower to him. Come on, this tunnel for the fresh air!'

Call this a city centre? She'd forgotten it was as small as this. OK, it had a lot of the shops she was used to. But the shopping area was so small they could get to the far side and back in a lunch-time. More like a market town. Where were the streets and streets of top-quality shops of the West End? She'd never needed to shop here for decent clothes before — young women supposed to be care assistants weren't expected to have enough money to dress well! Colin, now, he always dressed with — yes, with elegance. Perhaps she could ask him, without seeming to insult his native city.

'Clothes? Well, if you want smart but not trendy, there's all the shops-within-shops at Rackhams. Or if you want something more individual, we could high-tail it out to Kenilworth or Leamington. Have a nice girlie time,' he said, his voice suddenly camp. 'Or we could go to Merry Hell.'

'Sorry?'

'Merry Hill, dear. Out of town shopping. A whopping mall built on the site of Round Oak Steelworks. Heavy industry all round there, once. Now we Black Country lads have to look elsewhere for work. Mind you, duckie, I don't see me in a steelworks, for God's sake.' Camp again.

'So the Black Country —'

'Is just outside Brum. Come on, you remember: it's the birthplace of the Industrial Revolution, et cetera et cetera. And yours truly. And if you ever call me a Brummie it'll be the end of a lovely friendship!'

'I'm afraid they're a bit pale. I haven't got the flash sorted out yet.' Kate held a wad of Polaroid photos at what she hoped was the right distance for her aunt to focus on them. Aunt Cassie probably wouldn't be able to hold them herself.

'They're very small, aren't they? Don't they make them bigger?' The old woman pushed at them petulantly. She must be in a lot of pain.

It was a good job she'd come, though she could have thought of a thousand ways she'd have preferred to spend the evening. None of them to do with Kings Heath or Birmingham, come to think of it. Still, at least Halford's had come up with the goods, and the car had started first try.

'This is the size the camera churns them out. Have you ever seen one working? Look, here it is. I'll take a photo, just to show you how it works.' This was a ploy. She'd never had a photo of Cassie, who declared herself to be too ugly now to take pictures of.

'Hold your horses, young lady. How much do the photographs cost?'

Kate shook her head.

'Come, you must have bought a film. How much does it work out for each frame?'

'About a pound, I suppose.'

'And you're going to waste a pound just to show me how it works. Well, we know how long you'll keep your money.' Then one of the photos caught her eye. 'Is that my bedroom?'

'That's right. That's all new plaster. I've kept the grate because it's so elegant. I shall keep the others, too.'

'So what won't you keep?'

Perhaps talking would keep Cassie's mind off her pain.

'The airing cupboard. The central heating engineers said I ought to have a different sort of boiler, the sort that gives instant hot water without having to store it.'

'This is this new sort: I've read about them. Much more efficient. Good. And this is – what?'

'The bathroom. They're fitting the new bath tomorrow. I hope. I'm going for a white suite.'

'I thought you might have one of these new ones – they have such pretty colours,' she added wistfully. 'I always wanted a champagne one. Tiles?'

'Here.' Kate dug in her bag. 'I thought I'd have a border

of these, and one or two of this one scattered about. What do you think?'

'I think you chose a cheap bath and washbasin so you could have expensive tiles. That's what I think, young lady. And I wish you'd remember, you don't need to penny pinch. I've been working it out, the police must be going to pay you damages for letting your young man get himself killed.'

'No. It'll go to his children and –'

The old woman stared at her. 'And?'

'And his wife.'

'I thought they were divorced.'

'Separated. But she didn't want a divorce, so it takes five years, you see.' Kate writhed with embarrassment. She'd tried to conceal the worst of the truth from Cassie. She was old enough to be shocked, after all. Except – and the women exchanged a wry grin – hadn't Cassie been the Other Woman for years upon years.

'And you're going to let her have the lot?'

'What would you have done?' She'd never spoken to her like this, as an equal.

'Exactly what you're doing. After all, you had the pleasure of his company when he was alive. Except you seem to have supported him. Arthur supported me. Handsomely.' Her smile was at more than the hefty diamonds on her knuckles. 'I think you young women are worse off than you realise. I wish you could find a rich lover, dear. Have plenty of money. Enjoy spending it.'

Do what I say, not do what I did. Poor thing. Did she ever spend anything? But she couldn't ask her that, not straight out. Not yet.

'Honestly, I liked these so much –' Kate touched the tiles – 'I thought I'd have to have them even if it meant having a white suite: I don't think anything else would go.'

'Hmm. Now, there was some wet rot in the window –'

'There was wet rot in quite a number of the windows. So I thought I'd have them all ripped out and have double-glazing. Except –'

'Except you can't afford it. Talk to Mr Whatshisname, dear. Have some more out of the pot.' Aunt Cassie gestured expansively. 'Kate – they're slipping!'

Kate grabbed at the tiles and caught them.

'Put them back in that bag of yours. Don't want them broken.'

She did as she was told. 'No, Aunt Cassie. It's not money I need. It's advice. You've got that lovely Victorian window in the front bay – all that curved wood. I don't want to touch that. But the double-glazing people are saying I'll regret it if I don't.' No, she had no intention of letting them touch it: it was a matter of seeing how her aunt was reacting to the changes.

'Is the wood still sound?'

'Sound as a bell.'

'For goodness' sake leave it, then. Let them do the rest and leave that. Oh, and I'd always thought a door from the living room into the back garden would be useful. Let in more light. You'll find it's very dark in the winter. Humph, it is the winter, isn't it? You lose all sense of time and season in this place. They've got a room with special high-intensity lighting. They cart you down there and you're supposed to sit and chat with the others. Stop you getting depressed. The lights. Not the others. My God, there are some poor old dears here. Quite doo-lally and wee-ing themselves all the time. Which reminds me – is there any smell of pee in the entrance hall yet?'

'But you can't possibly live in a house in this condition,' Maz declared, her eyes widening in horror. She had arrived just as Kate squeezed her car into a space an inch too short for it. If what Kate really wanted was a hot bath and an early night, the next thing on her wish list might have been a friendly person dropping in.

'It'll be all right tomorrow: I shall be able to have a bath again.'

'It may be all right one day, but it certainly won't be tomorrow. Oh, Kate, why didn't you tell me? And come round to the manse for a bath, for goodness' sake.'

'There's nothing to tell. After all, I'm not here all that much. Most of the men come in when I've gone, leave before I get home. All I can see is the progress they've made. Which is considerable.'

'My God, what was it like when they started?' Maz looked around for somewhere to sit.

Kate grabbed a curtain she'd not yet consigned to the skip and rubbed it across a chair. It did little more than reorganise the plaster and brick dust that gave everything a dull orange sheen.

'It was the sort of place the National Trust should have taken over. Hardly any alterations to the original. Which is why part of me feels so guilty. It ought to be preserved. But I can't live in a museum. So what do I do?'

'Very much what you are doing, I should think. But don't let them double glaze that front door.'

'But the lead's breaking up, and some of the glass has gone. And leaded lights really are invitations to burglars.'

'Have it restored. There's a woman in Moseley who'll do it. Oh, it's an inner door, love. Keep a pit-bull terrier in that vestibule, if you insist, but save the door.'

'OK. If you can find this woman's address. Fancy a drink?' It was out before she could catch it. It was like in the old days, when you could have a glass of wine with a friend and not turn a hair. These days, it would be tough keeping it to one glass.

'Thought you'd never ask.'

'What'll you have? Not that there's much choice. Scotch or Irish malt?'

Maz raised her eyebrows a fraction. 'Hard stuff only? Irish, please. No water.'

Kate poured two. She gave Maz the larger. 'I'll bring my wine up when I've had the cellar painted! Actually, there's a cold shelf in the pantry I've earmarked for it. Here's to Aunt Cassie.'

Maz seemed to be about to say something. Instead, she took a deep breath. 'It was about Aunt Cassie I came. The Girls' Brigade have to do some sort of community service – visiting the sick or elderly. Or both. D'you think she'd like a visitor on a regular basis?'

Kate ran through several scenarios. One involved her asking her aunt. She dismissed that instantly. One involved a uniformed little girl turning up. She rejected that as child abuse. The third seemed a possibility. 'Tell you what, why don't you ask her? She's the most compos mentis person I know.' That way Aunt Cassie would get to meet Maz: she rather thought they'd both enjoy it.

The bathroom looked really pretty when she got in on Tuesday evening, apart from the fact that the tiler had managed to get one of the border tiles upside down. He looked at it in disbelief: 'Tell you what,' he said at last. 'I can't get it out, can I? So what I'll do is do you a freebie on the shower door.'

'Shower door?'

'Much neater than a curtain. Nice Victorian design. Save your carpet.' He pointed. 'Stop water splashing on your loo.'

'How much?'

'Fit it free. Got one or two in stock. Or you could go and have a look in Manjit Bros. That's were I get me materials from.'

'So would they be any different from yours?'

'I got mine from him.'

What a surprise. But perhaps a shower door would be better than a curtain. With a slight suspicion she was being conned she nodded. 'When?'

'Tomorrow evening.'

'Better be careful how I shower tonight, then!'

'Ooh, no. Can't use this for twelve hours at least. Twenty-four's better. See you tomorrow, Miss.'

She saw him out cheerfully enough. She managed to hold back the tears till she'd shut the front door and the leaded vestibule door. She made it as far as the stairs. And then she cried.

When at last she could see, when she could hold down the sobs and stop her hand shaking for long enough, she staggered to the kitchen. She didn't care which bottle. So long as there was enough in it to shut out the filthy house, the foul furniture and the fact she couldn't have a shower. Half a glass of Jameson's – that would do.

The phone. At first she meant to let it ring. Then she thought of Aunt Cassie, and snatched up the receiver.

'Hi! It's Paul. Paul Taylor. Is this a good time for me to pop round and have a word about the Brigade?'

'Not particularly. The house – bit of a mess.' She couldn't tell if her voice was slurred. All she could manage was not to sound sorry for herself.

Perhaps she didn't manage that.

'We'll go out for a drink, then.'

'No – honestly. I'm –'

'Kate – there's something wrong, isn't there? I'm on my way.'

Chapter Seven

Paul Taylor's shoulders filled the tiny vestibule: she had to back into the front room – she'd decided she'd call it her dining room – to let him through the equally tiny hall.

'Careful – where there isn't wet paint there's wet plaster. Go on through to the kitchen. I've just made some coffee.' She followed him, still talking. 'Would you like a cup? Only it'll have to be black: the builders have finished my milk. It probably wouldn't have kept till tomorrow anyway – as you can see, I don't have a fridge at the moment.'

'Kate – are you telling me you're *living* in these conditions?'

'Camping out. Oh, I know it's dreadful now, but they're laying the new floor tomorrow, and skimming the walls too, with a bit of luck, and then I can think about such luxuries as sinks and working surfaces.'

'As opposed to a camping stove on a windowsill. Goodness, woman, are you off your head? The police could surely have found you temporary accommodation. Or what about renting a place? Or B and B with a colleague?'

If only he'd shut up. He was right, of course, on all counts. She couldn't justify even to herself her decision to stay put. It didn't make sense. She was living out of suitcases anyway. Moving the suitcases to somewhere free of builder's dust, somewhere she could have a bath and boil a kettle – why on earth not?

'I didn't know it would be so bad,' she said at last. 'And I rather thought if I was around it might make them get a move on. But some of them work very strange hours. The plasterer never turns up before half four.'

'Doing foreigners. You know, moonlighting. No, I'll give the coffee a miss, I think. Look, go and put some things in a bag. Now. I'm taking you to Maz's. For tonight. You can argue with her. Go on.'

Too woozy from the whisky to argue, she went back to the living room and shoved tomorrow's undies and shirt into a carrier. Make-up. Shoes.

The car? She might be well over the limit. Wouldn't want to risk her licence. Not to mention her job. Get up early and walk back here to collect it, or go by bus. At last – the coffee might just be working.

'What's the rest of the place like?' Paul's question made her jump.

'Be my guest. Have a look round. But be careful – there are floor-boards up.'

She followed him up the stairs. 'The bathroom's nearly ready – but it's very small. I can't give you a conducted tour.'

He shrugged and went in. 'Hey, no door.'

'Didn't you notice – no doors anywhere! I'm having them dipped to get rid of the old paint. Then I shall wax them.' Her first positive statement. She must be sobering up.

'Lovely tiles. Oh, Kate,' Paul emerged. 'If the rest of the house ends up looking as good as this, you can be really proud of yourself. Which is your bedroom?'

'The big front one's nice. But with the school opposite it could be noisy. And Aunt Cassie's bedroom suite fits the middle bedroom so nicely – that's it, that pile of wood there. They had to take it apart to get it out so they could plaster. I suppose that was how they got it in in the first place, in pieces.'

Paul squeezed into the front room. 'It's nice in here,' he called. 'All those trees!'

'And all the mummies in their Volvos delivering their kiddie-winks because they're too little to walk.'

'Can you blame them? These missing kids, these abductions

– that little kid last week. Any news of him, by the way?' He picked his way back towards her.

'He's as well as can be expected,' she said. 'But no more than that.'

'What had they done to him?'

'Enough,' she said shortly. 'OK, Paul, there's only the end bedroom – the one that overlooks what claims to be a garden. I shall use it as my office. Careful! The floor's only staying up with faith and friction – they've not put the RSJ in underneath yet!'

She'd better stay where she was: walking along joists would be a worse test of being sober than walking the old white line. Penalty for failure – a rapid descent through the kitchen ceiling.

Even Paul slipped. Struggling for his balance, he dropped the leather-bound organiser he'd been carrying, more like some business executive than a down-to-earth college lecturer. Except down to earth was what he'd be if he wasn't careful.

'Wait – I'll get something we can pull it with. Hang on!' She started back down the corridor.

'No! It's OK. I've got it.'

Nearly, at least. It wouldn't do his jacket much good, lying across the floor like that.

'There!' He straightened, triumphant. 'Hey, there's something else, too.' He burrowed again. 'I can just reach it.'

At last he straightened.

'Are you OK?'

'Apart from filthy. Now, what have we here?'

'Hang on: I thought I heard something – did you drop anything?'

He flicked a quick eye over his organiser. 'Don't think so. It was probably the last of your rats abandoning a sinking ship. Come on, let's look at this.'

'The light's better downstairs.'

'You mean the lights *work* downstairs! Come on!' He flourished an oiled-silk package.

'Let's use my sleeping bag as a table, in case there's anything breakable.'

They knelt. He passed it to her. She untied the tape. Inside the silk was a little wash-leather purse.

'Well, you can't break those,' she said, her voice as prosaic as possible.

'Diamonds!' he breathed. 'Must be a small fortune.'

She pushed them back into the purse, running her finger tip along the stitching of the sleeping bag to make sure none was trapped. 'Let's say, they should keep Cassie in that nursing home a few more months. I wonder why she had cut diamonds: I'd have expected uncut ones.'

'I wouldn't have recognised them, then. You don't feel tempted – he straightened, and stood slowly – 'to help yourself to a couple – just to pay for the decorating and some decent furniture?'

He was joking. Of course he was joking. She'd better respond in kind. 'Save me having to go in for the Lottery, wouldn't it? I could do with a new car, too.' The purse was small enough to fit into the front pocket of her jeans. She shoved it down as far as it would go.

It was only when Paul let them into the Manse and called out, that she realised they'd never phoned Maz or Giles to find out how they'd feel about a stranger camping with them. She'd insisted on bringing her sleeping bag: she wouldn't cause them any extra washing and it meant they shouldn't feel guilty about offering her a sofa if there were no spare bed. Damn it, even a clean floor would be welcome, provided they could share their hot running water.

Maz appeared from the back of the house, a pencil stuck behind her ear. Giles came downstairs, in his dressing gown. Paul explained briefly – no doubt he'd tell them about Kate's boozing another time.

'Why on earth didn't you say? I could have bundled you up there and then!'

Kate shook her head like a child caught out in something stupid.

'Well, thank goodness Paul had more sense than I did. Come on.' She hugged her, not wincing despite the smell of whiskey which must have knocked her over.

They went into what appeared a well-rehearsed routine,

Giles to make cocoa and put the kettle on for a hot-water bottle, Maz to find bedclothes – the sleeping bag was vetoed. Well, they wouldn't want plaster dust on their mattresses for one thing, Kate supposed: there was a little sprinkling on the hall carpet where she'd parked it. Smiling, and kissing her on the cheek, Paul made his farewells.

She was halfway down the mug of cocoa before she remembered the purse. Giles was sitting at the kitchen table with her, Maz just dashing out of the door.

'Maz!' she called.

She stopped, halfway out. 'Is it important, love? Only it's Giles's night on duty on the domestic front, and I'm on the computer. Got to get this done for tomorrow.'

'Two minutes. But I want you both to see this. Paul and I found it under the floorboards. Have you got a sheet of paper? Yes, kitchen towel will do.' There was hardly any space: homework books jostled a pile of books. *Henry the Green Engine, Gordon the Blue Engine.* And there were some adult ones, all about locomotives.

'Tim's,' said Giles, as if there were any need for explanation. 'Just mad about railways. And he's too old for these and too young for these. Sorry.'

She undid the purse and tipped.

They both gasped. And sat at the table.

'Glory be! How much is that lot worth?' Giles asked. 'At least a new set of toilets, I should think.'

Maz snorted. 'Gold-plated loo seats! Any idea how many you've got, Kate?'

'Trust an accountant to want to know that sort of thing,' Giles said. 'OK, let's count.'

Out loud, like children, they chanted. 'Twenty-one. Twenty-two! Twenty-three! Twenty-four! *Twenty-five!*'

Kate pushed them around, watching the light play on them. 'Thank God Cassie's got all her marbles.' Realising what she'd said, she added, 'If not all her diamonds. She'll have far more idea of what to do with them than I've got. Hey, have you got a safe here, Giles? For collection money?'

'What sort of ministry do you think we have here? OK, we have a small one. I'll go and pop it in, shall I? Come on, I'd rather you watched me – the thought of gold-plated loos really does tempt me.'

'If,' Maz said, following too, 'you really did want to do a heist, can you think of three more unlikely criminals? A detective, an accountant and a lawyer turned Baptist minister. I should think with credentials like that we could get away with murder. How much – seriously – would they be worth?'

Did Giles flick a glance at her ringless finger? There'd never been enough money for anything like that, had there?

'How much do we insure your engagement ring for, love? Three and a half? We bought that when I was in practice, Kate. Every time we get a major bill I wonder when we'll have to hock it. Well, those stones were about the same size as yours. So, assuming the insurance value is slightly inflated, let's say each stone is worth a thousand pounds. Twenty-five times a thousand pounds is –'

'Twenty-five thousand. Even you should be able to work that out, Giles.'

'Hmm. Another year in the nursing home,' Kate said.

'Let's hope she lives to enjoy it,' Maz said.

'Or enjoys living it,' Giles amended, thoughtfully.

The safe was under the carpet in the room Maz had originally emerged from. Her computer was in screen-saver mode, but a pile of papers lay on the printer – a recent laser. The carpet was less new, and the curtains frankly shabby. But the chair was multi-adjustable and the desk looked more solid than the average flat-pack. The filing cabinets looked as if they meant business, too.

As did the safe.

'No,' said Kate. 'Don't let anyone see that combination. Even me.' Seeing their blank looks, she added, 'It has been known for the odd police officer to be bent!'

Chapter Eight

'Nothing,' Kate said, dropping her report apologetically on Graham Harvey's desk. 'Abso-bloody-lutely nothing. I've tried every database I could think of and then some. And – whatever field I've tried – there's nothing to suggest Chummie's on any register with any sort of form. So I reckon we must have a nasty new kid on the block.'

Graham leaned forward to pick up the thin sheaf of papers. 'These things happen,' he said, ruefully.

'All those hours wasted!'

'Nothing in police work is ever wasted. Surely you know that. All those names, all that form – it'll be in another computer now: yours!' He put his fingers on his forehead and smiled. 'Locked away until you need it. And look at it another way, you could have spent all that time on the streets in pouring rain and still come up with nothing. Next thing you'll say you'd rather have done that.'

'Well, since you ask me –' Kate grinned.

'All in good time. Tell me, are all your disks in place? Nothing gone walkabout?'

She looked him straight in the eye. 'No disks. But a notebook – no, anyone can pick up someone else's book by mistake.'

'True. And anyone can return it when they find someone else's writing in it. I shouldn't be having to ask you these questions: you should be volunteering the information, Kate.'

'As soon as I have proof positive. If ever I have proof positive, perhaps I should say.'

'I'm terribly afraid it'll be the former. OK.' He looked at his watch, half standing. 'You're looking pretty washed out. Are you all right?'

'Trouble with the house. No, delays, more like. So when they offered to let me sleep at the Manse, I jumped at the chance. I was daft not to ask earlier. Or go into digs or whatever.'

'Time for a pint before you go home?'

She flicked a glance at her watch. 'I'd love one.' God knew she'd like a whisky more. Or would she? Perhaps things were getting better. And she'd have liked a drink with him. Pity she had to add, 'But I'm talking to the chapel Boys' Brigade tonight: you know I've started to play the organ there. They need to know about the police for part of their community badge. The man who runs it's the minister's brother-in-law.' She could feel the excitement rising. 'Actually . . . look, I've got to tell someone, and –'

Graham settled down again. 'Tell someone what?'

Why was he controlling his voice so carefully? She checked the rush, and then let rip: 'I found a cache of diamonds at Cassie's last night! Twenty-five of them – this big!' She held her finger and thumb a centimetre apart. 'Or rather, Paul Taylor did – he's the brother-in-law – he found them. Under a floorboard.'

'My God! So what did you do?'

'Have them locked in the Manse safe. Well, they must be worth twenty-five grand or so. I phoned Cassie. She was quite casual about it. She had a long-standing relationship with someone in the jewellery trade: apparently he wanted to make them into a necklace for her but they had a falling out and by the time they'd made up again they'd forgotten all about the diamonds. Or he had. I'll bet she stashed them for a rainy day and kept mum. At least it'll keep her in that home another year.'

'Is she OK there?'

'Seems to be. I fancy she's running the place, actually.'

Graham laughed grimly: 'Yes, these old folks know a bit about management. My ma-in-law has us all dancing to her tune. But she won't survive on her own much longer. So we're keeping our eyes open for a good place.'

'I'd talk to Cassie, if I were you. She cased the lot before she settled on this one. Applied the pee test!'

'Pee test?'

'If the place smells of pee, you don't want to let her stay there.'

They were still laughing when they left the building. About other things. She couldn't have said what, had anyone cared to ask.

Cassie would have liked her to be a teacher, and had been shocked by her decision to do her Master's and then join the police. But after tonight she was quite sure she'd made the right decision. Paul had been vague about the ages and numbers involved: she'd rather expected thirty teenagers and had ended with twelve kids between ten and thirteen. None had seemed particularly interested, and she didn't know how to woo them. They perked up a little when it came to question time, asking for the gruesome details of any crimes she'd solved.

'It doesn't work like that,' she laughed. 'All this Morse and Lewis: it's not accurate. We work in teams, everyone dependent on everyone else. We need scene-of-crime officers, computer experts, not just a couple of bright men. Or women.'

They laughed, but weren't convinced. There was a lot of shuffling.

'My goodness, it's the big match tonight, isn't it? What time do they finish, Paul?'

He looked grim: 'They're supposed to have their own soccer practice tonight. We're bottom of the league, and I keep trying to get it home to them, watching Aston Villa or whoever isn't the same as training themselves! Trouble is, they've lost their coach, and I'm a rugby man.'

She laughed. 'Well, if they're desperate, I suppose – I've always been keen on soccer . . .'

'So there I was, offering to be their coach!' she said to Colin the next morning. 'They all look so weedy and unco-ordinated. God knows how long it'll take me to knock them into shape.'

'How do you propose to start? God, this coffee's worse than usual. Try some tea.' He slapped the dispenser. It produced a thin stream of muddy water and expired. 'Shit!'

'And when do you propose to start? I'll bring me binoculars, like.' Selby leered at the front of her shirt.

'Tonight. And after chapel on Sunday. Why don't you come along?'

'Fuck that: got better things to do of a Sunday morning.'

'Come on. I'm sure you'd like to see me at work on a big organ.' She turned her back on him: time she was back at her desk. Graham had asked her to read through the transcripts of all the statements, just in case. In case of what she wasn't sure. What she did suspect was that he was still protecting her. The trouble was his paternalism irritated the others. She wanted to pair up with someone, start seeing some action.

On impulse she phoned the CID team that were handling the Kings Heath rape. She couldn't have explained why, even to herself. Was it to talk to someone else who was stuck or to find out how the girl was getting on?

'Hi Kate! Ready to ID some more bums, are you?' This was Maureen, one of the women trained in dealing with rape victims.

'Maybe. Any news?'

'Only that the poor kid wouldn't go home. She's with some auntie in Leicester – more liberal than the rest of the family. My opposite number in Leicester's in touch with her now. Seems they didn't like her being out at night.'

'So why was she? It was past ten.'

'At the Central Library, studying. And then she had a drink at McDonald's in Paradise Forum. Poor kid, she's blaming herself–'

'What rape victim doesn't?'

'Well, it seems she was going against her family's wishes by going to college, compounding it by studying late in the Ref, and then committed the heinous sin of relaxing with a milk-shake. And then she goes and gets herself raped.'

'So the lads could have seen her in the library, in McDonald's or on the bus?'

'Or even at the Kings Heath bus-stop. And we're not much further forward. How's that cut of yours?'

'Fine. Tell you what, though, Maureen, it wasn't glass I cut it on. I went back and checked, me and the constable looking after the scene. I think it was a small knife. A little Stanley knife, something like that.' She'd have to talk to Mrs Mackenzie. Try to find out what she was so anxious about. And she'd bet a new carpet it would be something to do with young Royston.

So there she was, still avoiding the problem. But not for any longer. Time to get stuck in. Not that there wasn't a page of statement she hadn't read two and three times.

She snapped her fingers in irritation. There'd been something she'd wanted to look up, hadn't there? She'd written it down in that notebook that had gone walkabout. Something the kid had muttered in his sleep. Duck, that was it. Fancy forgetting that! Damn it all, they'd bought him that cuddly toy.

'You look as if you'd lost a bob and found a rusty button,' Sally said. 'Sorry, didn't mean to make you jump. You all right?'

'Fine.'

'No more trouble?' Sally jerked her head in the direction of Selby and Cope.

'Not recently. How are you? Not seen much of you for a bit.'

'Been liaising with Family Protection. But I'm coming off that now. Thing is,' she added, dropping her voice and looking around her, 'I'm leaving altogether. And now I'm expecting and all –'

'*Expecting!* That's –'

Sally shushed her. 'And then we had this win on the Lottery, see, me and Huw thought it'd be better if I became a full-time mum.'

'Win!' Kate mouthed. 'Wow!'

'Huw's in this syndicate, see. Two hundred thousand between them. So we get nearly seventy. And he's got a job with this micro-electronics place back home. So I told Graham, 'cause I thought he'd want to keep some continuity. I reckon he'll ask you to take over.'

'Me!'

'Well, since you and he are – you know.'

'I don't know.' Kate tried to keep her voice low.

Sally bit her lip. 'Sorry. But – come on, let's go to the loo.' She looked in Selby's direction. 'I'll swear that bugger can lip-read.'

Kate led the way. Sally followed. Neither spoke till the inner door was shut.

'Now what's this about me and Graham Harvey?' Kate asked, not quite failing to keep calm.

Sally looked at her wide-eyed. 'It's all round the squad, see. That you and he are – you know – having a relationship. I mean, he's good looking, and there's a lot of these blokes'll get their hands in your knickers with the promise of a quick promotion. I must say, I never thought it of Harvey.'

'Or of me, I hope.'

'Oh, I didn't mean – no, of course not. But they say that's how you got into CID. I mean, there's a long queue waiting to get in, and you come up and –'

So this was the cause of the hostility. She sighed. Still, if Sally was so adept at spreading information – or mis-information – she might as well use her to spread the honest truth. 'I was in CID before. Up here. They borrowed me from the Met to go undercover at an old folks' home. And when my bloke was killed, I found I couldn't work any longer with the guy who cocked up the whole operation and so I got transferred. I know it's not the usual way of doing things, but that's how it worked out.'

'OK, OK, keep your wool on. I just thought you should know, that's all. So you're not an item, after all, you and Graham?'

'Sorry to disappoint the rumour-mongers, but no. We've been trying to sort out a problem I've had with my computer. And his mother-in-law needs a residential home, like Cassie.'

Sally peered in the mirror. 'Poor bugger: I wonder if she's as dreadful as his wife. Real tartar *she* is. Has these migraines all the time. She *says*. I reckon it's just to get him dancing to her tune. Won't do this, can't do that. Won't come to any of our dos with him. Poor bugger. Deserves better. You're sure you don't. . .?' she asked almost wistfully. 'Ah, well.'

'Right.' Kate put a full-stop on the topic. 'Now, tell me about the baby. When's it due? And when will you be going?'

'Now, lads, I want you all to give it your best shot tonight,' Paul was saying. 'Remember Kate's not done this sort of thing before, and whatever happens we should be very grateful for her trying.'

Kate said nothing. This might not have been the sort of introduction she wanted, but to cavil publicly would only draw attention to what he'd said. She smiled. And then, hoping he but not the boys would pick up on her sarcasm, said. 'OK. Tonight I'm Glenda Hoddle. Right? And next match we play, we're going to score!'

The laughter wasn't much more than polite. But it was laughter, and they started on their stretches. Out of the corner of her eye she saw Paul disappearing into the church hall. Excellent. Without an audience, even an audience of one, the boys would be less self-conscious. And then he re-emerged.

'Hell, Paul, we're not ready for this sort of treatment, not yet. Nor for a long time,' she added so only he could hear. 'We're simply not ready to be videoed. They're self-conscious enough having a new trainer around without wanting a camera in on the action. Put the bloody thing away. Right, lads. This time we're going to jog and every ten steps we're going to stop and kick, stop and kick. OK?' She blew the whistle she'd found in a photographic shop, of all places, just off the High Street.

They jogged half-heartedly round the car park at the back of the chapel.

'Call that kicking? Wouldn't kick the skin off a rice pudding. Come on. Hell, now what?' She sprinted over to a red-haired lad at the back of the joggers. 'Marcus, you OK?'

'Asthma.' The kid's chest heaved.

'Got a spray?'

73

Paul was at his side. 'We keep one in the hall, don't we, Marcus? Come on, old son.'

Marcus pulled away.

'I'm sure you'd be better in the warm with me. Maybe football's not a good idea for asthmatics.'

'Lots of great sportsmen get asthma. People like Ian Botham. They just need their sprays. So just go and get it, would you, Paul? Now, Marcus, we'll soon have you OK. Paul? What are you waiting for?'

'I'll take him in. Come on, son.'

'He's not a baby. He just needs his spray. Now.' She tried for the boy's sake to keep the urgency out of her voice, but could hear herself failing.

'Yes, *sir*!' Paul saluted her aggressively and jogged off.

Marcus watched him out of sight.

'Had asthma long?' Kate asked conversationally. 'Come on, the rest of you: who told you to stop?'

'Ever since. I was a kid. Getting better. Bad when there's a cold wind.'

'D'you want to go in with Paul?' She'd forgotten what it was like to be small and miserable.

He shook his head violently. 'Stay here. Getting better.'

She was sure he wasn't. But Paul was strolling back, making a leisurely point, she thought. If only she could work out what the point was. Something to do with proving who was boss?

She took and shook the spray: not much left in there. Enough, maybe. 'Here you are, Marcus.'

'There isn't very —' Paul began.

'Shut up. If you want to be any use go and act as whipper in. Sheepdog, whatever.' She was surprised how angry she felt. 'Go on.' She turned back to the boy. 'How's that? Good, I can see it's working already. Right? Now, d'you feel like joining in the next bit? Because it's not running, it's kicking, very gently.'

He looked over her shoulder, eyes wide again. 'I won't have to go home, Miss?'

She turned. Paul was bustling back officiously.

'Not till you want to. And then I thought I might go with

74

you: remind your mum to let us have another spray. Ready? Right lads, I want you back over here. Now!' For Paul's ears only, she added, her voice oozing as much sarcasm as she could squeeze out of it, 'Provided that's all right with you?'

'Of course – I –'

'If you want me to run this session, I run it. My way.' She added more reasonably, 'If the boys think you're in charge they'll obey you. I have to have them doing what I say. All the time.'

'But I shall always be around.'

'That's as may be. But on the football pitch and in training what I say goes. Or it won't work. Now, are you going to join in?'

With ill-grace he joined in. Just short sideways passes. And she was glad to see Marcus was better at it than he was.

At the end of the session, she gathered them round her. 'Well done. You've worked very hard. I'll see you all again after the service on Sunday. Just half an hour. Don't want to make you miss your Sunday lunches. A little and often, that's what we want. Sweat shirts and tracksuits on now, please. And have a bath or a shower when you get home – stop you getting stiff. OK? And Marcus! Well done! It was very brave to keep going like that. And you've got good ball skills.'

She waited at the car park exit, and intercepted Marcus there. 'Shall I give you a lift?'

'I can take him, Kate, I know where he lives.'

'I've offered my prize striker a lift and I'll give him one if he wants one. Won't I, Marcus?'

'Yes, please, Miss.'

'Right. Mine's the Fiesta. Over there.' She zapped the alarm. 'Go and let yourself in.'

He trotted off.

She waved all the others off the premises, and locked the room, handing the keys with ostentatious deference to Paul. 'Yours. Your job the room, mine the team. OK?'

'Bloody hell, woman! What's got into you? Oh, don't tell me. PMT.' He turned and was locking the door. 'Or is it HRT?'

Could she be bothered to respond? She rather thought not, and strode off to her car.

Marcus directed her to a double-fronted house in a quiet part of Kings Heath protected by speed bumps. Apart from telling her where to turn and where to park, he'd said nothing. Accepting he might be shy, she'd not probed. Pulling in behind his and hers Volvos, she went to reach across to open the door for him, but he flinched. 'That lever there,' she said.

Both parents came to the front door. His father was old enough to be his grandfather, his mother scarcely thirty. They both looked at her oddly.

'Remember what I said about a bath or a shower, Marcus. I've been working them hard, Mrs – er –'

'Fulton. Melanie Fulton. This is Doug.'

They shook hands.

'I'm Kate Power. I'm the football team's new coach. Go on, Marcus – don't risk catching cold.' She waited until he was out of earshot. 'He had a bit of an attack, you see. Paul said the Boys' Brigade kept a spray on the premises, but it's nearly empty, and I wanted to make sure he brought a new one next time – you know what kids are like.'

Mrs Fulton turned an anxious face to her husband: 'I thought I sent one last week.'

He looked fondly back. 'You must have forgotten. In your condition.' His announcement was superfluous: 'We're expecting our second, Miss Power.'

Premature sibling rivalry? Was that what was eating Marcus? And had Paul known and was just trying to be kind to a confused kid?

'You'll make sure he brings one on Sunday? And gives it to me? Once his chest cleared he was very promising. I'd hate him not to join in.'

'I'll bring it myself and lay it in your own fair hands, my dear.'

'I know *them*,' Cassie said. 'He was her English teacher. Ever such a scandal there was. He lost his job, of course. But his mother dropped dead in the nick of time: left him everything. Such a boring man: never knew what she could see in him. So where are you sleeping these days? All this gadding off to the Manse.'

'The Manse. Just another couple of nights. Until they've sorted the problem with the kitchen. It's all stripped out and I've got a lovely new floor and the units will be delivered tomorrow. But no working surface. It's stuck somewhere in Sweden. And until that's fitted, no sink.'

'You've got the garden tap: you'll just have to make do with that.' Cassie spoke sharply: she was too tired for what seemed like complaints.

'That's right.' Best not to tell her she didn't have a cooker or a hob, either. 'Have you finished the crossword yet?'

'I should have thought,' Cassie said, 'that messing about with clues was your business.'

Chapter Nine

'I was hoping Kate and I could pair up for this job, Sir,' Colin was saying.

'Well, you can't. You're on with Selby. Miss Power, as everyone knows, is queen of the fucking keyboard. So she can stay put and work her way through this lot. If that suits you, Miss Power?' Cope leaned his beer belly towards her.

Snapping to rigid attention, she said, 'Anything you say, Sir. But I understood DCI Harvey might have other plans for me.' The liaison work with Family Protection.

'Well he might, Miss Power. But DCI Harvey isn't here to favour us with his thoughts, is he? He's on one of these nice high-powered – oh, dearie me, forgive the pun! – high-powered courses that our masters see fit to send us on from time to time. I bet you've been on a few yourself, a young high-flier like you? I'm sure we're all gasping to hear about every single one of them, aren't we, gents? No? So just cast your beadies over this lot and start tapping away. Selby, Roper – in my office, please.'

Kate switched on the computer. While it played its opening jingle, she stared unseeing at the pile of material Cope had dropped on her desk. Poor Colin. Though he'd never said anything, she had a suspicion she'd not voiced even to Harvey that Cope had his knife into him almost as deeply as into Kate herself. And she'd have liked to work with Colin: to renew her acquaintance with the streets of Brum. As it was – well, it looked horribly like more of the cross-referencing of databases she'd hoped she'd finished with. And it was: car theft from Newtown. Really vital stuff when there was a child molester out there. At least there might be something to report to Cope at the end of the day – that was the best she could hope for.

Meanwhile, she wondered what had happened to Graham. Deep down, somewhere she didn't like to think about, she was hurt he hadn't mentioned this course. Not told her all about it. Just mentioned it, in that comradely way of his. But he hadn't, any more than he'd told her about his sick wife. She pulled a face, and started on the first database.

It was terribly hard to have a row with a man who was cutting your front hedge without even being asked. There he was, Paul Taylor, clipping away with a pair of shears so rusty they must have come out of Cassie's shed.

He beamed when he saw her: 'I was a bit edgy yesterday – bad day at work. So this is a sort of sorry present. You did want it cut back, didn't you?'

'Want it cut back! Absolutely!'

He stepped back to consider his handiwork: the privet was so old and so overgrown that now he had trimmed back the top, all she had left was a collection of skeletal twigs.

'Perhaps it'll bush out in the spring,' she said, as if to cheer up a child. Her voice lacked conviction, largely because she'd hoped to root the whole lot out.

'And perhaps it won't. Oh dear, I did so want it to look nice for you.'

'Come on: the light's almost gone now. Let's have a coffee. I can guarantee milk this time.' She shook her Sainsbury's carrier. 'And chocolate biscuits.'

'I'll just get this lot swept up and into the skip. No! Not in those clothes you don't! Too smart for gardening. You go and get that coffee started.'

She unlocked the door, but turned to gather her bags of shopping. Paul was tidying up the cuttings, sure, but he was taking his time about it. Exasperated, she shoved the shopping into the vestibule, ready to help despite her suit, but he was working with a will by the time she'd straightened. A white cat oozed between the railings the far side of the playground. Paul speeded up again.

'You'll be staying here tonight?' Paul asked.

She shook her head. 'Tomorrow, maybe. I don't want to outstay my welcome at the Manse but I can't insult your sister by saying I'd rather stay in this pigsty. Still, it can't be long now. The kitchen seems to have arrived.'

He looked puzzled.

'All those flat-packs and boxes in the front room. There's certainly a sink there. But alas, no working surface that I can see. And until the working surface comes, they can't fix the sink.'

'Cheer up. It's getting better.' He put an arm round her shoulder, squeezing minutely, then distancing himself as quickly as he could. 'How's the upstairs?'

After a hug as perfunctory as that, she couldn't suspect him of wanting to get her into bed! 'Let's look.' Cupping her mug of coffee, she led the way. And was so pleased she could have hugged him. The two main bedrooms were carpeted, and the fitter had actually replaced the furniture. He'd come back to do other rooms as and when they were ready.

'Looks good.' Paul followed her into the middle room. 'Do you want to make up the bed?'

'I'll leave it to air one more night. And I'd want to dust and vac everywhere. All these rolls of fluff. I wonder –' *I wonder what Robin will say.* She made it to the bathroom, retching till there was nothing except bile. Hell. When would her body understand that there was no more Robin, and none of its protests could bring him back again? She slapped cold water on her face. But the towel was too filthy from workmen's inadequately washed hands to put anywhere near her face. At least they'd left some loo roll. Not much. Good job she'd bought a megapack tonight. As for the towel, it had better join the others in the bulging black sack she'd take to the laundrette. One evening.

Paul was calling.

'It's OK. I must have eaten something.' She rejoined him. 'Which bedroom will you have?'

'This, no traffic noise. And this suite just fits.'

'Georgian, isn't it? Must be worth a bomb.' He stroked the mahogany and the lighter wood of the inlay.

'Edwardian copy, Cassie says. Still worth a bit. Whereas the one that fits the front room is so naff I'd be surprised if even a charity shop will take it. Hey, do the Boys' Brigade have a bonfire? They could pop the guy on top of that dressing table!'

Paul looked shocked. 'Strip that down and put on a lighter varnish — it'd be fine.'

'The colour, yes. But not the shape. I never did like thirties shapes. Would you like it? To be honest I'd rather have the tackiest MFI than that.'

'You're serious?'

'Never more.'

'Thanks! I'll get some of the lads to help me collect it.'

'Can I operate this one, then?' Kate was in Tim's bedroom, which was almost entirely filled by a train set. Paul, claiming such matters were over his head, had gone home to attack a mountain of marking.

Tim nodded, not taking his eyes from the model he was fitting on to the track. 'This is my favourite,' he said. 'Flying Scotsman. Though I like King George, too. Can you see the bell on the front? That was from when he went to the States for a visit.' He looked up. 'Hey, those coaches are the wrong livery for King George. You need those over there. Great Western livery. See.'

So far as Kate was concerned they were just coaches. But she was spared an embarrassing confession by the arrival of Maz.

'And what sort of time d'you call this, Tim? Half an hour after lights out, I'd call it.'

'My fault,' Kate suggested, not quite truthfully. 'I love his layout.'

'Would you like to come and play properly tomorrow?' Tim asked. 'I'll show you which coaches to use and everything.'

Kate looked at Maz. 'Would you mind?'

'Mind! I should be delighted! Indeed, grateful. In fact, I was

going to ask you the most enormous favour. Night-night, love.
Dad'll be up to say your prayers with you as soon as you've
cleaned your teeth.' She kissed him and patted his bottom
affectionately.

Kate kissed him too. On the forehead. Like she'd kissed Robin's children. She hadn't realised how much she missed them.
She could hardly contact Kathleen and ask to see them.

'Are you all right?' Maz came back up the stairs and laid a
hand on her arm.

This time she wouldn't even try to pretend. 'Missing my
sort-of-step-children. Dan's about Tim's age, Emma about Jenny's. We used to have them some weekends.' She straightened.
'Now, what was the favour?'

'The kids. Someone's offered Giles and me tickets for
Symphony Hall for tomorrow night. Scenes from the opera.'

'And you'd like me to stay in with the kids? Fine.'

'All three? They can be a real pain if they think they can
get away with it. I could always get Paul to pop round, too.'

'No. Honestly. Paul says he's got a load of assignments to
correct, so I'd hate to bother him. No, just give me a set of
your ground rules and we'll be fine. Now, I know you said
not to bring any food in but they'd got this offer on smoked
salmon, and I thought we could all have a treat. To celebrate
Cassie's diamonds, maybe. I've brought a bottle, too.'

'Fresh bagels, cream cheese and smoked salmon, rounded off
with a couple of glasses of white wine. Perfection.' Giles sat
back smoothing his stomach. 'But you must have the last bagel,
Kate. Paul tells me you were ill before you set out.'

'It's ever since Robin's death,' she said quietly. 'My partner.
In both senses. Police and private. We were on a job. It was all
set up, supposedly. We were just going into this warehouse.
But we didn't know about the shooters. Until someone took
out the windscreen of one of our cars. The driver lost control
and slammed Robin and me into a wall. I was very lucky.
Robin pushed me, so all I got was a dislocated knee. But

he slipped sideways – trying to save me, I think – and was completely crushed. Except for his head.'

'My dear.' Maz took her hand.

'And since then, sometimes – and I can't even predict when – I think of something about him and I'm sick. Thought at first I might be pregnant,' she said. 'But I'm not. Anyway, tonight I was so pleased with the way my upstairs is looking, I wanted to show him. But I couldn't.'

For a dreadful moment she was afraid Giles would come out with the terrible cliché that maybe Robin could see everything, but he simply shook his head and poured the last of the wine into her glass.

'Don't think I haven't had support. The squad debriefing, the people in Welfare. Everyone's given me so much support. They even organised my transfer when I found I couldn't work with the guy who set up – or do I mean messed up – the operation without throwing up.' She managed a grim smile. 'Bit of a bummer, that. Literally sick of the sight of someone!'

'Have you had much support up here?' Maz asked.

'My DCI's very kind.'

'To me, that implies not all the others are!'

'They're having difficulties with what they see as an undeserved promotion. Hell! Excuse me!' She dug in her bag for her chirruping phone.

'Kate?' She could hardly hear his voice, it was so quiet. 'It's Colin here. Are you tied up?'

'Nothing I can't untie. What's up?'

'If I were you I'd get in here fast. Another missing kid. If anyone asks you saw it on TV. I'll explain when I can.' And the call was over.

'Another missing child,' she said briefly to Maz and Giles, who were looking at her with concern. 'I'm sorry. God knows what time I shall be back. I'll be as quiet as I can.'

Giles was on his feet. 'I'm taking you in. And you must take a taxi back. No point in courting trouble.'

Chapter Ten

There's a moment during the credits at the start of *Cagney and Lacey* where the two women surge into the office, only to be turned in mid-stride by the Lieutenant who wants them, presumably, to tackle another assignment. Kate was so struck by the similarity she would have laughed. But it was she who was being sent back and Cope who was doing it.

'What the fuck d'you think you're doing, swanning in at this time? We've been sweating our guts out since eight this evening and you think you can come in now. Just get out of my sight.'

She stood her ground: 'I didn't know until I heard it on the *News*.'

'Oh, she didn't know until she heard about it on the *News*. What about the phone call, Miss Power? When you promised you were on your way? Christ, you're as much use as a chocolate lavatory.'

'Sir –'

'Once more and you'll get a formal warning. Now just fuck off so I can get some work done. A missing child. And you don't get here till the others are searching the streets of Newtown.'

'Who phoned me, Sir?'

He turned on his heel.

'Sir? Who claims –' But she saw Colin and shut up.

He motioned her with a jerk of his head into the corridor. She was sure he mouthed *loo!*

Shaking with anger, she remembered what he'd said on the

phone. She waited between the inner and outer cloakroom doors. Sure enough, there was a gentle knocking.

'Interview room four in five minutes,' he mouthed.

'Did Selby phone you? Here, might as well sit down. Did he?' Colin sat too, leaning urgently forward.

'Of course not. It was supposed to be his job, was it?' Things were beginning to get unpleasantly clear.

'You're absolutely sure you had no call?'

'What else would you expect?'

'Shit! Kate, he's trying to drop you in it all the time. You're going to have to do something.'

'Is it him or Cope I've got to watch?'

'Cope?'

'I'm not exactly his blue-eyed girl, Colin. And don't forget how he *accidentally* pulled the plug on my lap-top. And I'm sure he's grassed me up to Graham.'

'Who has a soft spot for you.'

'Don't you bloody start!'

'Start what?'

'Oh, this rumour about me and Harvey, of course.'

'Ah. *That* rumour. Well, there'll always be rumours when two adults spend time together. The question is, friendship or sex? Gay or hetero?'

She looked at him, unable to keep the question from her eyes. 'Being gay can't be very comfortable in the Force.'

'Nor is it. Not when everyone thinks being gay equals being a paedophile. But I like you, Kate, and I don't want to work with you just for camouflage, just in case any nasty little rumour monger suggests that. And I want to help you sort out whoever's trying to shit on you from a great height.'

She took his hand and squeezed it lightly. 'Thanks. And thanks for – for trusting me.'

He smiled.

'And while we're at it, thanks for phoning. What the hell can I do, Colin?'

'Well, there's always the Skilled Helper option. You could go and pick up a phone and talk to someone now. A senior woman who'd listen to you.'

'Or?'

'Or you could document every single thing that goes wrong and talk to Harvey about it – when he gets back. In your position I'd do that. Evidence, Kate, that's what you need.'

'Evidence such as a print-out of all the phone calls going through the switchboard between the hours of – say seven and nine?'

'Evidence such as that. But it'd be my guess that you couldn't get that yourself. You'd need to ask Graham to authorise it.'

'When does he come back?'

'Next week. But it'd be my guess that Cope will try and nail you for that disciplinary before then. So watch your back.'

'He'll have to work bloody fast. OK, Colin: advice time. What would you do?'

'Just keep your nose clean – what else? Look, Cope'll be after me if I don't go back now. Wait another couple of minutes and then come up too. Get your things and scoot if that seems appropriate. Or occupy yourself with whatever you were supposed to be doing earlier today. I don't know. Play it by the proverbial ear.'

She'd rather be working. That was easy. Just in case a job needed doing and there was no one else available. So she waited a count of a hundred, and went slowly back upstairs.

She'd almost expected it: the file of material she was preparing on the missing cars had gone from her desk. Despite herself, she quivered with anger. All those hours' work casually purloined. Something else to record in her log for Graham Harvey. Colin came into the room with Cope. With a witness, she might risk it.

Standing to the sort of attention he'd demanded before, she coughed. 'Sir!'

'I thought I'd told you to fuck off home.'

'I thought you'd want this first, Sir. It's what I've been working on today.' Bending, she unlocked her desk, and fished in the drawer she'd ear-marked for personal things – photos, tights, tampons. There was the missing file's duplicate. Smiling, she passed it across. 'Sir, I know you're busy, but I wonder if you'd just check it's OK. Only I've been having trouble with my computer, and I've lost some information. I might not be able to run off another copy.' She didn't catch Colin's eye. Later on, if he wanted to be a witness he could: she didn't want to implicate him at this stage, not with Cope's sharp little eyes missing nothing.

He flicked open the file. She watched his eyes flickering down the page.

'What's this stuff down here?' He jabbed a stubby forefinger.

'That? Oh, that's just the file number, Sir. How it's saved on my hard disk.' *And on a floppy disk in my desk, and another at home.*

'I thought you said you were having trouble with the computer?'

'I did, Sir. Perhaps it just needs servicing or something.' *Or perhaps I'm assuming you know very little about computers.* If she hadn't been standing rigidly upright, she'd have crossed her fingers.

'Hmph. I thought you'd been on all these courses – don't come cheap, you know.'

'No, Sir.'

'Right. Now you're here, get on the blower to the lads: I've sent out a radio call but there's still some not answering.'

'What shall I tell them, Sir?'

'To fuck off home. They've found the kid. Looks like it was all a false alarm. Looks like he was playing up. Well, he won't play up no more.'

'Sir?'

'Because he's run under the wheels of a bloody juggernaut heading for Spaghetti Junction, that's why. Chasing a fucking football.' He turned away. She was sure he was in tears.

Perhaps she was mistaken. He was facing her again. 'Tell you what, Power. You *can* do something useful for a change. You can go and tell the parents.'

★

There was no point in arguing. In vain to point out that they'd be expecting the friendly face from the local nick, the kindly man or woman who'd taken down details and been bright enough to bring CID in quickly. They'd get Kate and – yes, Colin was grabbing his jacket and coming too. At least they'd have someone from Family Support with them by now, someone to turn to when she'd delivered the news and had left for home.

The parents – Janice and Alan Butler – were doing their best with a modern terrace in a tired council estate. They'd put up hanging baskets of winter pansies, and when the security light came on, Kate could see the wallflowers waiting in neat rows to greet the spring. They might have to wait a long time.

Alan Butler let her in. He'd found some manual work somewhere in this city of a thousand dying trades: there was oil round and under his finger nails. He sat heavily, covering Janice's red-tipped fingers with his ham of a hand. They broke the news. The woman sergeant who was supporting them found tissues, made the right noises.

'Chasing his ball?' He repeated at last, picking out from all Colin's words the one thing he seemed able to take in. 'A ball?'

'Seems like it, Alan. You know what kids are like. And – Colin hesitated, as if groping for the right words – 'the only consolation is that it would have been very quick. He wouldn't have known, wouldn't have suffered.'

Kate opened her mouth to ask something, and closed it again. Very gently, she picked up a framed photo of a toothy eight-year-old. 'That's him?'

No one seemed able to say the boy's name out loud. Danny. Danny Butler.

'I told Lesley, here,' Janice began, gesturing vaguely at the sergeant. 'He was going to need a brace, see. In a few years.'

'Lovely hair.' It was classically golden and curly. Those big blue eyes and he was a ready-made cherub.

'Took after Alan's Dad, you see. Oh – I haven't offered you a cup of tea. Don't know what I'm thinking of.'

'Would you like one?' Lesley was on her feet.

'Oh, I never drink tea at night. Stops me sleeping.' And then she realised she might have a much greater reason for not sleeping, and at last she burst into tears.

Alan stared at her helplessly.

'I think we should call your GP – your family doctor,' Lesley said. 'Get something to help her sleep. Help both of you sleep. Why don't you give me the number?'

Kate held Janice's shaking shoulders. Damn Cope for dropping this on her: all she wanted to do was sit and cry with her. Cry for Danny, cry for Darren and cry most of all for Robin. And then, as if a voice called her from a distant planet, she remembered that something had worried Alan.

'Alan: this ball. You seemed surprised he was playing with a ball.'

'His ball's there.' He pointed to a stack of plastic boxes – Lego in one, books in another, videos in a third. Top but one basket held cuddly toys, the topmost a ball. 'Don't tell me he's been thieving again!' He half-rose, as if to yell the question at his son. He subsided. 'Only there was some trouble, see. They thought it was clever to nick things. These kids of eight and nine, shoplifting. Little cars, sweets. I made him take me with him to each shop and give them the cars back. Took his birthday money to pay for the sweets. Don't tell me he's been and nicked a bloody football.'

The front door bell. Kate responded to the chimes: a sari-wearing Indian woman in her late fifties with the kindest eyes Kate had seen for years. She carried an old-fashioned doctor's bag.

In the end, Colin ran her home.

'But it must be miles out of your way. Where is it you live? Blackheath?'

'What's a couple of miles at two in the morning when it's pissing down and a kid's been killed?'

'I wonder what the post mortem'll show up.'

'Being squashed by very big tyres, I'd have thought.'

'Too convenient. Why should a kid from the same school as young Darren Goss go missing? Same age, same appearance? You know what I'm expecting?'

'No.'

'Same anal damage. That's what I'm expecting.'

'Why?' He slowed for the lights by the county cricket ground.

'Because – just, because. But I could be wrong. Pray God I'm wrong.'

'Amen. Jesus, what do the bastards get out of it? Shoving their ugly great pricks into innocent kids?'

'And unidentified metal objects? They haven't found what went up young Darren, have they? Right at the island.'

'No. But whoever put it there was sick, I tell you, Kate, bloody sick.'

'Right. Now, what I want to do tomorrow is check out that football story. Talk to his friends, the school, local shops. See if he really did nick it. Or . . .'

'Or?' Colin prompted.

'Or if it came into his possession some other way. I don't know.'

'I think you do. But I'll tell you something for free, our Kate. Cope'll try and block whatever you want to do. A fiver on it.'

'No takers. Tell you what, maybe I could do it without him knowing. Lunch-time or something. Or even do the sensible thing for a change and wait for the PM results.'

Chapter Eleven

By nine the following morning, Kate's common sense seemed to be making a weary come-back. There was no way she could sneak out in her odd spare moments to go and play the great detective. She had work to do here, for a start: someone new to the patch seemed to be making a determined effort to break into all the doctors' surgeries, pharmacies and even vets' they could find. What that called for was another morning tapping into databases and liaison with her colleagues in Drugs. But since she was clearly going to spend a good deal of time on the phone, she might as well call Danny's local nick: find out who'd dealt with the case when the Butlers reported him missing and, more important, who'd attended the fatal accident. The ball business still worried her.

The constable who'd dealt with the accident itself wouldn't come back on duty for hours yet, but at least she'd left meticulous notes. Dark; wet road; heavy traffic. A couple of well spoken pedestrians who'd done what little they could but had melted away into the scenery as soon as the paramedics had arrived. No names or addresses. And no ball. She left a message for PC Kaur to phone her. No harm in double checking.

And then back to the databases, and a couple of promising leads from Leicester and Bradford to report to a silent and unappreciative Cope.

Lunch-time. She looked in Colin's direction. He was looking as depressed as Cope, not at all as if he'd want to eat out, but certainly as if he ought to. She strolled across.

'A quick half somewhere?' In spite of herself she grinned.
'What's up?'

She threw him his raincoat. 'Tell you outside.'

'Now. No one's about.'

'It's just that I offered you a drink. When I came I hardly dared. I was into whisky in a very big way. And somehow I've forgotten I needed it.'

He looked at her very hard. 'You're sure?'

'I know. Once an alcoholic always an alcoholic. But last night I found myself drinking socially. When you phoned me, I just put down the glass and walked away. All right. One swallow doesn't make a summer.'

'Depends on the sort of swallow.'

'How about a coffee and baguette?'

'Fine by me. And I'll show you a suit you should try on in Rackhams.'

'Fine by me. Provided that –'

'Provided what?'

'That you tell me why you looked so miserable back there.'

'Tell you over that baguette.'

The underpass which had once housed the back entrance to a big department store and now accommodated the Citizens' Advice Bureau was foul with pigeon droppings: they'd evidently moved there from the Cathedral Close, which was where she remembered them.

'Depressing sort of place,' she said, forgetting her earlier glee. 'There are times I wonder why I came back.'

'Oh, but there are the new developments! Come on, pedestrianisation and all that stuff out by the ICC: Birmingham's really becoming a city!'

'You could have fooled me.'

'You haven't been to Waterside yet?'

'Not even Symphony Hall.'

'We'll have to fix that. And you can wear that new suit.'

'I haven't even seen it yet! Neither, of course, have you explained your glum face.'

He sighed. She'd pitched it wrong.

They walked on in silence.

'Tell you what,' he said at last, 'there's a really nice cookery shop you ought to see. Be lovely for stocking your new kitchen. Tomorrow lunch-time, maybe.'

'You're on. Just to look at this stage, mind. Nowhere to put so much as a teaspoon at the moment.'

Silence again. They were in Corporation Street, and he'd speeded up, only to come to a halt in front of a window display. The suit, presumably. There were several.

'Selby. It has to be Selby,' he said. 'Every bloody time it's Selby that gets the course. Computers, this time. I mean, he's a Neanderthal, doesn't know his Apple Mac from his arse, and now he's off at Tally-Ho! being taught all sorts of clever gizmos.'

There was a sensible observation to make: that Selby was clearly in need of a course. But that would have been the wrong one. She groped feebly for something else. 'At least with Selby we'll get living proof of the old computer adage: GIGO.'

'He only puts garbage in so he'll only get garbage out?' He managed a pale grin; but she hadn't expected much more. 'That turquoise one over there: it'd set off your hair something lovely.'

'Hmm. Trouble is, that skirt'd set Selby off something shocking!'

She called into what she ought to call home before going on to the Manse. She'd asked Maz if she could put a load through their washing machine while she baby-sat, she was so short of clothes. The workmen were just locking up.

'Glad I caught you,' said the foreman. 'Only I'd like to talk to you about that back door.'

Nodding, she gestured him ahead of her.

'Rotten, you see.' He jabbed with a horny nail. 'And if the rest of the place has been double-glazed it'd be a sin just to lick paint on this and forget it. I'd organise it myself but you'd probably get a better deal from the firm that did your windows.'

He was middle aged and could probably have done with the money.

'You're right,' she said. 'Tell you what, I know it's the wrong time of the year, but how are you on fences? Look at that!'

'Flapping like a line of washing, isn't it? Now, are you asking me as part of Buildsure or you asking me?'

'Alf, I'm asking you.'

He smiled. 'Thanks. Now, tell me one thing. Why don't you ever open your mail? Me and the lads are putting it safe, but –'

'Where?'

'In the front room. On the fireplace. There you are.'

She pounced with more glee than manners.

'And I'll let you have a quote, like, for that fence?' he prompted her.

'I'm so sorry. Yes please!'

She shoved the whole bundle into a carrier ready to take to the Manse. She couldn't spoil their evening by keeping them waiting. And there was the washing to sort and bag, too. Five minutes of frantic activity, three carriers of laundry, one of post and one of clean clothes for the following day – she'd promised to sleep over so Maz and Giles could make a night of it if they wanted – she was ready. OK, so it was Saturday – a whole weekend – ahead, but that didn't mean she wouldn't be at work by eight: she'd give Cope not the slightest excuse to rebuke her. And if that meant putting in a twelve-hour stint so that she could legitimately take time off on Sunday, so be it.

'There's a list –' Maz flapped her hands frantically

'Kate, there are dozens of lists,' said Giles. 'How to operate the washing machine. Medication for Lynn. Prayers. TV programmes they may and may not watch. It's my fault. We don't get out often enough together and Maz has got to the stage where she's convinced the world will end if one of us isn't there to tuck them up.'

'A palpable hit,' Maz conceded. 'OK, there's the remains of a casserole: all you have to do to work out the microwave –'

'One of the kids'll show me, won't they?'

'Look – we'll never be able to park if we don't go now.'

'So go! I can cope, honestly. Tim'll help me with the washing first, because he and I are going to operate his trains – that's right, isn't it, Tim?' She remembered in her Latin lessons at school – were there any schools left in the country that still routinely offered Latin? – that there were some questions that were open, and others that, by the speaker's choice of words, suggested an answer. Her question clearly demanded the answer 'yes', though by his face Tim was not specially keen to give it. She'd always pretended to Robin's children that she needed help with technology, though she always showed she was quick to learn: stereotyping herself as the useless blonde had never been part of her remit. She adopted the same technique for Tim.

'So I've got some white things that want a hot wash, and some coloured ones that might run. So what do we do?' Maybe she'd qualify for parenthood one day. Not something to undertake lightly in this job, though. And certainly not singly, not as far as she was concerned.

The washing machine was programmed and a ball of liquid solemnly placed on top of the shirts; Tim switched it on. No problems. Nor with the microwave: he even showed her how to microwave a couple of potatoes to go with the casserole.

Lynn floated in at this point: 'Mum said to help you cook your tea. And show you how to use the washer.'

'*I* did it.'

'You don't know how.'

'I do!'

Et cetera.

'OK, kids. Your dad said something about TV. Is it worth watching or shall I eat my tea in peace in here?'

'But what about my train set? There's only half an hour before bed-time.'

She'd come to play trains: play trains was what she had to

do. She followed Tim to his bedroom leaving her supper on its plate on the table.

'What we'll do,' Tim said, 'is this. You see all those carriages: we'll shunt those into that siding. And then we'll couple the British Rail livery ones to Flying Scotsman. And we could have a goods train, too. We could shunt some wagons together. You see that little diesel shunter: you could use that.'

Kate had seen that coming. 'I couldn't use this one instead?' She pointed to a maroon steam loco.

'Duchess of Hamilton! No! She's a passenger locomotive. Tell you what, you could have my new loco if you like.' Tim switched some points and turned on the power. A pannier tank bowled out of the engine shed. Great Western livery. Very smart.

'You haven't got a Thomas the Tank Engine?' Kate asked.

Tim looked shocked. 'You mean with a face? That's kids' stuff! Mind you,' he conceded, 'I call this one Duck, although it's in the books, because –'

'Duck? Did you say Duck?' She tried not to shout.

But he was wide eyed.

'Tim: please – tell me about Duck.'

'That's what he's called in the engine books. The Reverend Awdrey. And I thought – well, it sort of suits – I know it's a bit babyish.'

'Babyish? But it's a sort of duck shape, isn't it?' She picked it up and traced the outline with her finger. 'The water tanks look like a duck's wings. And with no cylinders to conceal the wheels when you're looking at it from the front, maybe it waddles a bit. Let's set it off. Yes, those big hub things going up and down, up and down on opposite sides – it does waddle! It's GWR livery, isn't it?' She was trying not to talk too fast, trying not to yell with joy at finding what she suspected was a vital piece of the Darren Goss jigsaw. And there was nothing she could do about it now, not while she was supposed to be putting Tim and his sisters to bed. And who to tell anyway? Cope would laugh in her face, or worse.

'Yes. Which trucks do you want?'

Kate chose idly, her mind still racing. 'That Kit-Kat one. And the Cadbury's.'

Tim laughed. 'You *do* like chocolate! Would you like some of mine? It's all right. It's allowed. So long as I've eaten my tea and so long as I clean my teeth.'

'Which you'll be doing soon anyway. Let's have a couple of chugs round the track first. I've hardly seen anything moving, yet.'

'We could eat the chocolate while we watch.'

This was indisputable. It was good chocolate, too. Swiss. 'Uncle Paul gave me this. He always buys nice sweets.'

'You don't think he'll mind your sharing with me?'

Tim considered. 'Not if you don't have too much.'

At last the locomotives and the rolling stock had completed their adventures, going through level crossings and over what looked like an old Triang bridge. There were a little mirror lake, and farm and a fire and ambulance station. Plots of what might become a village were roughly sketched near the fire station: Tim had clear priorities.

And then it was bed-time. Absolutely.

'Right: we'll shunt the wagons into those sidings, and then you can run the passenger train just once more. And then it's a wash and your teeth and bed!'

So there he was, in his pyjamas, snuggling under his duvet. A couple of teddy bears rapidly joined him. He looked so cute, she wanted to hug him. When she kissed him on the forehead, he solved any problem of what she should do by putting his arms round her neck and hugging her. He smelt warm and clean, slightly minty from his toothpaste. She hugged him back.

As she backed out of the room, ready to switch off the light, something caught her eye. A ball. And her heart contracted. There was a family over in Newtown with no child to tuck up tonight.

★

Washing. Better put the next load in. And then the post. And all the time, the question buzzing in her head: what to do about Duck?

Chapter Twelve

And then there were the girls. She'd ignored them, believing that with one theoretically asleep and the other doing homework all would be well. Perhaps just checking would allow somewhere in her mind to throw up some answers on the Duck problem. She tiptoed into Jenny's room: seraphically asleep. Possibly. But quiet and breathing and alive. Lynn was tapping away at the computer in the study when she finally ran her to earth. Not a game: there was a lot of text which disappeared from the screen as soon as Kate hove into view.

Coughing gently, Kate raised an enquiring eyebrow.

'It's all right. I've saved it.' Lynn was defensive, dismissive.

'School work?'

Lynn said nothing.

'I reckoned you'd got another half hour before your parents wanted you in bed.'

'That's OK. I'll have a shower and read in bed.'

'And you'll need something to eat with your antibiotics? Hell! I never ate that casserole! Or the baked spuds! I got caught up with the train set. D'you fancy a baked potato? I can do another one for me.'

Lynn's expression was opaque, but since she removed the disk from the computer, pocketing it, and closed the system down for the night, perhaps this was an affirmative.

Still no ideas. If she spoke to Cope the idea would be ridiculed or mysteriously lost. Blast Graham Harvey and his wretched course.

And damn him for not leaving a contact number: bullying and crime weren't going to take a holiday just because he wasn't there.

The baked potatoes were cold, but she warmed them. Without speaking, Lynn burrowed in the fridge, producing a bowl of coleslaw.

'Home-made,' she said briefly.

'Smells good. No thanks, I don't think it'll go well with the casserole.' But she didn't want to stop Lynn communicating, so she said, 'I know Jenny wants to join the Girls' Brigade and equally Tim refuses to join the Boys'. I don't remember whether you were a member.'

'For a bit. But I had too much work for school. And I'm not keen on badges and things.' She added some butter to the potato and coleslaw. She took a few desultory scoops. 'Right. I'll go and have my shower. Goodnight.'

'Hang on. The antibiotic. Here you go.' Kate undid the childproof top with difficulty. 'My God: you wonder how they chose their colours. Best to have a swig of water. Don't want you coughing and shooting someone.'

Lynn nodded briefly to acknowledge and dismiss her attempt at humour, picked up a book from a pile by the phone and went off.

By now Kate was ready to tear her hair. All the silly stupid demands on her time. Washing. To hell with the environment: she'd have to tumble it dry, and make sure the rent she intended to pay the no doubt unwilling Maz covered the electricity. And she'd have to put another load in. And she was hungry: the smell of the wasted supper proved that. And there was the post. God, she'd like a drink. They wouldn't begrudge her a gin. Or two.

She slammed the microwave door harder than necessary. Potatoes and casserole coming up.

Post. The envelopes slithered on to the kitchen table from the carrier. She checked inside it. Nothing left. OK. Sort them into piles. Bills, junk and others.

Bills. Thank goodness for telephone banking. Except she didn't like the sound of her balance. Junk. They kept a carrier in the pantry for paperbank paper. And now the proper mail: just three interesting-looking envelopes.

The microwave pinged as if on cue. She couldn't expect the casserole to endure another reheating, so she reached the plate out, forgetting the steam would scald.

Nothing serious. Nothing to come between her food and between her and the mail.

'That smells wicked.'

She nearly shoved the fork down her throat. 'Tim! I had this idea you were in bed.'

'Can't sleep. I'm – he looked at her plate – I'm hungry.'

'And you fancy a bit of a natter? Look, we had a great time with the engines, but you should be in bed. Here, get yourself a plate, and you can have a little chicken and half a potato. Then it's clean your teeth again and bed. OK? And not a further whisper. Or I don't ever come back and play with your set. Not even to drive Flying Scotsman. Get it?'

Tim got it. But he ate the chicken so enthusiastically she was tempted to believe his claim that he was hungry.

'There's some of Mum's semolina pudding left.'

Since when did kids like semolina? But there was something odd about this one. She sniffed it as she reached it from the fridge. 'Hmm. This smells good.'

'It's Mum. She's got this really bad recipe with coconut milk. Try some.' He produced two dishes, two spoons, knocking one of her letters on to the floor.

She tasted. 'Brilliant. Now eat up and push off. I'll be up in three minutes to check you've cleaned those teeth again. And I don't remember hearing you say your prayers.'

She finished her semolina slowly, and opened the first letter. Yes! At last, a long-term let. And the possibility the tenant might want to buy, she liked it so much.

The next one was junk dressed up as genuine. Her garage asking her if she'd like a new car and reminding her a service was overdue. Service? It was all she could do to park the car within walking distance of her house, let alone think of driving it enough for a service. In any case, she'd better find a garage in Birmingham. Someone at work would be able to advise.

There was a scream from upstairs. Going up two at a time,

she reminded herself that children did scream, even for things like spiders or broken hair slides. But then there was another, and another.

Jenny's room. It said so on the door. She burst in, ready to kill anyone so much as touching her. But Jenny was still asleep, if very restless. Now what? Wake her? Or let her settle?

Lynn sauntered in, hair damp, dressing-gown tied tight. 'Having one of her dreams, is she? She'll be all right. Gives the rest of us the screaming habdabs, and never wakes up herself. Look, she's back to normal now. Tell Tim he can clean his teeth now, will you?'

Exit Lynn, leaving Kate holding a teddy bear and her temper. If Lynn was like this at eleven, what would she become when she was a fully-fledged teenager?

Tim was reading, of course. An adult book about diesel engines.

'Go on. Clean your teeth, there's a good boy. And not another peep, then.'

'Can't I even scream, like Jenny?' He smiled, scrabbling from the duvet.

'Especially not scream like Jenny.'

OK, no gin, but certainly a coffee. How on earth did parents with full-time jobs cope? Especially when the phone started ringing when you were halfway down the stairs. She took the last few at a gallop, only to have the phone stop as she reached the kitchen.

Which wasn't surprising, because someone had answered it. The someone who was standing with his back to her, his right hand idly playing with an envelope.

The man was Paul and she had a nasty suspicion that the envelope he was now slitting open was the one she'd forgotten to pick up: certainly there was nothing under the table except a few crumbs.

Paul wrote down a message, repeated it to the caller, and replaced the handset.

'Good evening,' she said coolly. She'd had a lot of practice, not letting her voice quaver no matter how hard her heart might be pumping. At the moment she wasn't sure whether it was the shock of finding him there, or the anger that he should still have her post in his hand.

'Hi there! I thought you might need some moral support.'

'I'd have liked some sort of warning you were here. Oh, and I'd like my letter, please.' She stuck out a hand for it.

'Not until you ask me nicely. Here I am with some hooch and a video and all you do is yell at me.' He smiled in what was no doubt supposed to be a playful, indeed flirtatious way, and held her letter above his head.

'What do you expect?' *No, better lighten up.* 'I come down here, find a strange man in Maz's kitchen and get into combat mode, ready to defend her semolina pudding against all comers. Of course I'm yelling. But I would like my letter, please.' Her hand stayed forward. She touched her thumb to her fingers a couple of times.

He held the letter higher. 'Pretty please?'

'Most beautiful please.' And she sprang, wresting it from his grasp before he realised what she was doing. Thank goodness for netball.

Except he grabbed her round the waist. 'Come on,' he said, and started to kiss her on the mouth.

She laid her hands on his, as if clamping them to her waist. And then pulled back his little fingers, stopping only when he yelled.

She stepped back, ostentatiously sitting at the kitchen table and removing the letter from the envelope he'd started to open.

'Come on, Kate.' He sat opposite her. 'What's up? Lost your sense of humour?'

'No. Nor, before you ask is it the wrong time of the month. I just don't want to play games at the moment, Paul. I told you, you should have let me know you were here. And you certainly shouldn't have opened this.'

'I always let myself in.' He shook a bunch of keys at her. 'And I'm sorry about the letter. I just did it automatically.' He sat down opposite her. 'Hell, you didn't half tweak my fingers.'

She grinned. Perhaps she had over-reacted. 'It was either that or hurt you! Now, I'd love to watch a video with you, but I shall have to iron my shirts while I watch.'

The rest of the evening had started pleasantly enough. She'd brought the tumble-dried washing in from the utility room to find him washing up and putting on the kettle, and then he carried through the ironing board into the living room. When she found the video was *Shadowlands* she decided to acquit him of any salacious intent. No doubt he behaved like an over-age teenager because he spent so much time with teenagers. And of course, this was his sister's home, and he was no doubt used to coming and going as he pleased. And yes, she'd been rattled anyway. No reason, when she'd hung the last shirt on its hanger and put away the iron, why she shouldn't join him on the sofa, if not closely. They were both crying so hard at the end of the movie that any remaining lust must be completely extinguished. And then she found she couldn't stop crying, and didn't think she ever would again. *Oh, Robin.*

Kate came back into the kitchen to catch Maz in mid-torrent: 'Damn it, Paul – she lost her lover only three months ago, and you make her watch *that*? I know it's wonderful, but haven't you any imagination? Come, love: have a brandy. One won't hurt you.'

'Very small. How was the concert?'

'Brilliant. Absolutely wonderful. And the hall's perfect. You must go.'

'I'll get some tickets – make up for tonight,' Paul said. 'I really am so sorry, Kate. I just didn't think.'

At last, still shaking, she went to bed. Giles had produced homeopathic sleeping pills and a hot-water bottle. It wasn't until she took off her trousers she remembered the letter in the pocket. She smoothed it out.

Dear Kate

Just a note to explain about this course. It was dropped on me at absolutely the last minute. I'm concerned about what may happen to you at work while I'm away and my office door locked. If necessary post stuff to me at the above address. If anything crops up phone me, for goodness' sake. I know mobile phones are inventions of the devil, but there we are.

Kindest regards
Yours
Graham Harvey

Midnight. Well, he wouldn't welcome a call now. But tomorrow! And before she knew it, Kate had fallen asleep.

Chapter Thirteen

No need for an alarm this morning! Kate was awake, surging with enough energy for a long run, just after six. Time for a shower before the family took over the bathroom.

But she had done no more than set the breakfast table when Maz appeared, bleary and, without make-up, looking old. For all her smart day clothes, her dressing gown was embarrassingly bald.

'Better this morning? Funny how a good cry can clear you out, set you up again. Is that kettle for anything special?'

'Tea for you and Giles. Unless you'd prefer coffee? I was going to bring it up to you. I still could. Go on: when did you last have tea in bed?' *And when did I? Our last morning, that's when. But don't think of that now. There will be good times. One day. One day.* 'Off you go. I'll start the breakfast. But I'll nip off early. I want to make a couple of phone calls before things get too hectic.'

'Make them from here?' Maz gathered her dressing gown skirt, as if to start upstairs. But she dropped it again, and started to reach out for breakfast cereals.

'Tea. There you are. And now push off. It's Saturday, isn't it? Day of rest. Now, I've promised to come and play with the train set again, but I'm not sure when. I think I might be on to something at work, so goodness knows what time I shall be finished. And I have this yen to sleep in my own bed.'

'Have you got a new mattress for it or are you sticking with your aunt's?'

Kate gasped. 'I'd completely forgotten . . . Still, I'm sure I can get someone to deliver a mattress this weekend.'

'See you sometime this evening,' Maz said dryly. She picked up the tray. 'Everything OK last night, by the way?'

Kate omitted Tim's excursions, but touched on Jenny's nightmare and Lynn's quietness.

'Starting her teens early, my poor Lynn. Hogs the computer to record Her Thoughts and Feelings. And Jenny does get these dreadful nights. The doctor suggested sleeping tablets of all things.'

'Have you thought about hypnosis?'

'Oh, I'm not sure . . . Maybe she'll grow out of them.'

What time could she decently phone Graham? They probably got them up early on these courses, so she might try soon after seven. Or what if he was at home? He'd not indicated how long the course was to last. You couldn't drag an innocent man from his slumber at this hour, not at the weekend. But he might want her to. She'd have to try, but not from the bus. Perhaps she should take her clean clothes home and try from there. What about the workmen? There'd be a room. And it might be worth taking her car in, she was so early.

She was half way up her road when she remembered she hadn't phoned PC Kaur. How could she have forgotten something as important as that? She'd have to jot it down.

'You all right, Kate?' Her neighbour was putting out milk bottles so thoroughly washed Kate could see bubbles of detergent in the bottoms of them.

'Hi, Mrs Mackenzie! Miles away, wasn't I? Yes, I'm fine. And the house is coming on nicely. Oh, my God: I've still got your casserole, haven't I? Can I give it you now? I'm so sorry. Come on in.' Why couldn't she stop the words pouring out? It wasn't just guilt over the casserole – it was her fears about Royston. What would that sort of accusation do to the family?

'Don't you worry, love. When the Lord made time, he made plenty of it.'

By some miracle, the casserole was still in the bathroom, where she'd taken it to wash it, and no one had yet got round to using it as an ash tray. She ran downstairs with it.

'You're right: this place is coming on a treat. My Lord, what's all this in here?'

'Kitchen units. Flat packs. I've got a bloke coming to fix them, but he can't do anything until the work surface comes. So I'm staying at the Manse.'

Mrs Mackenzie raised an eyebrow. 'Which chapel you going to?'

'That funny big one down by the park.'

'We used to go there. Royston was in the BB. Now we prefer C of E. Kind, good people,' she added with a certain emphasis.

Perhaps she and her family had had to endure the pettiness of some of those old women.

'Did you find –' Kate began.

'We all go. A family that prays together stays together.'

There was no reply to that. She had to find one, of sorts. 'Royston too?'

'Sometimes.'

'I've started to coach the BB football team. Trying to get them off the bottom of the league.'

'We all have our crosses to bear,' Mrs Mackenzie observed. And, taking the casserole, she left.

Alf arrived. His pick-up, across the road, was laden with wood. 'I got this job lot, Kate, me love. So I've taken the liberty – I mean, here's the quote I prepared.' He dug in his trousers. 'And I'll put this lot in for you at fifty quid below that.'

'It's not back of a lorry stuff, is it, Alf?' The question was out before she could stop it.

'Would I do that? Someone ordered extra, tried to get the wholesalers to take it back, and when they wouldn't, I stuck my oar in, and here we are.'

'I'm sorry. Comes with the job. You know, the police.'

He stared, round eyed. 'You a lady policeman?'

'CID. That's why you don't see me in a uniform.'

'Well, you don't look like one, that's all I'll say.'

So what did he expect? Size ten feet? Involuntarily, she dropped her eyes to her neat four-and-a-halves.

'I'll leave this lot in the entry, shall I? And get on with your wiring and that in the kitchen. Have everything where you want it today, I should think.'

She sat on the floor, her back supported by Aunt Cassie's magnificent wardrobe. My God: when had she last visited Cassie? She'd have to try and fit it in this evening, if things were slack at work. But perhaps it was up to Graham to say how busy she'd be.

She dialled. A long wait. And then a woman's voice. 'Yes?'

It was not encouraging.

'May I speak to DCI Harvey, please?'

'You people think you own him. For your information he's out cleaning the car.'

At eight in the morning?

'Could you ask him to phone me back? It's quite urgent.'

'Certainly not. You hang on. Then it'll be your phone bill, not ours.'

No wonder Sally wanted Graham to have a fling! The footsteps took for ever to recede, and then she heard more urgent ones coming back. Why hadn't the woman taken the phone to him? It was his mobile, for goodness' sake!

'Hello?'

'Graham, it's Kate!' She couldn't disguise the pleasure and relief in her voice. It was so good to make contact with a solid island of sanity in what seemed a very heavy sea.

'Give me your number,' he said quietly. 'I'll call you back. Ordinary phone, for preference.'

There was only one telephone, and that was in the living room. Maybe it would reach halfway up the stairs, away from the worst of Alf's noise – he had a penchant for Radio Two.

She ran, gathered it, stretching the cable carefully, and perched it on her knee. Panting slightly, she snatched up the receiver first ring.

'Problems?' he asked. No preliminaries.

'Maybe solutions.' She too could be terse. 'Duck, for a start. You remember Darren and his duck? There's a railway engine in a children's book called Duck. And you can get models.'

'Abnormal damage – Jesus Christ, are you thinking what I'm thinking?' His voice shook with anger.

'I think I probably am. And what I really want to know is if a little boy who was smashed by a juggernaut the other night has similar damage.'

'Boy? Don't know anything about this.'

'He went missing in Newtown – Cope had just mobilised everyone – everyone except me, incidentally: I never received the phone call someone was supposed to make – when we heard he'd been killed in an RTA. But there are things about the accident – I don't know.'

'It sounds to me very much as if you do, Kate.' His voice became warm with approval. She could see his slow smile in her mind's eye. 'What are your plans for today?'

'Some time today I have to buy a mattress and I have to see Cassie. But I thought I'd go into work, see if I could make sense of one or two things.'

There was a pause. 'Hmm. Now, I've got to take my wife to her hairdresser's this morning. But I shall come in as soon as I can. Go and sort out your mattress now, Kate. And I'll be with you about eleven.' He put the phone down.

Yes! She punched the air and sprang to her feet, grinning. And then she sat down. Why all this fuss? She was simply going to talk to her boss about some particularly vicious crimes. But it was so nice, so very nice, to be taken seriously, to have your judgment trusted.

She'd take the car. Although it was a lovely autumn day, sunny and quite warm, the streets were still almost empty. Saturday rush hours came later, perhaps.

The phone again. Should she leave it? But she decided to take the call.

'Kate? Graham. Did you say you wanted a mattress?'

'Yes: I've got an old-fashioned bed with a metal frame and

springs. Sooner or later I'm going to have to get a modern one and attach the headboard and footboard but I haven't time . . .'

'There's a spare in my garage. Ma-in-law bought it and then didn't like it. All we've got to do is transport it.'

'I'll think of something,' she said.

'Good. We'll sort it out later. See you, Kate.'

'See you!' And, as he put down the phone, she yelled, 'Alf?'

If it hadn't been for the sun slanting across her desk, she wouldn't have noticed her memo pad. The top page was clean, but that wasn't surprising. She wasn't a doodler, and once she'd dealt with a message she tended to scrap the paper and start afresh. What was surprising was the depth of the indentations on this new top page: someone had scribbled in a hurry, underscoring something. If she looked at it face on, there was nothing to see. If she slanted it even more, so the light caught it at an even more oblique angle, she might be able to work it out. Not quite. Not quite.

Someone else was coming in: instinctively, she shoved the pad into her tights drawer. She was sitting down, casually reaching another from her top drawer when Cope saw her.

'What are you doing here?' The question wasn't hostile, more surprised.

She stood. 'Trying to catch up on some of my back-log, Sir.'

He nodded her back to her seat. 'Fair enough. Looks like you'll have a lot more to do soon, me wench.' He slapped the file he was carrying. 'That kid as was run over. Young –' He stopped to check.

'Danny Butler, Sir.'

'Right. Well, he wasn't just run over. He'd got a sore arse, too. Like young Darren.'

She shut her mouth on what she wanted to say: that at least they now knew what had done the damage. Far better for Harvey to say that. What she could do was ask, 'Does this mean we've got a murder on our hands, Sir?'

'Murder?'

'Did he fall or was he pushed?' Surely Cope must be testing her in some way. He wouldn't have missed anything as obvious as that. Bully he might be, he couldn't be thick to have got that far in the Force.

'You know what kids are. Shove the Green Cross Code into them till it comes out of their ears and they still run across the road two yards from a crossing.'

'Especially if they're running away from something. Or someone,' she said. 'Like the two mysterious bystanders who called the paramedics. And then disappeared.'

'Some stupid WPC didn't know she should take a statement,' Cope said. 'There's been some more pharmacy break-ins. Ladywood, they've started on now. Here's the reports.' He slung them on to her desk.

No slinging them back; no pointing out they'd got sick bastards out there ruining and maybe ending young lives. Just routine until Graham arrived. Pulling the papers towards her, she sighed. Looked like another morning on the phone.

She heard Graham's brisk, light footsteps coming down the corridor. She was smiling her professional smile when she looked up, but as he came into the room, she could feel her dimples insisting on making an appearance.

'How's it going?' he said, coming to peer at her computer screen.

'The pharmacy break-ins, Sir? I think we –

'Bloody hell, woman – I thought we'd got a murder on our hands. Don't you have a sense of priorities?'

She shrugged. Still without saying anything, she reached in her tights drawer, and handed him the memo-pad, slanting it so that the sun fingered the impressions in the paper. He took it in silence, tilting it backwards and forwards. Then he looked her straight in the eye. 'My room. Five minutes,' he mouthed.

She nodded. He took the pad with him.

Tapping at his door, she found him at his desk, head bent over a sheet of paper.

He looked up briefly, then returned to his task – scraping a pencil lead into fine dust. 'Shades of Biggles,' he said tersely. 'There.' He tipped the graphite on to her pad, shaking and blowing so it filled the indentations.

WPC Harjit Kaur: definitely no ball.

Graham looked at her: 'I'm sure this means something to you!'

She sat down, nodding. 'The lorry driver who ran over young Danny was convinced he was chasing a ball. His parents are equally convinced his ball was in his toy rack, and if he'd got another he must have nicked it. What I'd have liked to do was check the local shops, just in case.'

'But you don't expect any of them to have lost one on Thursday?'

'No. Not now the result of the PM has come in. I think someone – mutilated – him, and wanted him dead. Pushed him under that juggernaut and sent a ball bowling along as well.'

'Quite an imagination you've got, Kate.'

She nodded. 'I know. But there's the hard fact that the two men who dialled nine nine nine beat it as soon as we turned up. Harjit Kaur.'

'The woman the message is from.'

'I hoped to speak to her in person. Forgot to phone her last night, I'm afraid. But at least she was on the ball enough to phone me. Oh. Oh, I'm sorry.'

He gave a bark of dry laughter. 'Sounds as if you could use a cup of tea.'

She got up to make it, but the kettle was empty. 'Back in two ticks.' She took the large polythene bottle, his back-up supply, too.

As she headed for the loo, she wondered how much more she should mention. Was it grassing? Or was it what a loyal officer and friend – friend! – should do? She rolled the word round her head. Well, that was how she thought of Graham, but she'd really been thinking of Colin. Funny how things got mixed up when you weren't thinking about them properly. She washed out the bottle and kettle, and then filled them both. Before she left, though, she put them down so she could tuck up her hair which was escaping from the clips. That was better. No point in looking a total mess.

The room was empty when she got back, the door ajar. She plugged the kettle in, and noticed the mugs. Dirty. Another trip to the loo.

Graham was back when she returned. He was by the kettle, flourishing a plastic cup of milk. 'Sorry: should have washed those before I went.'

'Was it a good course?'

He selected an Assam tea bag. She nodded – she'd share it.

'Not bad. Someone dropped out at the last moment and my name must have come out the hat. Crowd control. May be useful one day, I suppose.' His smile was ironic. 'Come on, Kate, what's been going on? Young Colin's out there with a face like a wet week. Any reason?'

'Only that he didn't get a place on a course.'

'And someone else did?'

She nodded, fishing his tea bag out and dropping into the other mug. He dribbled in milk.

'And?' He wandered over to the window.

'Someone took a file off my desk. By some stroke of good fortune I'd prepared two. And I've kept the information not just on my computer but on two disks, one of which is in my desk, the other at home.'

'That's dodgy, Kate. Taking stuff home. Could lay yourself open to suspicion there.' Then his smile erased the grimness.

'Though of course my room was locked, and my desk ditto. Hmm. I don't like this.'

She stared at the traffic in the street below. An ambulance was trying to push its way through. Another sick kid maybe. Another Danny or Darren.

'You may not like something else I did. I left some bait. I left the computer file number on each sheet, and then told the officer in question I was having trouble with my computer. Maybe the file will wipe itself, Sir.'

'Witness?'

'Another officer. Absolutely reliable. Though he might not like what I'm doing, either.' No, Colin had enough problems of his own.

He said, so quietly she could hardly hear, 'Leave your tea and go and sit on the hard chair. Fast.'

She obeyed. Had her hands in her lap looking penitent by the time the door was fully open. Cope.

'– if it keeps playing up, get it seen to, for goodness' sake,' Graham was saying. The man deserved an Oscar. 'OK?'

Dismissed. Well, she'd had a sip of tea. She nodded, and was at the door herself, held for her by Cope, when Graham added, 'I'll talk to you about the other matter later. Did you fix transport?'

'Yes, Sir. All arranged.'

No, she wasn't proud of being part of a conspiracy, but her pulse was racing with excitement. Never could a series of routine phone calls about attempted break-ins have been made with a warmer, more concerned voice. Yes, she was beginning to love her job again.

Chapter Fourteen

Alf backed his pick-up carefully into a space a few inches too short for it. Kate smiled grimly: on a Saturday afternoon in her road, most parking spaces would be too short. Graham merely parked on the yellow zigzag lines by the school gates. The two men wrestled the double mattress, heaving and wobbling as if in the throes of a giant passion, off the pick-up and into the house. They dropped it in the tiny hall and caught their breath.

Graham peered. 'Where are your stairs?'

'Through the living room. Before you get to the kitchen. And there's a very sharp bend.'

'May need me tow-rope – tie it up, like.' Alf disappeared.

'Kate: are you seriously telling me you've been trying to do a day's work while coping with this lot?' He looked at her and the house with infinite concern.

She wasn't sure how to react. She tried smiling: 'It's getting better every day. But I told you I was staying at the Manse: this is the reason.'

'No place to call your own, and you've come in to work to be subjected to bullying and harassment.' He shook his head 'Yes, that's what we need. Excellent. Have you somewhere flat we can lay this, Kate? Like a floor?' He looked in at the front room and shuddered.

'Living room. It's not too dirty – they found rot and insect infestation and had to put in a new floor.'

Alf sniffed. 'Got a clean dust-sheet in the cab.' He trudged off to get it.

Graham inspected the new door, the old mantelpiece. 'I suppose – one day – but Kate, why on earth didn't you show some sense?'

'I was a bit low on sense altogether. Maybe it's coming back. And the good news is I've let my place in Croydon. And the tenant may even want to buy. So my funds are thawing. Not that Cassie hasn't been extremely generous –'

'Given you a pig in a poke, more like,' Alf said.

Between them they trussed the mattress.

'Bit of good stuff this,' Alf said. 'This weight's springs – none of your foam rubber. Good for your back, Kate.'

'But not for yours or Graham's trying to get it up those stairs.'

As if on cue, before either could protest, a man's voice called from the hall. 'Kate? Anyone at home?'

'Must have forgotten to shut the door,' Alf muttered.

Paul erupted into the room. 'Hi, gorgeous. I kept my promise: tickets for Symphony Hall tomorrow. Oh.' He paused theatrically.

'Alf. Graham. Paul.'

They shook hands solemnly.

'Wonderful timing, Paul. You're a rugby man, you say.' Kate gestured. She was relieved. Alf might be tough, but he wasn't young. And Graham had those rounded shoulders which must put his back at risk if he tried hefting anything as heavy as this.

The older men hadn't been exactly fulsome in their welcome: she thought she'd heard Alf sniff with what seemed horribly like disapproval. And Graham wasn't exactly a bundle of smiles. She hadn't got an outbreak of antler-locking on her hands, had she? Well, if they all wanted to show off their masculinity, there was no better way than getting the mattress round that awkward bend without damaging her nice new paint. And their backs.

She appointed herself guide, peering down at them from the landing. Alf joined her, reaching down to steer. Graham and Paul combined their efforts underneath. And within moments they were stuck.

'Hang on!' Alf leaned down and tightened the rope. 'Not

so fast, young fellow-me-lad – never heard the one about the tortoise and the hare? Well then. Nice and easy. Let us old uns set the pace.'

Kate had spread the old springs with a thick – and even older – blanket: she didn't want this mattress damaged. And although she'd dusted and indeed wiped the springs and the frame, it would never be pristine again. She held it flat while they laid the mattress down, and straightened it as they untied the rope. Yes.

'Perfect. Thank you all so much. Now, I think you all deserve coffee.'

'Coffee? I can think of better things! But perhaps we'd better wait until we're on our own.'

Alf raised an eyebrow.

'Like that guy going for a walk in the snow, it may be some time. I see you've started on that fence, Alf.'

'Got the weather for it, haven't we? Don't mind a bit of overtime on a day like this.' He led the way downstairs. Graham made sure that Paul went next. Kate was left to bring up the rear.

She organised them onto deckchairs the canvas of which made her fear for their lives it was so thin, leaving them to what would no doubt be laddish chat if Paul had anything to do with it. Or would he leave them to it, on the pretext of helping her? Yes: so she'd better beat him to it, by scooping everything on to a tray as fast as she could.

But the footsteps on the path outside were Graham's. 'Anything I can do?'

'In the short term, open these biscuits. In the long, we may have to devise a way of getting rid of Paul, there. Sticks like a leech.'

So it was foolish of her to mention later that she was going to visit Cassie that evening.

'That's the old lady that Maz is so taken with?' Paul asked.

'That's right. My aunt.' She raised her mug at the chaos of the garden, which probably exceeded that of the house at its worst. Or maybe not. But it was bad enough. Cutting the sycamore trees down had crushed any grass and shrubs that might have survived the recent years of neglect. The shed was on its knees, ready to collapse. 'Funny to think that my childhood memory of this garden is of a fairy-tale garden. Pretty little paths, edged with fancy bricks. Secret places under trees.'

'Plenty of them,' Alf said. 'Now, if you'll excuse me' – he set his mug on the tray and returned to his saw horse. 'Only I want to have a clear run tomorrow – I don't want to leave you with no fence any longer than I can help. News soon gets around.'

'Ah, but you'll be guarding the place again tonight, won't you? Now you've got a proper bed?' Paul prompted her.

'If you want my opinion,' Graham said, sounding like a caricature of a policeman, 'you'll give that mattress a good airing before you sleep on it. It's been in my garage for months.'

'But I bet it's a very solid garage,' said Paul.

'Don't want you going down with rheumatism, Kate,' Alf said. 'Now, I'm afraid I need your room more than your company.'

'And we need to talk shop, Kate.' Graham got to his feet, folded his deckchair and Alf's, and held his hand out for Paul's.

'No, I'll hang them back in the entry on my way out.' So he could take hints. 'What time shall I pick you up tonight, Kate?'

'Tonight? I thought it was tomorrow we were going out? He's got tickets for Symphony Hall – can't wait to see it, I've heard so much about it,' she said to Graham, conscious that she sounded as if she was offering the excuse she was.

'Yes, but we're seeing Cassie tonight. If she's agreed to let the Brigade kids visit her, the least I can do is thank her. And I can hardly swan in when you're not there.'

That was true.

'Are you going anywhere near the Manse? Because you could tell them I shouldn't be late.' She rather thought honours were even.

Graham looked at his watch. 'I suppose you haven't any shopping to do?'

'I've got a week's to do. Why?'

'I promised my wife I'd bring some things in. And Sainsbury's is practically your corner shop. We could talk while we walked.'

She wasn't surprised he seemed embarrassed, but grabbed her bag, checked for her keys, and yelled to Alf to lock up if she wasn't back.

He stopped to look at the privet skeletons in the front garden. 'Oh dear.'

'I know. I shall have to get them out. But if I so much as think about it, Paul will be round there excavating them and telling me what I should do with the garden. Not so much telling as doing it, in fact.'

'Well, what it needs is reducing to ground level, and then double digging with gravel and fertiliser. Sounds just the sort of job an outdoor type like him would love.'

'But would I love him to do it?' She set them in motion down the road.

He looked at her sideways, a question in his eyebrows.

'He's such an overgrown teenager. Doesn't know where to draw the line.'

'You have to draw it for him?'

'Precisely. But he's such a public-spirited sort – devotes himself utterly to the BB. Hasn't had time for girlfriends to civilise him, perhaps.'

Graham snorted. 'Are you telling me you're doing a course of advanced community education for him?'

'He'd love to hear you say that! Him a teacher – sorry, *lecturer*! – in some college.'

'Talk about the blind leading the blind.'

'Quite. And now I've got myself landed with him this evening. On top of tomorrow!' she wailed. 'Just when I wanted a nice girlie chinwag with Cassie. Though she's terribly tetchy these days.'

'Is he planning to enlist hordes of boys and girls from the Brigade to improve her shining hour?'

'Maz – his sister – is on to that. In any case, it's Cassie

who'll improve theirs. Especially if it comes to manners.' They'd reached the High Street. 'You know, I really think we should cross at the pelican – it wouldn't look good in an incident report, two police officers flattened in the same RTA.'

They'd got as far as the delicatessen counter before he opened up. And then it was hesitant. 'So now what?' he asked.

It took her a second to realise he was talking about work. 'Have you had time to look at the PM results?'

'It's the interpretation that's the problem. If I were absolutely convinced I wouldn't be standing here agonising over Camembert and Brie. I'd be mobilising everyone.'

'Not convinced?' Her voice rose in disbelief. She controlled it with an effort.

As if he hadn't heard her, he continued, 'I want to talk to the lorry driver, for a start. He's stuck in Calais until the barricades are lifted. Then young whatshername – the local PC –

'Harjit Kaur?'

'Right. And she's at a wedding – in Delhi. I'm talking to the parents as soon as Family Support think they're up to it. I want the disappearing Samaritans. And all the local newsagents and corner shops selling balls. They're being done now. No point in Uniform not earning a living.'

'The ones that interest me most are the disappearing Samaritans. Any sort of ID at all from the paramedics?' She took her number from the dispenser. 107. The number now being served was 96.

'I'd better get some bread,' he said. 'Any for you? Or are you at the Manse for the duration?' He didn't sound pleased with the prospect.

'I want to move into my home,' she said, surprising herself. Did she really think of that dump as home? 'But I'm in a quandary. Would Maz and Giles see it as an insult if I wanted to return to what's basically a building site? Or would they be relieved to be lodger-free at last?'

'Have you got a freezer yet?' he asked.

She blinked. It didn't seem an answer to her question.

'And,' he pursued, moving to one side to let a stream of trolley-pushers through, 'a fridge and a cooker and a washing machine and a TV and all the other adjuncts of civilised living? Because I'd start acquiring them. Then as soon as all your floors are safe and your units are in, you can move in properly. Meanwhile, if this is a murder inquiry – and I'm sure in my bunions it is, even if I haven't managed to convince Superintendent Gordon yet – then you'll be working all hours God sends and then some.' He bent over the brown sliceds. She thought he added, 'Nest while you can, Kate!'

It didn't seem to be an answer to her question, but her number was coming up and she shuffled into the queue.

At the check-out, they carefully separated the contents of the trolley – mostly his, of course, despite her claim she had a week's worth to do. It was all so familiar – except there was no friendly bicker over paying – that she bit her lip to stop the tears coming. If that wasn't bad enough, someone in the straggle behind them was wearing Robin's cologne.

Cassie wasn't in her room when Kate and Paul tapped at the door.

They stared, Kate for some reason more nonplussed than she felt she ought to be.

'Some sort of emergency, I suppose,' Paul said. 'Why don't you sit down – I'll check it out for you.'

She shook her head. 'Card room more like.' Her voice was flat and prosaic. But despite herself there was a sharp tug of guilt. What if Cassie were ill? All this time she'd never made the effort to go and see her! Even if she couldn't see her every day, the least she could do was contact her regularly. 'Come on – it's this way.'

Paul's face was stubbornly concerned. 'Nurse! Nurse!' he called. 'The old lady – is she all right?'

The 'nurse' was a tea-lady. 'We got a lot of old ladies. Which one would you be meaning?'

'Cassie Whitethorn,' Kate said. She pointed to the door.

'Oh, the one who plays cards all the time. Patience. You her niece? Always talking about you, she is. Sun shines out of your ears, like.'

'Is she all right,' Paul prompted, his voice urgent.

The woman shrugged. 'Far as I know she is. Why don't you try the Card Room? She says the TV lounge is full of silly old buggers losing their marbles.'

Was the charm pure or applied? Whichever it was, Cassie and Paul got on as if they were aunt and favourite nephew. Kate watched with interest, aware that some of her aunt's gracious behaviour to a stranger might be to punish her for her absence. It was certainly on Paul's arm that Cassie leaned when they escorted her back to her room, and when she had to rest on one of the strategically-placed chairs, it was Paul who settled her as if she were the Queen Mother. He told her about his students and his houseplants, his Boys' Brigade and his love of boating. He flirted and he teased.

Cassie was entranced.

Kate let him get on with it. His energy seemed inexhaustible, whereas hers was ebbing fast tonight. She'd be glad of the Manse bed. And soon – as soon as she could fix it – her bed. Graham's mother-in-law's bed.

They drove back to the Manse in silence, and he made no attempt to come in. Well, he'd learned something. Perhaps now she could think about thawing a bit – at least to the level of politeness. Perhaps she'd over-reacted, been a bit puritanical, all this keeping him at arm's length.

But on the whole, she decided, as she pulled herself wearily up the stairs, arm's length was precisely where she wanted to keep him.

Chapter Fifteen

Giles's Sunday morning sermon had been particularly good, about the nature of charity. On a good day, he was clear and lucid, like a really good teacher. She'd managed to persuade the choir to rise above a dirge, too, and was generally feeling good about life. True, she'd be going into work later, but Graham would have told anyone interested that she had a right to religious observance. Whether God would class half an hour's goal-shooting practice as religious observance she couldn't say. But she certainly felt it was a social obligation.

If supermarkets used music to vary the pace of the punters, she didn't see why she shouldn't use a brisk voluntary to speed the dawdling worshippers out of the church. She tried to be subtle: no need to go round antagonising people. But – more quickly than she'd hoped – the chapel was empty and she was free to scuttle off and change her sober suit for a tracksuit.

Twirling her whistle on its cord, she stepped out into the sun, which was strong and low enough to dazzle. The lads were already charging round with enthusiasm, young Marcus among them. She waved cheerily, but then realised that two tall men were stepping between her and her team.

'My goodness, this is what being arrested must feel like!' she said.

But their faces didn't produce answering smiles. It took her a moment to realise that embarrassment was one of their main emotions. For the life of her she couldn't remember their names, although she remembered them clearly. They'd been sherry drinkers. Attached, that was right, to one of the chilly women.

'I'm Alec Walters,' said the elder. 'And this is my son Derek.'

'Of course – we met the other day, didn't we? How can I help? But first I'd like to get the boys doing something purposeful – can you give me two minutes?'

They exchanged looks. Reluctant agreement, she would say. Before they could change their minds, she gathered the boys into a circle and explained what they had to do. No problems understanding or implementing her ideas. Off they went, belting the balls into the white rectangle painted onto the wall.

'Now, Miss Power – er, Kate – this is very awkward,' Alec said. 'We can see you're doing a great job with these lads, but – but you see, there are procedures and if you're to be a BB officer we have to abide by them. You'll forgive me – but you should have filled in a form and supplied references. And we should have taken them up before we let you anywhere near the boys.'

Derek nodded. 'We have to protect them. That's our absolute priority. Anyone wanting to be an officer has to go through the proper vetting and training.'

'There are some nasty people around,' she agreed. 'Look: I did some undercover work at a children's home a few years back: why don't you contact the people in the Met who organised that? They investigated me thoroughly, believe me.'

'Isn't there anyone local we can talk to – to speed things up a bit?' Alec suggested.

'I've only been here five minutes – I wouldn't think anyone knows me well enough to give the sort of assurances you need. Except my aunt, and I suppose family wouldn't count. You'd need long-term, in-depth knowledge of a person to be able to testify they weren't a danger to children.'

The men looked taken aback: perhaps she'd taken the words out of their mouths.

'Look, I've seen what the wrong sort of person, shall we say, can do – it's part of my job. I wouldn't want *anyone* taken at face value if I were a parent. Any more than I'm sure you would. Now, the question is, what are we going to do with

these boys while you check me out? By the way, I don't want
to be an officer. I don't want to be involved in anything but
this. I couldn't do the BB justice, not with a job like mine.
Coaching I can commit to. Nothing else.'

The men shifted awkwardly.

It was time to cut the Gordian knot. She beamed: 'Tell you
what, why don't you train with them? That way you can keep
an eye on me and get fit at the same time.'

'It's a matter of time, isn't it? I mean, we've got a business
to run.'

'Take it in turns? Hang on!'

A skirmish had broken out. She whistled for silence and
stillness, and got neither. She tried again, and yelled, producing
the sort of volume that she used in street brawls. Instant success.
'I thought you were supposed to be training? I thought you were
supposed to be improving your ball skills?' She eye-contacted
each boy in turn. 'Or do you want the team to hold up the
league as long as you're in it? A bit of success, wouldn't that
be nice? A goal or two? Right! Get on with it. Now.'

Alec and Derek – now she came to think of it, more like
brothers than father and son with their matching names – were
deep in whispered conversation when she turned. She gave them
a minute or two to finish. No point in harrying. When, however,
she heard the name Paul Taylor her ears did prick. There was no
way she was going to have him in her training group. The man
liked to dominate people. And there was no way he could play
second fiddle, no matter how good his intentions.

Alec looked up, catching her eye. 'I gather you're on very
good terms with Paul Taylor –'

'With all his family,' she added quickly. 'I'm staying with
Maz and Giles, after all.' She might pre-empt them. 'He's a
rugby man, unfortunately.'

Alec looked crestfallen; Derek missed her point. 'Wouldn't
he want to be involved – after all, he's been in the Brigade
years. Lives for it.'

'As I said, a rugby man. No, he wouldn't want to train
with the boys either.' And if he did, he wasn't going to

get the chance. She hoped her voice was regretful enough. 'So it looks as if we're stuck. Pity. The kids need the help.'

'Couldn't we just bend the rules for once?' Derek appealed to his father.

'No,' she said firmly. 'I know the majority of people who interfere with children are men, but there are women involved too. I spend my life enforcing rules. I wouldn't want to bend someone else's myself. We'll suspend activities until I've got clearance – I'm sure the Met will respond quickly.'

'I'll turn up this week,' Alec said. 'Keep an eye on things. OK? And you need this.' He produced a glossy folded card. 'This is our Code of Practice. I'd be grateful if you read it and made sure you observed the contents. Especially the part about physical contact with the boys. An incident like last week's must not be allowed to recur, Kate. For whatever reason.'

She stared: last week's incident? Marcus's asthma! But she'd been as careful as if these guidelines had been branded on her forehead not to touch him. Indeed, she'd done everything she could not to let Paul crowd him. She said nothing, waiting to be prompted.

'With the asthmatic lad. Taking him home – that sort of thing shows – well, favouritism,' Alec continued.

What she wanted to do was ask what the hell she was supposed to do with an asthmatic child with no inhaler. What she needed to know was the source of his information. But the last thing she should do was bridle and deny.

'He was quite poorly,' she said at last, 'and his spray was almost empty. I didn't want him to have an attack on the bus home.'

Derek stepped in: 'You should have left it to the officer in charge. Not tried to deal with it yourself.'

Despite all her first aid training? Despite her experience with Robin's wheezy children? And, most of all, despite her suspicion that Marcus wanted nothing at all to do with a man?

She took a deep breath, swallowing all she wanted to say. 'OK. He's got a new spray now: Paul's put it in his desk, so we know it's full when we need it. And if one of you is with

me during the sessions and there's an emergency, you can deal
with it?'

The men exchange glances, but nodded.

'Fine. So I'll carry on as usual, under supervision, and you'll
check me out. Now: I really must get back to those kids. Calm
them down with a bit of ball control!'

If anyone needed calming down it was her, of course. All
these men wanting control! But if there was one thing being a
police officer taught you it was to obey rules even when they
seemed stupid. And this little Code of Practice wasn't stupid.
A glance was enough to show her that sensible, but sensitive
minds had been at work on it. She tucked it in her pocket,
and turned to the boys.

'Of course we take the issues seriously,' Giles was saying, as he
carved roast pork. 'An organisation like the BB's like the Scouts
– a magnet for the little-boy-fancying weirdos of this world.'

'I wish they were weirdos,' Paul said seriously. 'The trouble is,
they don't all come with dirty macs and staring eyes. Respectable
people, most of them.' He turned to Kate. 'There's even some
in the police, one hears.'

She wouldn't bite. 'I'm sure you're right. We've got paedophiles, wife-beaters, the lot. Wherever you've got people,
you've got problems. You've probably got them in colleges
like yours.'

He tore his hair: 'We've got nasty teachers? Don't tell the
media! At least the police don't have the media on their backs
all the time. The way the press go on you'd think all the world's
ills can be laid at the door of teachers. And the minister of
education's leading the pack! All we want is a bit of support.
Oh, and a bit of pay, too. We really are the Cinderella of the
education world. You'll see what I mean when I show you
round my college!'

Maz looked at Giles: Kate could see it was a significant
and meaningful look. Well, she'd evaded marriage arrangers
for years enough. Though she did seem to be playing into

their hands by going to this concert with him. Time to break the growing silence. She thought she could detect an unusual stuffing for the pork: she could ask about that.

Graham greeted her arrival with a smile. 'How was the football?'

'Nearly non-existent.' She explained.

'Good to know one organisation's taking the issue seriously.' He took the folded card and scanned it. 'Hmm. Good for the BB. But it puts a hell of a responsibility on the Captain or the Minister.'

'Both of whom would be trained,' she said.

'Good.' He passed back the card.

'Any developments?' she asked, sitting down opposite him. 'Like keeping an eye on the school the kids went to?'

'Volunteering? Yes, there's a team set up to keep obbo. Don't want a third victim. Though my bet would be that we're wasting our time. Chummie will already have moved to another source for kids to groom. But we'll do it anyway. And I'd like you to go in there tomorrow and sort out the names and addresses of any other angelic-looking kids. We can get Family Protection to question them – see if any approaches have been made. Of whatever sort. And you could check with the staff if there are any obvious targets.'

'The quiet ones, you mean? Few friends to confide in?'

'Right. And just keep your ears open generally. You're looking very smart, by the way.' His eyes said, *very attractive.*

'Hmm. Not exactly working clothes, are they? But I've got to go to Symphony Hall, remember – Paul's got the tickets – so I thought I'd look the part. And I haven't got many clothes up here to choose from. Now I've got wardrobe space, I could do with a trip to the Smoke to collect some things.'

'Is that a request for some time off?' His face became tightly official.

'Hardly! Not until this lot's sorted. But I shall have to sneak an hour to get some curtains, Graham. Not just warmth, decency. You don't want me arrested for exposing myself to the denizens of Kings Heath.'

Paul was as proud of Birmingham's new city centre as if he'd designed and built it himself.

'I can't believe you haven't made the effort to come and see it before this,' he said, gesturing. 'I mean, it isn't as if you work in Solihull or somewhere. You're practically here. Why haven't you been in your lunch hour or after work?'

'We tend to work through lunch when we're busy. Which is most of the time. And my memories of Brum are of a nasty dirty place devoted to the car. But this – it must look lovely by daylight.'

'Even better by night, I reckon. Look at the lights in that cascade. Isn't it magic?'

She had to agree it was.

'Now, we'll walk through the Forum past the Rep to Symphony Hall. Good job it isn't raining.'

Paradise Forum had to be the naffest bit of civic development in years – what other public place would have as its focal point the Lottery stand! – and she wasn't sure about the squiggles of coloured lights on the face of Symphony Hall, but she fell for the ICC interior, suave and elegant compared with the scruffiness she remembered of the old Town Hall. And the acoustics were all they were cracked up to be. Although Paul had booked seats right up in the highest tier, the sound was excellent.

'You're not bothered by the height?'

She shook her head.

'Only some people say it's bad for vertigo. I was afraid you might find it made you dizzy.'

It would have been sensible to check before he'd booked them, then, wouldn't it. But she'd abseiled down post office towers with the best of them, and had never understood – though never doubted – that grown men and women could be reduced to shaking and gibbering at the thought of going up a ladder. She settled back to enjoy the concert.

So would Maz and Giles still be up watching TV when they got back to the Manse or would they have beaten a tactful and tactical retreat so Kate would have the pleasure of Paul's company solo?

A compromise. They were drinking coffee in the kitchen. So it would be in the kitchen that Kate would sit. And she would discover the need for an early night.

Maz and Giles were in the middle of an argument, however. Not the raised voices and slamming fists she'd so often seen. But she sensed there was some passion, nonetheless. Field sports, and whether they should be made illegal. Kate had her own views, which involved the impossibility of forcing big silly men on bigger, sillier horses to do what the law wanted them to do. Or not to do.

'And if you ban hunting, are you going to ban other sports that involve killing?' Giles demanded. 'Pigeon-shooting? Angling?'

'You'll have to forgive my husband, Kate – he's country born and bred and try as I might I can't civilise him. Yes, I'd ban angling, Giles. All those maggots. Imagine coming home and finding your husband or son had left a tin of maggots open! Happened to a friend of mine once – came down in the night for a drink, thought she was walking on sugar and found – well, I can't go on,' Maz laughed.

Kate was laughing too. Oh, yes. Very funny.

'They'd be very sleepy,' Paul said. 'Apparently if you want to make them lively enough to be any use you have to put them in your mouth.'

'And remember not to eat your sandwiches!' Giles cackled. 'Actually, when my Gran was young, if you had earache, you put a maggot in your ear.'

Kate forced herself to speak: 'Haven't they started to treat bad bruises with leeches again?'

Paul nodded. 'And they're using maggots to clear wounds

which have become gangrenous – just like in the First World War. I wonder if you'd feel them, munching away –'

Maz shuddered dramatically. 'Enough!'

Giles grinned. 'OK, I'll ban fishing – but only because of the maggots. And it's townies that fish.'

Say something or go and be sick. She swallowed her saliva and tried: 'I'd ban the townie-fishermen.' Yes, she had her voice under control. Nearly. 'They're like darts players – all beer-gut and no muscle.'

'Like slugs,' Paul suggested.

Kate thought he shot a look at her.

'Far worse,' Maz laughed. 'At least slugs have no choice. Fancy allowing your body to – ugh! More coffee, anyone? Biscuit?'

The men patted their trim waistlines, preening. Kate, to take the taste from her mouth, took two.

The biscuits didn't work. But at least she kept them down until Paul had kissed her a public and affectionate goodnight. And then she'd just reached the loo in time.

'You all right?' It was Tim, pink and ruffled in his pyjamas.

'Fine,' she whispered, wiping her mouth.

'Something you ate,' he said wisely.

'Something I ate,' she agreed.

'Better have a drop of Dad's brandy.'

'No: we mustn't disturb anyone.'

'You sure?'

'Sure. Off you go to bed. I'm fine, now.'

'You sure?' At last he seemed to accept it, and padded off.

Before she'd even closed her bedroom door, there was a gentle scratching.

'Tim! You should be in bed!'

He produced a shapeless teddy bear. 'He's not my best one. But he always used to look after me when I was ill.'

'And he'll look after me now? Tim, you're a sweetie. Night-night!' She kissed his cheek.

Getting into bed, she surveyed the bear. How many germs, viruses and microbes had it had to deal with in its lifetime? Perhaps it could deal with a phobia too.

Chapter Sixteen

Kate had phoned the headmistress to ask if she and Colin could slip into the school assembly. At one level it would be easier than scanning pages of posed photographs, searching for children who might attract unwanted attention. At another, she wanted to see for herself the little community which had been so cruelly bereaved. Darren was back. They were trying to see if everyday life would help him recover. But he was still not speaking.

'Not much therapy finding one of your mates is dead,' Colin said, unfastening his seat belt.

'But they don't know quite how he died. Any more than we do.' She cut the ignition.

'Come on: you feel it in the twitching of your thumbs!'

She nodded, then added, 'Supposed to bring bad luck, quoting that play.' She was crossing her fingers despite herself.

On their way in, they walked past their colleagues, spending the day in what appeared to be a ordinary decorator's van. Not a nice day, either. Hot in even the autumn sun. Cramped and smelly. And Sally only a couple of weeks before she left – was mixing with the young mothers. Was there anyone watching the children who didn't seem to have brought a child? Anyone, in other words, prospecting for a victim?

The children washed and swirled round the playground, busy in their own worlds. Colin and Kate slowed to watch, penned behind a chainlink fence separating children from the adult entrance. The school had done its best with security. And even as she turned to speak to Colin, an adult approached them.

'Can I help?' No one was getting into her school without good reason, her voice and posture said.

Kate resisted the urge to be equally officious, and she put her hand on Colin's arm. Flashing IDs would be too melodramatic.

'Mrs Hassan's expecting us,' she said.

'Ah.' The monosyllable spoke volumes.

'Nice artwork,' Colin ventured as they followed their guide. It was. The walls were bright with huge autumn leaves. There were photos of all the staff: they were following Mrs Williams, who was also photographed surrounded by her class. Four W. Kate caught Colin's eye. And looked meaningfully at the other class photographs.

'If you'll sit down and wait,' Mrs Williams said, 'I'll see when Mrs Hassan can see you.'

'Wasted here,' Colin whispered, as they watched her disappear into the Head's office, closing the door ostentatiously behind her. 'Ought to be a GP's receptionist.'

'She might not be the only thing that's wasted. Our time might be, too. Notice the kids? I thought perhaps the white kids were being kept away or something.'

He nodded. 'Well, it is Newtown. Most of the kids'll be African-Caribbean or Asian. Unusual to have an Asian Head, though.'

But the woman who opened the door with a friendly smile was a middle-aged European, her blonde hair fading slightly to grey. She was three or four inches shorter than Kate, and was still slim. For some reason she'd chosen to wear a shapeless pinafore-dress in an unflattering grey-brown. The material looked horribly like crimplene. And why had she chosen those trainers to go with it? Surely a woman on her salary could do better than that – after all, she was a role model for all these children. A little make-up wouldn't have hurt, either.

'I'm Detective Sergeant Kate Power. And this is Detective Constable Colin Roper.' Kate always liked to make it plain who was answerable to whom.

Mrs Hassan nodded. Maybe she too had been taken for a

colleague's junior, simply because he was a man. 'Tea or coffee?' she asked. Her voice must once have been low and pleasant, but had been coarsened by all those years yelling across windy playgrounds. 'I can't start the day without my caffeine fix, so I don't expect anyone else to either. But there's herbal tea if you'd prefer.'

They opted for coffee. Mrs Hassan put her head round another door and spoke.

Then she came and sat opposite them. 'Tell me how I can help.'

Kate smiled. 'As I said on the phone, we have no evidence at all that any of your children are at risk. But it's better to be safe than sorry in these cases. And now there's Danny.'

Mrs Hassan nodded. 'But Danny was run over. Wasn't he?' She looked sharply at Colin.

Kate answered. 'In absolute confidence, Mrs Hassan, there is evidence that Danny may have been assaulted, too.'

She went so white that Kate was afraid she was going to keel over. But from somewhere – all those years in control of herself and others, perhaps – Mrs Hassan found some words. Her voice was so tight they had to struggle to hear what she said. 'And was murdered to keep him quiet?'

Kate kept her voice flat, normal. 'I didn't say that, Mrs Hassan. All we know is that he was run over. The lorry driver swears he was chasing a ball. But we're taking the case very seriously, very seriously indeed.'

Mrs Hassan raised a finger to silence her. 'Come in! Ah, thanks, Parmjit. Just put it on the table here, please. Thanks.' She waited till her secretary had left. 'Now, is there any relevance in the fact that both Danny and Darren are blond, blue-eyed cherubs? Were. Oh, whatever.' She seized a fistful of tissues from the box on her desk. 'You get so fond of them. I've got to go and take assembly and I can't stop crying. Been like this all weekend. Kept thinking if only I'd hammered road safety just one more time it might – But now you're saying –?'

Colin's turn: 'We're not saying anything, Mrs Hassan. Like you, we're just playing around with pieces of the puzzle. But if there's anything we can humanly do to prevent another child suffering in any way –'

'I think you'll find life can devise any number of ways of making people suffer,' she said drily. 'Especially when their childhoods are as deprived as these children's.' She stood up, more stiffly than Kate would have expected of someone of her weight and build. 'OK. Time for assembly. And you can look at all our records. But I can tell you both now, Sergeant, that you won't find many other Darrens or Dannys in my school.'

Nor did they. Colin watched the dark heads bobbing out of the room, like ducklings on a pond. 'At least they should be safe from our bloke.'

'If not from the problems of poor housing and poor diets. I wonder how many will make it to university, for instance. But we mustn't let ourselves get blinkered, Colin. Just because two pretty white kids have been victims, that doesn't mean the next can't be a pretty black kid. So we do what we came here for: to look at photos.' In the end they got together a list of possibilities. 'I'll pass this on to Family Protection as soon as I've bought a decent cup of coffee,' Kate said. 'And a cake.'

'Eh?' Colin pretended to faint with shock.

'Coffee break. Nice day. Fresh air. Time to breathe.'

'Why all this luxury?'

'It occurred to me yesterday just how many lunch-times we've had to work. Do you realise, I didn't get as far as the new city centre till yesterday.'

'Hell! I was going to get tickets for Symphony Hall, wasn't I? Forgot all about it. I'll get a programme.'

There was a knock at the door.

Mrs Hassan's head appeared. 'If you've finished, can I have my office back? I've got a couple of confidential phone calls to make.'

Kate got to her feet. 'We shall need the names and addresses of these children.' She picked up her list. 'I'd rather not ask your secretary.'

Mrs Hassan grimaced. 'Parmjit's safer than the Bank of England. But give it to me if you prefer. I'll get them off the computer for you.'

★

'But you don't think he'll be surveying that school again?'
Graham sat on the desk at the front of the Incident Room,
his back to the photos of the two boys pinned to the wall.

'In the first place, if he's picked those two, he's already had
time to select any other victim he might fancy, and can simply
wait for the hoo-ha to die down before he moves in. In the
second, as the headmistress pointed out, if his taste's for blue
eyes and golden curls, there aren't many that fit the bill. But
there are some beautiful children there: African-Caribbeans with
huge eyes and curls; Asians with huge eyes and little top-knots. If
you want red heads, there are a tough-looking couple I wouldn't
want in my class if I had the misfortune to be a teacher. And
there's a cluster of loud Irish kids with hair that's every colour
except gold.'

Graham slipped off the desk, crumpling a styrofoam cup.
'I'm awash with water!' He added more quietly, 'Fancy a decent
cup of tea?'

'I'll phone these names and addresses through to Family
Protection, shall I?' She glanced quickly in the direction of
Cope. He was flicking through a file, his shoulders hunched
and his face drawn. Anyone else and she'd have described him as
depressed. In a far corner, Selby was hard at work on a computer,
moving and clicking his mouse with slow determination. He
was so deeply engrossed he didn't even look up when Graham
left. She picked up a phone.

And thought better of it. If the only witnesses to her
conversation were that unholy duo, she'd rather use the phone
in the main office.

Colin was working through a file on an old case – he was
due in court the following day, and Graham had threatened
murder if anyone made a hash of their evidence.

She made her call. As she left for Graham's office, she stopped
by the door. 'I see Selby's profited by that computer course,' she
said. 'He can't tear himself away from the bloody thing.'

'Have to set a mouse-trap,' he said idly. 'He does seem
quite hooked, though. Perhaps it'll keep his mind off us for a
bit. I mean, you and me separately, if you see what I mean.'

He flushed. 'Hell, just wait till he decides that we're an item. Kate – you don't really mind being my beard, do you?'

She stared blankly.

He made a great show of donning false whiskers, hooking them behind his ears and smoothing them down.

At last the penny dropped. 'Ah! I'm your disguise!'

'And maybe,' he continued, smiling, 'I'm yours.'

Alf was still at work on her fence when she got back. She made a couple of mugs of tea, and took them through to the garden before doing anything else. Even before inspecting the front garden again.

'Tea break,' she announced, passing him a mug, handle first. 'You've earned it twice over!'

'That lot wasn't me,' he said, jerking his head towards the front. 'That teacher. Paul. Said you'd asked him to do it, so I wasn't going to argue. And it makes sense, like he said, for me to burn the privet when I have the bonfire for this lot.' He gestured with his mug at the rotten fencing. 'All that extra soil! He's barrowed it all through here – see, that heap, over there.'

Paul had certainly been busy. Not a skeletal bush remained, and he'd levelled the bank from which the hedge had grown down to path height.

'Lot of clay at the front,' Alf said. 'Needs double digging – put in a load of gravel for drainage. And compost, too, if you ever want anything to grow. What'll you plant there?'

Kate shook her head. It was one thing to get rid of something, another to know what to put in its place. And that applied to the back garden even more. Without its monster trees, all she had was a patch of inadequate grass – she could hardly dignify it by the title *lawn*.

'Only I know this woman, see. Done some work for her, as a matter of fact. She does it for a living, designing gardens.'

Kate laughed. 'This is too small for a design, surely!'

'Now that's where you're wrong. A big garden, there's

room for mistakes. One this size and you can't hide it. Same as with your kitchen. Only now it's a nice space, you could afford to put something in the wrong place. Except as far as I can see from your plan, you haven't. Nice job there, Kate.'

'Not me. Well, I suppose I had the ideas. But it's all done by computer. They give you all these different views so you can see what it'll look like. Absolute magic.'

'Ah. The only thing they don't give you is your working surface, of course. And until we get that, we're stuck. You're stuck. No sink, no hob. Good job your aunt had that tap fitted out here. So long as you remember to turn it off inside in the winter.'

Kate nodded. 'Tell you what, Alf. There is something else I should have thought of. A security light. Is it too late to rig one up now? Over the back door?'

'No point in having one at the front, that's for sure. Be on and off all night. Yes, I'll sort something out for you. It'll mean getting the floorboards up again, in that little back room of yours.'

'Let's hope you find another packet of diamonds!' And she told him about Paul's find. It was time she did something about selling the stones. No doubt Aunt Cassie would tell her who to approach. Perhaps she should call in for a few minutes this evening. Without Paul.

'Not just one, but two young men in tow, eh?' Cassie cackled.

'Two?' Kate repeated.

'Well, there's the handsome one you brought on Saturday. Paul, that's him, isn't it? And — hey presto! — who should interrupt *Neighbours* this tea time but another man claiming to be a friend of yours. Not a boyfriend, he didn't use that word. But then, he wouldn't, would he, since he's hardly a boy.'

Kate found herself blushing. If it was Graham, no, he was hardly a boy. Nor a boyfriend either, of course. Friend, that was how she'd describe Graham. And forget *boyfriend* for Paul, too. Better get some plain talking done: that would appeal to Cassie, who certainly didn't consider herself too old for a spot of girls' talk.

'So this not young, not boyfriend, Cassie: did he have a name?' She pulled a chair closer to the bed. She wouldn't look at her watch: she knew without that that she was tired and hungry. But she'd neglected Cassie recently, and if she wanted a long talk, she deserved one. All that kindness needed repaying. And yes, however irritating Cassie might be, Kate was fond of her.

Cassie twinkled. 'I'd have thought you'd be telling me that! All these admirers –'

'And Robin hardly cold in his grave,' Kate cut in, trying to restore sense with a little brutality. 'Paul seems to have a bit of a crush on me. He's terribly Boy Scoutish – he's just dug out that front hedge. Not a word beforehand. Just whipped it out. And he's moved most of the earth to the back garden, just where I don't want it. Still, Alf – he's doing a spot of moonlighting for me – he'll be able to burn the bushes.'

'Alf? Not another one!'

'Alf's old enough to be my dad. He's constituted himself my looker-after-in-chief. And he doesn't like Paul at all. Neither does Graham.'

'That's the man that was here earlier. Must have been handsome when he was younger.'

He still is! But she bit that back in time. 'Always makes me think of a schoolteacher,' she said instead. 'What did he want, anyway?'

'Advice. He said you'd told him I'd investigated all the places he was considering for his mother-in-law, and could I tell him what he should be looking out for. I gave him the file I'd kept. See that he lets you have it back. Or better still, send him with it. I like a bit of male company, especially when it comes with eyes as blue as that.' Cassie leaned back. Kate thought her laugh sounded forced. Perhaps the pain was bad. Cassie opened her eyes again. 'Though why he didn't get his wife to sort things out I don't know. Her mother, after all. Not his. And it doesn't sound as if there's much love lost between them, him and the mother-in-law, that is. How does he get on with his wife?'

'I don't know – I've never met her.'

'Come, now – there must be office gossip. They say bread's the staff of life, but believe me, at my age, it's other people. I like a little foible or two.' She closed her eyes again, and fidgeted with the bedcover. 'But men like that never leave their wives. Yes, I know about your Robin. But this Graham's been with her too long – he'll stay for comfort and convenience. A young woman like you wants a husband and children. You stick to young Paul. Good-looking, fit, healthy. You can convert that – what did you call it, *boy-scoutishness* to being good at do-it-yourself. Save you a fortune on decorating bills. And shoulders like those would be useful about the garden. Nice little bottom, too. We weren't supposed to say such things when I was a girl, but I've been reading all those magazines in the library downstairs. A real education, some of them. Not the things they tell you to do – there's nothing new under the sun – but *writing* about them. In books that aren't literature with a capital L. Some of these Mills and Boon novels. I'd never read one until last week. But they're light in your hands compared with some of these heavy tomes. Now, get me a gin, Kate, and tell me how things are going.'

'Gin!'

'In that bureau. The only problem is keeping the ice, but little Zeena fills up that Thermos after tea every night. And she's bought me tonic that's supposed to taste of lemon. Go on, a stiff one. And one for yourself.'

And why not? Cassie was paying well for her accommodation, and with it the facilities. And if there wasn't a bar – now, that was an idea for someone building sheltered accommodation! – why shouldn't she have her own supply? Her own TV was accepted, and the music centre, not to mention the filing cabinet with all her life neatly docketed.

Kate poured one stiff, one very weak gin. 'I keep forgetting,' she said, helping Cassie into a more upright position, 'about your diamonds. They're still in the Manse safe. But they're not earning you interest or adding to your capital there. What would you like me to do about them?'

'They haven't gone rusty, have they? Well, leave them there. Or if the minister – what's his name, Giles? – finds the responsibility too much, pop them into a bank. No, they'll charge you for looking after them. Ridiculous. You could always pop them back under the floorboards.'

'Could, but won't. I prefer proper safety. I was hoping you might tell me where I could sell them.' Kate looked at her sideways. 'You must have some contacts?'

Cassie returned the look. 'I might be able to make some telephone calls. Twenty, we'll sell twenty. The rest you'll have for an engagement ring. And a pair of ear studs. Time you had your ears pierced. What have I said?'

Kate shook her head. 'Don't fancy that. I'm happy with clip-ons.'

'You couldn't trust diamonds on clip-ons! One yank and –'

'Better that than torn ears. When I was on the beat, the yobs had this great game – tear the earrings from Asian women. And it spread – to African-Caribbean and then to white women. That's when I decided. OK, I've lost one or two I treasured. But no blood. And believe me, you can lose a lot from a torn lobe.'

'Humph. You wouldn't have to wear them on duty. Just sleepers. No one would want those. There's a hairdresser just off the High Street who'll do them very cheap. Let me see – what are they called?'

Kate sipped her gin. All she had to do was change the subject.

'I'm hoping to move in properly in the next couple of days.'

'In? Properly? Where are you now, then?' Cassie fixed her coldly.

'I thought I'd told you. At the Manse. The work on the double-glazing made such a mess. And the kitchen's not quite ready. But Graham's promised me an hour off to get some curtains –'

'Is he going to help choose them?' The eyes were several degrees warmer again.

'That'd be nice,' she said unthinking. 'But I dare say I shall ask Colin – he's a detective constable – to help. He's got brilliant taste.'

Cassie's grin was predatory. But then her mouth turned down. 'Only a constable?'

Kate nodded. 'Only a constable. And very, very gay.'

Chapter Seventeen

Idly, not too keen on getting up, Kate flicked on the radio. The headline she caught on the *Today* programme was like a blow to her stomach. Another missing boy! This one lived in Liverpool, but her alarm bells started ringing. At least the media hadn't yet put two and two together to make half a dozen, but they would, soon enough, Kate thought grimly. And perhaps they'd be right to. All she could think about during the long bus journey was the innocent heads of the Newtown school kids.

When she reached the Incident Room, Selby was already on the computer, shifting the mouse and clicking with some determination, and definitely increased speed. She was impressed, and would have told him so, had not Cope hove into view, followed by the rest of the team. Brainstorming time. If there were any brains amongst them. Graham and Colin would be out – they were giving evidence in a court case – and for a moment she felt isolated. But she'd not crossed swords with anyone for a while, and it would be good to have to make an effort to get along with the others. She sat next to one of the older men, just back from his annual leave.

'You must be Kate,' he said affably. 'Reg Tanner. I've been down in Oz for a couple of months, seeing my son get married.'

They shook hands.

'How are you settling in? Everything all right?'

'Fine, thanks. I've been made very welcome.' *By most, if not all.*

'I bet you have, nice-looking wench like you. Ah, better hush-up.' He turned towards Cope, leading in Graham's absence.

He didn't do a bad job, really. He reviewed all the evidence so far and the on-going activities. The main problems were a total lack of witnesses to Danny's RTA and Darren's continued silence. He spoke with anger of the injuries and the possible cause of the damage – a Hornby 00 gauge railway engine.

'Has anyone shown one to Darren – to get his reaction?' Reg asked.

'Not as far as I know,' Cope replied. 'That's up to the medics, isn't it? We can't go interfering.'

'Has anyone asked the medics?' Reg pursued.

'They have been contacted, with what result I'm unable to say.'

'There's your answer,' Reg muttered to Kate. 'Bet that would open the floodgates. Bloody hell, there's some nasty pieces of knitting around.'

She nodded. 'Have house-to-house inquiries brought up anything, Sir?' she asked aloud.

'Only a lot of mish-mashed notes. Maybe you'd care to help decipher them and make a report, Power. At your convenience, of course.'

Which would teach her to keep her mouth shut. While the others tossed ideas back and forth – none of them greeted with much enthusiasm by Cope, but none received with such hostility – Kate tried to close her mind to the noise of the room. There was something, wasn't there? Something she ought to remember. And as it came to her, she knew it was nothing she wanted to share with Cope. Except she was part of a team. She'd float it gently, and if Cope shot it down, she'd take the rest to Graham. Or start herself. 'I suppose,' she said hesitantly, 'they must take the poor little devils somewhere. Their safe house. There's no reports at local nicks by neighbours of odd behaviour, I suppose?'

Cope didn't even bother to sneer. 'Safe house? Of course. But you don't suppose they'd be so daft as to behave strangely. We're working with cunning buggers here.'

No one laughed at the grotesque pun.

The next question was from Reg: had they warned boys' clubs and other organisations.

'I think you can rest assured that that's underway, Reg. Just because you've been away the world hasn't stopped turning.'

And Reg took it. Not a murmur. And yet he was probably even older than Cope, still a DC so not one of the ambitious ones. But a solid, reliable-looking man. Solid in both senses, come to think of it – the sort of man who might have boxed, played rugby, in his younger days.

No, she wasn't going to push the idea of the safe house. She wasn't going to mention that conversation she'd heard on the bus that wet morning about a mysteriously under-occupied suburban house. She was going to find the house.

'Is anyone going up to talk to the scousers?' Sally asked.

'Fancy a trip up the M6, do you? Well, sorry to spoil your plans, but you'll be staying down here. DCI Harvey'll be going up soon as he's finished in court. Provided you have no objection, Power?'

Pretend not to have heard? Certainly she couldn't ask why she should object – that'd be asking for trouble.

'Eh, Power?'

Bastard! 'Can't think of anyone better, Sir,' she said sunnily.

As soon as they'd been dismissed, she and Reg drifted over to the water dispenser to join Sally: a mutual licking of wounds was due, perhaps.

'Jesus, Sally, me love, he hasn't got any better, has he?' Reg took a plastic cup and filled it, passing it to Sally. 'And what's this about you leaving?'

'I won't say it's all down to His Nibs,' Sally said. 'But it was a factor, Reg. These bloody moods of his – he's worse than my mam, and she's going through the Change. Must be a Male Menopause, like they say.'

'If he goes on like this much longer,' said Kate, 'I'll ask for a transfer to Traffic.'

Someone yelled for Sally to come to the phone.

'You'd better get stuck in too, my wench. And I'll get me a date with my computer. Got to get this bleeder. Hey – what was that you were saying about safe houses and that?'

'Just a hunch. They must take the poor kids somewhere. And it'd have to be detached. Plenty of parking,' she added, thinking about her own house. 'Somewhere where people are out at work all day, and prefer to keep themselves to themselves.'

'You're describing loads of places, aren't you?'

'But if someone had got nosy – *had* contacted their local nick . . .' She tailed off. Cope was back in the room. Back to a morning tapping keys.

Today, despite all the pressures to get on, she scheduled herself a lunch break. Not to buy curtains: she wanted a plan of Birmingham's bus routes and a large scale street map. OK, it meant another night at the Manse, but at least there she'd have a floor large enough to spread out her new maps.

The first problem of course was remembering which bus she'd got on. Any number ran along the High Street into town, but they joined it – and therefore left it – at different points. So unless she knew her number, she couldn't trace the route backwards, couldn't hope to find that rather nice cul-de-sac the women had spoken about. The one with the house where all sounds were suppressed and a flap of felt kept prying eyes from the letter box.

The traffic was so bad, she decided on impulse to stop off at the Kings Heath nick to find out the latest on the rape she'd interrupted. She found Maureen, the WPC she'd dealt with before, slumped over a coffee in the canteen. The only sign of life was from her left hand, stirring in sugar. Kate collected a cup of tea and joined her.

'How are you settling in?' Maureen demanded, straightening up. 'There's a rumour you're going out with a vicar.'

Kate grinned, but shook her head. 'I'm not going out with anyone, Maureen, much as everyone would love to pair me up with someone or other. My bloke was killed this summer, remember. I don't want a relationship. Sorry,' she added.

'Don't worry. Everyone treats me like an agony aunt. Last

time I was at a conference I got this Chief Superintendent telling me he was afraid he was a transsexual. He thought a bonk with me might help him decide.'

'I won't ask if it did! Any news, by the way, of the lads who didn't have that sort of excuse for bonking? Those young rapists I disturbed?'

'The girl's being tested for STDs, poor kid. Nearly hysterical. But she's not pregnant. And she thinks she might prefer to go and live in Leicester permanently, auntie permitting. And her family over here seem glad to be shot of her. But as to her assailants, no, we've got nothing yet. They would have to be sodding Afro-Caribbean – can't interrogate anyone without being accused of racial harassment and damaging community relations. As if raping a sixteen-year-old isn't pretty harmful to community relations.'

The women sat in silence for a bit. Then Kate asked, 'What time do you finish today? Fancy a pizza or something?'

'You mean you haven't got to dash off to your vicar?'

'Avoid his brother-in-law, more like. Which is not always easy when you're staying at the Manse.'

'I shan't be off shift till ten. By which time all my tum wants is an omelette. So we'd better take a rain-check. Unless you fancy eating here? Oh, it's not that bad!'

'OK: what do you recommend?' Kate pushed up from the table with what she hoped looked like enthusiasm. She cannoned into a tall, bespectacled man.

'OK, Sarge,' Maureen said. You haven't come all up here just to ask me what time it is. Problem?'

'Hole in one, Mo. We've got a girl in tears at the desk. No idea what's the matter – she won't talk to a man.'

'Sounds like they're playing my tune,' Maureen said, getting up. 'We'll have that pizza another time, Kate. Specially if you make it a balti – there's a good place in York Road.'

So that was that. The traffic was still solid, so she left her car where it was and walked down the High Street towards her home. What she had to do was find out that bus number. And by far the easiest way was on foot. She could pick up supplies at one of the supermarkets, too. And window shop. Yes, those curtains looked good. It'd be nice to shop locally, rather than using the big city centre shops. Provided she could get out here while the local shops were still open.

She'd caught that bus at a stop by the parish church. That's it. Two shelters, one nearer the lights than the other. Had she got on at the first or the second? For the life of her she couldn't remember. And clearly it mattered. She'd got on a double-decker, surely. And as she watched, a double-decker came up the main road. And a single pulled in from Vicarage Road, the 35. Were all 35s single-decker? Were any 50s single-decker? And now, since both buses had filled up and pulled out, there was no one to ask.

Suddenly homesick, she crossed at the lights and headed for her house. Just to see the progress, just to see when she could call it hers. That was all.

And she nearly walked past it. She'd forgotten there'd be no hedge and Alf's team had moved to the front of the house: Aunt Cassie's dispiriting black was under an even more dispiriting dark grey undercoat. And light grey round the window, which would soon be white.

She let herself in. They'd started on the skeleton of the kitchen now, though nothing could be finished till that working surface came. Not even a slot for her microwave. Upstairs to reassure herself that there was progress somewhere. Her bedroom. Not Aunt Cassie's now, hers. This weekend she'd put some pictures on the wall, that'd be better. And those curtains in the High Street shop would be just the ticket. If not just the size. She slipped back downstairs to find a tape measure. Working quickly, but, she hoped, accurately, she jotted down the dimensions of each room, including the windows, in her organiser. Right! Ready to build a home.

And ready for some supper. Too late to cook, especially in someone else's kitchen. She'd get one of those magnificent chicken tikka naans from the chip shop she'd tried before.

The assistant greeted her like an old friend. 'How many d'you want, chick?'

'Just the one, thanks.'

'Only one! But it was three last time!'

She couldn't explain, could she? 'I've already eaten,' she lied cheerfully. 'This is just a snack!'

Paul was washing up when she arrived. He dried his hands, and made much of finding her a clean plate and pressing salt, pepper and any other condiment on her. At last she convinced him there was spice enough in the chicken, and that she needed no more than a plate and a knife and fork.

'Thanks for all your efforts in my front garden,' she said, belatedly. 'You've really opened things up. D'you think the wall's all right? It doesn't seem to have much in the way of foundations.'

'Last as long as you, that wall. I thought some cotoneaster would look nice against it – I'll look out for some. But nothing by the window or you'll get damp in your foundations.'

She nodded. 'Maybe a clematis up the side of the bay window. And a hanging basket: I've always liked hanging baskets.' Though for this she'd have to consult her neighbours – they shared the wall, after all. Another chance to talk to Mrs Mackenzie, and possibly the charming Royston.

Although he sat and watched her eat, he got up as soon as she'd finished. 'I'm sorry,' he said. 'I've got these piles of marking. Have to love you and leave you.'

'No problem,' she said, realising too late she had not made the most tactful response. 'I've got a load of work to get through myself.'

She was running George V round the track when she asked Tim if he ever travelled by bus.

'Everyone does,' he said, watching it round a couple of circuits. 'Dad says it's better to use buses for going to town and that, because of the parking.'

'So which do you catch?'

'Any of those on the High Street,' he said. 'They all stop by the hot dog stall. The West Midlands Transport ones and the Your Bus ones. Though Dad says West Midlands took over Your Bus.'

'Which are best?'

'I like the double-deckers best. Except they do sway about a bit.'

She reversed George V into a siding. 'Which one now? So are the double-deckers on all the routes?'

'Let's get an HST running. No. Only the West Midlands ones. The big blue-and-silver ones. Except some are blue and cream – that's their old livery. They're on the fifty route.'

'Nothing else?'

'No. The rest are all single. Why?'

'Just that I got on one when I first arrived and I couldn't remember which it was.'

He nodded, as if that was explanation enough. 'Let's do some shunting,' he said. 'Come on: it's time Duck earned his keep.' He picked it up: 'Nice little engine,' he said, as if it were a pet hamster.

She looked at his blue eyes and blond curls and prayed that he'd never have cause to think it otherwise.

Chapter Eighteen

Kneeling on the floor of her room at the Manse, Kate spread the street plan and bus route maps in front of her. Her Kings Heath bus-stop had been roughly halfway along a very long route, with lots of culs-de-sac that might be possibilities. If she extended her search to allow for women prepared to tackle a stiff walk, there were even more. How many hours' work to find the right one – more to the point, how on earth would she know it was the right one? One long shot would be to phone all the local nicks just to check whether the well-dressed woman had been public spirited – or plain nosy – enough to report her suspicions. An even longer one would be to start travelling by bus. And to do that efficiently she would have to cover each bus-stop along the route, for the salient time each morning, hoping to see the women she'd overheard.

If she approached Cope she'd get a flat denial and public ridicule. Graham was the only one she could ask. And he was in Liverpool. He'd have his mobile phone with him. Why not phone him – it was only half past ten? But he might be back the following morning: she could ask him then. Except that would postpone action for another day.

Inaction, rather. This could be a long, slow and ultimately unrewarding slog.

Go on: phone him.

What she could do was go in by bus next morning – the traffic was so bad she wouldn't lose much time. And she would phone all the police stations within the area, just on the off-chance.

She was late, of course, and as she ran from the bus-stop in town kicked herself doubly: the morning she'd overheard those women she'd been even later than this. It must have been after eight when she'd reached the High Street, and here she was, trying in vain to make that seven-thirty start everyone honoured.

At least she was on the phone, obviously talking to a police colleague, when Cope peered round the door; he'd have to postpone his bollocking, though she couldn't imagine him cancelling it altogether. She asked, waited, had nil returns. So much for that idea. So when she spoke to Graham she'd try not to overplay the significance of the rest of the plan.

Colin breezed in just as she was brewing some coffee. He put his hand up to give a friendly five: 'We got him! Sent down for four years.'

'Is that long enough?'

'I'd have said seven; Graham said we were lucky to get more than two. So that's fine.'

'I thought Graham was off to Merseyside?'

He wagged a finger: 'Nosy! Yes, he set off last night, must have been about six. All that lovely traffic on the M6. I told him to hang on an hour – wouldn't make all that much difference to the time he arrived there, after all – but that would have meant going back to Mrs H, and Graham doesn't like going back to Mrs H if he can avoid it.'

'Why does he? There's such a thing as divorce – God knows enough of us end up with broken marriages.'

'Don't ask me, ducky – not my scene at all.' He returned his voice to normal: 'Thing is, he's got religion, see? Serious stuff. Not just your C of E on your next-of-kin form. Something unlikely. Seventh Day Adventist or Mormon or something. And divorce is Frowned Upon. Poor bastard. Get him to talk to you. He needs all the shoulders he can find to cry on.'

'He doesn't strike me as the sort of bloke who'd cry publicly.'

'You know what I mean. I only know because – well, there was a WPC he fancied. Almost as much as she fancied him. He'd just made it to Inspector. Oh, out in West Bromwich or somewhere. I knew her – even went out with her before I realised honesty was the best policy. Anyway, she and I keep in touch. I heard all about it from her.'

'She might have been biased,' Kate said mildly. 'Like me and Robin's wife,' she managed to add. 'Even if she'd walked on water I couldn't have thought any good of her.'

He smiled, as if acknowledging the effort she'd made. 'Oh – but you piece things together.'

'Does he still see your friend?'

'Clean break. She's got another bloke, now. University lecturer she met when she was on a course. Right: back to the grindstone. Did I miss much yesterday?'

The team that had been watching the school had seen no one suspicious. None of the families contacted by Family Protection and social workers reported any of their children being approached. It was a gloomy and dispirited team that sat in the Incident Room.

'We've drawn blanks everywhere,' Cope concluded. 'But there's news that a kid somewhere in Devon, Dawley or some such –'

'Dawlish, Sir?' Sally put in.

'Dawlish, is it? I didn't realise you were one of our intellectual high-flyers, Sally. DS Power, now, we all know she's got letters after her name – didn't know you had, too. So now we know it's Dawlish. Little one-horse seaside town. Anyway, this lad's been approached by a man and a woman. I thought we should go and take a gander. Power, how soon can you be there?'

'By tea-time, gaffer. But I'll need to go and pick up my car – it's back in Kings Heath.'

'No. I won't ask why. I'm sure there's some explanation you're dying to favour us with, but frankly, I haven't time.

Take one from the pound, for Christ's sake. Stay as long as you need. You're not much use here.'

Swallow it. She had to swallow it. 'I shall be back by tea tomorrow, Sir. I coach a football team on Thursdays. Can't miss that.'

There was a guffaw. 'Oh, neither can we, Power, neither can we. All these women running round.' He joggled imaginary breasts. 'Tell me when your next game is.'

'Saturday, Sir. Boys' Brigade Junior League. I coach little boys.'

As an exit line it wasn't bad. It covered the seething frustration she felt. No curtains – well, she'd survive. No chance to start searching for that crucial cul-de-sac. No chance of checking her theory with Graham.

She collected the file Cope had put together, reached for the overnight bag she kept as a matter of habit in her locker, and remembered in time to phone the Manse. She didn't like leaving her message on their answerphone – they deserved a more personal explanation – but neither Maz nor Giles was at home. And then she was on her way.

She picked up the M6, and then peeled off on to the M5. Spectacular views of the once industrial, still tatty West Midlands. Someone somewhere ought to be pouring money into the area. It was the heart of the industrial revolution, if not the birthplace – that honour belonged to Ironbridge, didn't it? Mecca for school trips. She still remembered Blist's Hill in the pouring rain, then, only an hour later, Blist's Hill in quite savage sun. Weird, the British weather. Like now: even though you'd have thought the bright Indian summer weather general over the country, she was running into skeins of mist. And that could mean fog.

Near the M4 turn off, she ran into it. Thick, mucky stuff. She switched on every sensible light, and dropped speed dramatically. At last, she decided she might be safe at thirty. And people were hurtling past her at eighty, ninety.

Just as she was bracing herself to remember all her first-aid skills, the fog lifted. Brilliant sunshine, as if she'd been imagining everything.

Time to take a break in any case. She pulled off at Gordano, wondering how on earth it acquired such a name: wasn't it originally Peter-in-Gordano, or something equally obscure? Easton! That was it. Easton-in-Gordano. No need to speculate why they'd changed it.

In the cafeteria tea queue, she fell in behind two patrol car drivers. Were they discussing the latest evasive driving techniques?

'Assam or Darjeeling?' one asked.

'In this weather Earl Grey with lemon might be nice. No, I'll settle for Darjeeling. What about you?'

She'd enjoy reporting that to Graham when she saw him.

There was no reason to avoid or to join them. But when they all tried to reach for the same teaspoon, she laughed, and introduced herself.

'Fancy an escort for a few miles? Burn a bit of rubber?' asked the younger, a lad of about twenty-five.

'Look, they measure our petrol by the eye-dropper: if I use more than my inspector thinks I should, they'll have me valeting cars until he reckons I've paid for it. Until the millennium, probably. Any news,' she added, 'of any nasty weather? I came through a patch of fog, earlier. No warning. No warning messages, either.' Might as well get in an inter-departmental dig.

'That's because we haven't seen any fog. You sure you didn't fall asleep, love?'

Jesus! Could she have been nodding off?

'Better have a bun or something – raise your blood sugar level. Going far?'

'Exeter,' she said. 'Been some trouble in Dawlish – my inspector thought there might be some connection with a case we've got – abduction of little boys.'

'Dawlish! That's that picture book little place with the railway running along the front. Big red cliffs. Nothing ever happens there!'

'There was the time the heavies from Taunton used to go there to have pitched fights on the grass near the river –' his colleague put in.

'The Lawn, they call it. Very respectable place, Dawlish. Heart of the Costa Geriatrica. Well, good luck to you. But mind you stay awake, eh, my love?'

Perhaps Exeter was starting its rush hour exceptionally early, or perhaps it was still recovering from the morning rush. It took Kate an hour to fight her way through, only to find every single parking slot near police headquarters occupied. But when she announced herself at reception, she was greeted cordially enough, and shown straight to the DCI in charge of the Dawlish case, an iron-grey woman in her fifties, who offered her tea.

'I shall have to get rid of the motorway tea first, Ma'am: could you point me to a loo?'

Iron-grey looked at her askance: presumably in her book bladders came after crime fighting. 'Leave me the file. Can start flicking through it. OK?'

'Yes, Ma'am.' She kicked herself for having been so casual.

When she came back, she waited till she was told to sit. The tea was regulation foul, in the thickest of regulation mugs. DCI Earnshaw regarded her and Cope's file with equal distaste.

'I hope you had a good journey,' she said.

'Ma'am?'

'Because you'll soon be making it back. Why you should bother me with *this* I don't know.'

'Ma'am?'

DCI Earnshaw leaned across the desk. 'DS Power, we all try to make connections between crimes. That's good policing. But why you should nag your inspector into letting you come all the way down here to bother me with the most tenuous connections, you alone know. Yes, we had an attempted abduction in Dawlish. An eighteen-year-old girl. And the abductor was her ex-fiancé. I really don't see too many connections with some sick old man buggering little boys, do you?'

'No, Ma'am.' And then, despite herself, her chin came up. 'Ma'am, may I ask why you think it should be a bee in my bonnet, no one else's?'

'My dear girl −' and then Earnshaw's voice softened. 'My dear girl, are you saying this expedition wasn't your idea?'

'I'd rather be in Birmingham hanging curtains, Ma'am.'

'I think you'd be better employed doing that! All right, Kate. I shan't show you the letter from DI Cope, because, as you no doubt observed, it's confidential. But I will favour him with a note, similarly confidential. Meanwhile, it's well after six, and I for one am going home. Tell me, do you have any accommodation booked?'

'No, Ma'am.'

'There's some sort of Festival on. Accommodation could be tricky. If you want you can fetch up in my spare room.'

Despite her awesome facade, DCI Earnshaw − she never thawed beyond the *Ma'am* stage − produced omelettes and salad, with an absolutely solid − organic? − brown loaf. Apples and underripe pears for sweet. The house − it called itself a cottage but was in fact a double fronted affair with four bedrooms − had once overlooked the Exe estuary. Now the view was somewhat interrupted by the motorway.

Over a perfunctory coffee, Earnshaw pushed Cope's file at her. 'I've got work to do. I'd suggest you read this file from cover to cover. Note any sins of omission or commission. That sort of thing.'

'I will, Ma'am. But can't I wash up for you?' She got to her feet.

Earnshaw looked amused. 'Can if you want. My weekly woman usually does it. If you shift that lot, she can wash my nets instead.'

Kate had never heard of anyone saving washing up. But Earnshaw did. Stacks of plates, turrets of saucepans. Nor did there seem to be any hot water. No point in looking for rubber gloves, presumably. In the end, having boiled the kettle eight or nine times − she lost count − and having soaked four tea towels, she felt she'd earned her bed and board.

Indeed, they seemed to be related. There were hard beds

and hard beds. This was somewhere in the premier league of hard beds. But there was a good bedside light – the overhead one might have made it to sixty watts, just, but in any case the shade prevented much light escaping. And Kate, wrapping herself tight in her travelling dressing gown, settled down to read.

'Well?'

They were eating surprisingly creamy porridge in Earnshaw's kitchen.

'There is a surprising omission,' Kate said. 'The MO. As far as I can see, nowhere in that file is there any reference to the way the boys are damaged.'

'Which is?'

'The perpetrator uses a toy railway engine.'

'Jesus Christ! Pretty significant. Well, you go back and tell your DI from me – no, you can't, can you? Because your DI chooses to send you on a wild goose chase. So what are we going to do?'

'Do?'

Earnshaw sighed with exasperation, and plonked the bread on the table. 'You can't let him get away with it. Oh, the bullying, you can, if you want to show the guts of a flea. But not the bad police work. Come on, Kate, get your thinking cap on.'

Kate played for time, attacking the bread with a blunt bread knife.

'Give it here, girl – you're playing at it. No, what you'll do is leave the file with me. You've got all the original documentation, but we'll copy it before you go. Evidence, girl, evidence. If you ever choose to use it. And I shall send it back – eventually – with a note commending your impeccable intelligence. And meanwhile we'll both plot. Tell you what, you pop into Dingles before you go back – should get some nice curtains there.'

Chapter Nineteen

Kate left a short, formal note on Cope's desk, telling him that she had passed on all the information in the file to the Devon and Cornwall Constabulary. She did not favour him with her feelings about being sent on a round trip of three hundred miles – at the tax payer's expense – at a time when she could have been doing things that were infinitely more productive. Except that omission – that was surely as significant as anything else. What the hell was Cope up to?

It was a matter of yards down the corridor to Graham's room. It was locked.

To do them justice both Derek and Alec were on duty for her practice session. Both were in good shape, sporting natty tracksuits. But they were low on stamina – perhaps too much working on weights, not enough aerobic work, Kate thought. They deferred almost too much to her authority, but she and the boys just got on with the training anyway. At the end of the evening Kate was exhausted.

'You work yourself very hard,' Alec said, coming up to her as they watched the boys being collected.

'You can't ask anyone to do what you can't manage yourself, can you? Well, I suppose you can. I've never kicked a ball before except on the beach. All I'm doing is basic keep fit with a few ball skills thrown in.'

'You're not a soccer fan, then?' Derek sounded surprised.

She wrinkled her nose. 'Never miss a Cup Final on TV, but I'm not the sort of person who goes to the terraces whatever the weather.'

'I've got a spare ticket for the Blues on Saturday afternoon if you're interested,' Derek said. 'Dad can't use it. And it'd be nice to see some professionals kicking a ball around, as opposed to us lot, I mean! Saturday morning's the Big One, isn't it? Needle match. And your first as coach.'

'I'd love to come,' she said. 'Depends on work, though. If I'm committed to the team in the morning, there shouldn't be a problem. But I may have to compensate by going in later.'

'But it's a Saturday!'

'Free time doesn't exist when there's a panic on, and that seems to be most of the time. But let's assume it's OK for now, shall we? Tell me all about it.'

Using people again! She stirred a coffee, dropping the spoon into Maz's sink, not specially pleased with herself. She'd no idea yet how Derek saw Saturday – a date? or just someone to be friendly with? She hoped it was the latter. As a man he didn't register with her: he wasn't much more than twenty-three or four, and though he certainly wasn't bad looking, he lacked whatever it was that might attract. Maybe it wasn't a minus, may be it was the plus of that Boy Scout factor that irritated her in Paul. No matter. It would be good to do something quite different from the norm for once, no matter how hard her house called to be cleaned and rehabilitated. Not to mention the garden.

'You're looking very serious,' Maz said, dumping an executive briefcase on the kitchen table. 'How are things, Kate? We hardly see you.' She looked at the coffee. 'Fancy a brandy with that? I know I do.'

Kate shook her head. 'No thanks. Maybe later.' She smiled. 'The booze seems to have given me up, doesn't it? I tell you, Maz, if it hadn't been for you and Giles I'd be an alkie by now. No, seriously: if I'd been stuck out in my house there'd have been nothing for it.'

'You'd have been OK!'

Kate shook her head. 'I frightened myself, Maz. It was bloody close, I tell you. It's an occupational risk in the Force – drink and divorce, in whichever order. My fault, thinking I could deal with it all. But I should be able to move home soon.'

'Oh, stay until it's all sorted out,' Maz said. But her voice wasn't as enthusiastic as usual, perhaps. Perhaps she heard the difference, too. 'I mean, you're not in the way. We hardly see you, and when you're here you're looking after Tim. And the next occupant of the spare room could be a teenage drop-out or a visiting preacher with a taste for smelly pipes. And –' she dropped her voice and grinned conspiratorially, 'at least I get to see my kid brother now you're here. I'd love to see Paul settle down,' she added, sitting at the table.

Kate passed her a coffee. 'But not with me, Maz. Not after Robin.' But that was evasive. 'Paul's a nice young man, but he's not my type. I mean, he's so – so *young*.'

'Immature, you mean? Well, he's the youngest by ten years. An afterthought baby. So he had Mum, and me, and my two elder sisters – all of us mothering him like mad. And then we were surprised when he liked it.'

'Has he had many girlfriends?'

'Loads. Well, you'd expect it, wouldn't you? He's such a stunner, though I says so as shouldn't, as they say round here. But he's never got deeply involved. We've always said anyone taking him on would have to take on the BB as well.'

'He's being very kind to me,' Kate said apologetically. 'I wouldn't want him to – you know, think I was falling for him in return.'

'Likes helping people. Always has. Always on at me to let him look after the kids. Always doing bits of DIY – well, Giles is hopeless. He's a nice kid, my Paul. No, don't look so guilty. I never match-make. Too risky. But if you want to freeze him off, you'll have to do that yourself – I'm not into being a go-between, either.'

'Tell me about Derek Walters,' Kate said. 'He and I are going to watch Birmingham City play on Saturday.'

'Another devoted BB young man. He and his Dad. Funny pair. Very serious. But – hell, Kate, you're not really thinking –'

'Soccer match full-stop,' Kate said. 'I'm not into cradle-snatching. Just want a handle on him, that's all.'

Maz shrugged. 'They're both accountants. No shortage of money. Both stalwarts of the chapel. Both good men. Both bore the hide off me. OK?'

'OK! So if Blues have a nil-nil draw I could be in for a truly exciting afternoon!' She yawned. 'Sorry. All this exercise and fresh air.'

'Fresh? In the car park?'

'All right. Fresh-ish. But I'll have a quick shower and turn in, if it's OK with you.' It was the travelling, she supposed. To Devon and back. As if she'd been in some time warp.

It was a nightmare, she told herself. She was having a nightmare. She wasn't buried alive, maggots already crawling over her. She was alive and having a nightmare. She must wake herself up.

The scream continued after she woke. Hers. But as she forced herself to stop, another continued, wild, desperate. Terrified she might have an attack, her heart was pounding so hard, she was on her feet and dragging at the bedroom door before she realised she could hear Maz's voice, calm, kind. 'Mummy's coming! Only one of your dreams, love. Wake up! Only a nightmare!'

Only! My God, was there anything worse? Kate padded downstairs to start cocoa for anyone who might want it – she certainly did! It was bad enough having them at her age, when in the warmth of the kitchen she could analyse them away. But for Jenny, a kid, just knowing the terror was as real as anything in 'real' life – that didn't bear thinking of.

'You all right?' Colin peered at her. 'Here, I'll make you a coffee.'

'Thanks. No, not a night on the beer or anything. My landlady's kid had a series of nightmares.'

'Series? One's bad enough!'

'Twelve-thirty, one-thirty, and – just for good measure – four-thirty. Poor little mite.'

'Poor little Kate, by the look of you.'

'Oh, I just gave up. Actually, I've started a one-woman hunt for that safe-house, Colin. And what better time to crawl round the streets of suburbia than five?'

He glanced about him. 'What are you on about? Oh, some of you may be able to manage on Thatcher-rations of sleep – I need my eight hours before my brain gets into gear. And I went clubbing last night. In Manchester.'

'And you say you haven't got stamina! Hey, you can join my football team.' She too looked around. No one in the office. 'Look,' she said, dropping her voice, 'I ought to tell Graham what I'm up to. Why don't you come along when I tell him? What have I said?' She stared. Her hand gripped his forearm.

Colin put his arm round her, steered her to the corner of the office. 'Sit.' He remained standing, so he could see over her head. 'You obviously haven't heard. No, don't look like that. Nothing major. You know that motorway pile-up – Wednesday, was it? – on the M6. Well, Graham was in it. No, no!' He took her hands. 'Nothing serious, I promise. Listen – would I lie to you? It's just bruises. He was trying to get someone out of a car when someone hit about five cars back. So most of the impact was absorbed by the other vehicles. But even though it means him having to spend a few days with Mrs H, he's got to take time off.' His voice changed. 'So put your dosh in the envelope, there's a good girl. And – Good morning, Sir!' He straightened.

Kate got to her feet, turning as she did so. 'Morning, Sir.'

Cope nodded. 'Tell you what, Power. If you want to

do something useful, you can drop the envelope round to the DCI.'

She nodded. 'What d'you want me to buy, Sir?'

'For fuck's sake, how should I know? Just give him the money!'

She looked at Colin, who took her cue. 'I wondered about a book, Sir,' he suggested. 'I know he likes walking – maybe –'

'Got that, Power? Get the man a book on walking. And drop it round. But maybe first you'd better grace us with your presence in the Incident Room. There's been another development. If you're interested, that is.'

He stomped off. Colin held Kate back. 'The trouble is with Cope, you never know what his motives are. Does he think going to see Graham is a penance? Or does he suspect you like Graham and relishes the prospect of your being at the receiving end of Mrs H's ire?'

'Ire? That's a very literary word! Sort of thing I came across in Shakespeare once. Colin, if you hear anything else –'

They were by the door. No, Cope wasn't lying in wait for them. She stopped. 'I'm not having an affair with him, Colin. Hang that on the grapevine, will you, and hang a few fairy lights round it, just so everyone sees.'

The development was small, but Cope was right to regard it as serious. A paperboy from Hockley had told his teacher he thought a man had been following him during his evening round on Wednesday. Kate and Colin were to go to the school to do a repeat of Monday morning's activities. No argument with that. Nor with the news that surveillance was now extended to this school. Yes, it had been scaled down at the first.

Kate and Colin set off. The brightness of the recent days had been replaced by a steady drizzle. The windscreen wipers smeared screen-washer backwards and forwards, with little effect.

'Time you got some new blades,' Colin said. 'And putting

this through a car-wash wouldn't do it any harm. Come on –
there's one over there.'

'No. We might miss assembly. On the way back –
promise.'

They watched the giant rubber rollers gear themselves for
action, and braced themselves for the noisy impact.

'A bit more work for someone there,' Colin said, releasing his
seat belt and stretching. 'Ever thought of applying for training to
work with kids?' He skewed round in his seat to look at her.

The car started to shake under the blue and red rollers.

'Oh, I always thought of it as Women's Work,' Kate said
dourly. 'In any case, I'm not sure I could hack it. Jenny's
nightmares are bad enough. Dealing with kids who've been
raped or buggered – no, that's too tough for me. Give me a
good clean murder any day. Or a spot of fraud – now, that
could be interesting.'

'Take years off your life – just think of the paperwork,
Kate, and all those years the trials take.'

'With the inevitable "not guilty" verdict, because the
jury can't understand all the evidence. OK. You've convinced me.'

'In any case, it'll be desk work for you, won't it? This
accelerated promotion scheme – you're not destined to spend
the rest of your life legging it round the streets. You'll be
organising the rest of us.'

'I could end up like Cope!'

'Hardly. He was never going to be a star. Someone
thought you would be, though. Inspector within the next
two years, eh?'

'I doubt it. Not the way things are going. I need to put
in a spot of study, Colin. And that means having a room to
do it in. Hell! I just want to get my house straight. Live in
it. I'm sick of camping.'

'You and me both, sweetie!'

Chapter Twenty

Clutching a card signed by everyone she could find – from Selby to the women on reception – a gift-wrapped set of Wainwright's *Walks* and a potted plant, Kate presented herself at the Harveys' front gate. The house was in the sort of residential area she rather aspired to: no problems parking your car when you had a double garage – no doubt the one that had housed her mattress – and a wide fancily-bricked area in front of the house itself. There were some token winter pansies in terracotta pots. She'd rather expected Graham would be a lush lawn man: perhaps the back garden would be more inspired. In any case, this wasn't the time of year any garden would be at its best. Except she fancied some shrubs, even in her tiny patch, to give all-year colour.

She pushed open the gate, shutting it carefully – if at some peril to her gifts.

The house itself was probably late eighties: built for status. Why two people should have decided they needed so much space – Graham had never mentioned children – was beyond her. But the trouble was, of course, that houses tended to get nicer as they got bigger. Like cars. Except at least you could now buy a snazzy small car, like hers. She'd like a house that was the equivalent of a sixteen-valve Fiesta one day.

The doorbell chimed rather pretentiously. Why was she so judgmental? It wasn't as if she'd made any particular effort for the visit. Just her usual working clothes – today, given the gloom of the weather, a skirt and waistcoat in a rather nice dark red which set off her hair, come to think of it. A dark jacket. And yes, she had taken extra care with her make-up.

Movement behind the frosted glass: prepare to meet the dragon.

If she was a dragon, Graham's wife looked remarkably human. She was about Kate's height, dark-haired, though hers was beginning to go grey. Her skin was startlingly clear, setting off good regular features: a classic English rose. She'd age as well as Cassie, with bones like that. She was slimmer than Kate – yes, slender to the point of thinness – and neatly dressed. Her skirt was a good deal longer than Kate's, but not fashionably long – reaching that unkind spot where the calf is at its thickest. And she wore a twinset.

Kate smiled: 'You must be Mrs Harvey. I'm one of Mr Harvey's colleagues. DI Cope's sent me to –'

'To pester my husband. Well, I can tell you now, he's not at all well.'

Couldn't she see the armful of presents, for goodness' sake?

'I've brought a card from the squad. And these.' Kate nodded at her armful.

'You'd better come in. You can have five minutes. This way.' Mrs Harvey paused: Kate realised she hadn't wiped her feet, and proceeded to do so, with some fervour, before following her through a square hall into a long living room.

'Come into the lounge,' Mrs Harvey said, over her shoulder. 'I'll get him.' She disappeared through another door – perhaps one to the kitchen.

Kate looked around her. Careful good taste in here: the carpets, suite, curtains and wall-paper all co-ordinated. An expensive looking Afghan rug held the whole lot together with a pattern of the rather acid blues and pinks of the rest of the room on a deep red ground. Kate felt covetous. Her house was too small for anything other than plain carpets, plain walls. She hovered. She hadn't been invited to sit, and yet to look at the pictures might be construed as prying. She looked anyway: English landscapes, too pretty for her taste. On the hearth and on what looked like a home for a CD collection were some dried flower arrangements, the sort of thing that came out like the foundations of bonfires if she tried them. These looked like those in the glossy magazines she avoided even at the hairdressers.

'Kate!'

The voice came from that other door. She turned. Involuntarily she stepped towards him. Graham's face was puffed to a caricature of itself, with two lovely black eyes. There was a raw-looking bruise down his right cheek.

As if to give her time, he smiled: 'You should have seen the others.'

'That'll teach you to pick on someone your own size,' Kate said. The presents grew awkward in her arms. 'We had a bit of whip round for you.' She realised that Graham had left the door open, that Mrs Harvey was somewhere behind it. Perhaps she was making tea.

Graham reached for them.

She could see how blood-shot the right eye was. 'Whatever happened?'

'There was this pile-up. Mid-afternoon, Wednesday. Broad daylight. You'd expect the fog to have cleared by then. But just north of Stafford – yes, I was nearly home! – it came down like a hand. I mean, I was cruising at seventy – no problem. Anyway, I saw the crashes in front. I managed to get on to the hard shoulder, call for assistance. I was trying to help this teenager in a beat-up old van when there was another series of crashes. And the car behind shunted into this kid's van.'

'Is he all right?'

'I managed to get him out before the fires started. And a few others. Didn't realise I was hurt until the meat-wagon people told me to get in.' He took the pot plant. 'This must be terribly hard for you, Kate,' he said, his voice gentle. 'After –'

After Robin. After her own injuries. That was what he meant. She straightened and passed him the books. He looked around helplessly. This was not a room you just dumped things in.

'Is there a mat we could put that plant on?' Kate asked. 'Or the hearth –?'

But the marble of that was polished. No, not even a newspaper she could spread.

'Maybe the kitchen,' he began.

'Your five minutes are up, I'm afraid.' Mrs Harvey had materialised. 'Doctor's orders, dear. You know what he said.'

'Of course. I'm sorry. I didn't realise.' Kate was still holding the card. 'I'd forgotten this. Look after –'

'I'll look after him, all right.' Mrs Harvey took the plant, sniffing disparagingly. Or perhaps it was just to see if there was any scent. Not with hot-house azaleas, though. There never was.

Kate headed for the door. Graham followed. She turned: 'I could do with some advice. There's a major problem at work.'

'Well, you'll just have to solve it without him, won't you?' Mrs Harvey said. 'Can't you see he's sick?'

'I'll be in on Monday,' Graham mouthed.

She opened her eyes extra wide, pulled a face: would he be fit?

He managed a smile – not a wink. 'Thanks for coming round,' he said. 'Send everyone my thanks. Tell them I'll be back as soon as I can be.'

'When the doctor says it's all right,' Mrs Harvey's voice over-rode his.

'Goodbye then.' She peered round his shoulder. Mrs Harvey regarded her. 'Nice to have met you,' Kate said, like a kid at a party.

On impulse, she went home, not to the Manse. Thank God for chicken tikka naan. She ate it on her lap in her bedroom. Then, slowly at first, and then maniacally, she started to clean her windows. Her bedroom. The back room. The bathroom. The landing. The front bedroom. She might even do those downstairs. The new doors. The windows. And at last, opening the front room door – the room that was to be her dining room – she was hit by the smell of paint. Primer to be precise.

She sat down on a pile of cardboard boxes – her kitchen in chrysalis form – and stared. Someone had started to rub down and prepare the bay window.

★

How long she'd been sitting there she'd no idea. At last it dawned on her that the phone was ringing, and she sprinted to it.

'I was afraid you might be at the Manse,' Graham said.

'I come home sometimes.'

'Not often. I tried to get you a couple of times. How are things?'

'Cope's weird. Sent me on a wild-goose chase to Devon. But I've got this bee in my bonnet, Graham. I haven't dared tell anyone yet.' She trusted him to interpret her silence correctly: that she knew she could trust him.

'Shoot.'

'One day — just after I started — I was very late in —'

'I bollocked you, if I remember rightly.'

'I wouldn't call that a bollocking. Anyway, on the bus on my way in I overhead these two women talking about a house in their cul-de-sac. Seems the people using it went to ridiculous lengths to maintain their privacy. Graham, it's the longest of shots — but I want to find that house. May be nothing to do with this case.'

'May be everything in the world to do with another one. OK, Kate. Find it. Kate. Before I forget. If ever the phone rings back immediately after I've put it down, ignore it. You can always one four seven one it. And I'd be grateful, if you ever phone me here, if you dial one four one first.' His voice writhed with embarrassment.

She didn't need to ask why. God, another conspiracy. Just so she could talk to her boss. All that just so she could talk to her boss.

'This house, Graham. It might take a long time to find.' She told him what she was looking for.

'I only wish I could help. But there's no way I can drive for another couple of days. She's taken my keys, just to make sure.' He laughed. An embarrassed schoolboy laugh.

'Any ideas how I could clear it with Cope?'

'You can't, can you? Because he'd veto it as a waste of time. It'll have to wait till I'm back, Colin. But thanks for the call. Always nice to hear from you lads.'

End of call. He wouldn't win any Oscars for that performance, though.

The phone rang. And rang. She sat on her hands in her effort not to answer. At last it stopped. It started immediately. She went to the loo. At last, she returned, and checked the origin of her call. Graham's number.

Find it, the man had said. She'd give it till twelve tonight. Couldn't go on too late and risk being knackered for tomorrow's match, could she? Match*es*, she corrected herself. She went back upstairs to retrieve warm, sensible clothes – her thickest tracksuit, and warm cords and sweater for the afternoon. There. But it would be so nice to live in just one house. Picking up her coat and the *A-Z* she let herself out of her house, locking the door behind her.

'You look like you could do with your weekend.'

Kate jumped. Literally. 'Mrs Mackenzie! I was miles away! I'm so sorry.'

'That's all right. House coming on?'

'Slowly. Even when it's finished, I shall never be able to get it clean.'

'You want cleaners? I know cleaners.'

'Would they want to tackle a job like this?'

'Is the Pope Catholic? You just tell me when. You got a job, they want a job. You got money, they want money. Symbiosis.' Mrs Mackenzie grinned. 'Fancy a coffee?'

All those plans for prowling the suburbs!

'Love one. But –' she gestured ineffectually at her house.

'My place. I only like grounds with my coffee, not grit.' She let them in. The house was silent, apart from the irritating tinkle of a central heating radiator. It still smelt of paint.

Kate followed her into the immaculate kitchen. Shedding her coat, Mrs Mackenzie fished beans from the fridge. She pulled a face while she ground them, but then grinned. 'Got this new espresso machine,' she said. 'Black or white?'

Kate tossed up: which did she need more, a good night's sleep or wakefulness for her suburban patrol? 'White, please.

Didn't sleep too well last night. Jenny gets these nightmares and shares them.'

'Jenny?'

'The younger daughter at the Manse. Screams in her sleep, poor little mite.'

Mrs Mackenzie nodded: 'My Royston had a phase of that. Never think it to look at him, but he was a timid child. Bullied. That's one reason we moved churches. Kate – you don't mind if I call you Kate, do you? I'm Zenia. Seems my parents wanted to call me after some flower and couldn't bloody spell it. Pardon my French. Don't swear, except it's been a bit of a day. Got this woman on the ward – I tell you she hasn't a bit of skin left on her.'

Kate looked up sharply.

'Oh, natural causes. Eczema. Only you feel so helpless. Been dabbling in this herbal stuff. Just because it grows natural, they think it must be good. Well, whatever she was on wasn't.'

Kate waited. The coffee-maker belched. The smell was making her salivate. 'You say Royston was bullied? At the chapel?'

Zenia bubbled the coffee into the tiny white china cups she'd reached out. 'Help yourself to sugar. Bullied at school – that's for definite. But there was something at the chapel he wouldn't ever tell us about. Never has.'

Kate looked up sharply. 'Any ideas?'

'None. I looked for the obvious things – including sexual abuse, before you ask. Nothing I could see. Tried to talk to him. Had a discreet word with the officers. Maybe some racism, they thought. It's a very white, middle-class chapel, that one. And he's much happier now we've left it. Happier! Lord, when was a teenage boy ever happy?'

'How old is he? Hmm, this is good!'

'Fifteen. Working for his GCSEs. And doing well, his teachers say. I suppose it's best for him to be polite at school, rude at home, if he's got to be rude. Get a GCSE in swearing, I sometimes think. Bad company. There's him in the A stream of a grammar school and he chooses friends dropping out of the comp. That's kids for you. I sometimes wonder if it's because I work.'

'I doubt it. I think trouble's something all teenagers are prone to – like a virus.'

Zenia bridled. 'Trouble? I didn't say anything about trouble. But you never know what they get up to, do you. Watch and pray, that's what they say. Except the watching's hard when they dash off the second they've done their homework.'

'Tell you what, if he's still doing his homework, I shouldn't think you've got all that much to worry about!'

Zenia laughed, but her voice was soon serious. 'I hope you're right. That's all I can say.' She made an obvious effort. 'Now, tell me all about this handsome young man my husband tells me he keeps seeing at your house.'

Kate sighed. 'Handsome pain in the arse, more like.'

Zenia shook her head. 'When you get past forty, no handsome young man can ever be a pain in the arse. Ever.'

'This one can. Oh, he means well. But he's at my house more than I am, doing little jobs.'

'And big ones – digging out that garden took him a good while.'

'He's painting my front window, now. Not now this minute. Now his current job. Except he's got a job. He's supposed to be a college lecturer – he doesn't seem to be spending a lot of time lecturing.'

'Skivers in every walk of life. Don't tell me you haven't got some policemen who sit on their backsides and let the others do the work? Anyway, when you're in love, what's a little thing like work? And that young man's got to be in love.' As if sensing Kate had had enough of the subject, she got up. 'Now, I want an honest opinion. I've got a bit of a promotion at work, and I saw this outfit in town. And I fell for it. Well, we've got a wedding to go to. Joseph's niece. I haven't shown it to Joseph, yet.'

'Let's see. Go and put it on.' Kate waved her out of the room. She might as well give up the safe-house search for tonight. She was too weary. In any case she deserved a break

and it was good to get to know her neighbour. At first she'd
assumed she was just another middle-aged woman. Now – she
gasped as Zenia returned.

'My God – you look absolutely stunning.'

'You don't think it's OTT?' Zenia turned slowly.

'Not a scrap. The cut – it's absolutely lovely.'

'Cost me a bomb.'

'It shows. Turn round again.'

Zenia was transformed from a slightly dumpy forty plus into
a queen.

'Is your hair long enough to put up properly? Go on, try!
And a hat?'

She didn't leave till nearly eleven. They'd had more coffee,
and Zenia had produced cakes from her deep-freezer. They'd
had a feast.

'You all right, girl?' Zenia peered at her under the
hall light.

'Be nice just to go home, wouldn't it. Not have to zap off
to the Manse. Though I don't know why I'm moaning. It's
not all that far.'

'You know as well as I do it's nothing to do with
distance. It's your roots, Kate. You're looking for somewhere
to plant them.'

Chapter Twenty-One

The turn-out for the match was gratifying, to put it mildly. When Kate arrived with Giles, Alec and Derek were just walking from the carpark. Most of the boys seemed to have at least one parent in support – both Marcus's were there, with an asthma spray, she discovered. Paul arrived just as they were about to kick off; he too waved an asthma spray at Kate, who nodded gratefully – he couldn't have known there'd be another one. A minute later he was followed by Colin, who gave her a highly public hug. 'Thought you might need a beard,' he whispered.

Kate made perfunctory introductions, and then gave her concentration to the game. The pitch wasn't bad – on playing fields belonging to a college for blind people in Harborne. A strong wind cut across it. Her tracksuit, despite the layers underneath, wasn't nearly up to the job. Clearly she would have to make time to go down to Croydon to retrieve the rest of her clothes. Not to mention the books and other personal things she'd crammed into the box-room. Her new lodger was paying a reduced rent until she'd got the whole house. It was to everyone's advantage to get things sorted out as soon as possible. But dashing off to the Smoke would take time away from the more urgent matters that were filling her life. Maybe she could just manage the double journey after church tomorrow – especially if Colin were free and would co-drive. Fingers crossed there were no new developments at work and they both had the whole weekend free.

'Sure,' he said loudly and cheerfully. 'We'll go in my car – hatchbacks hold more and are easier to load.'

'Mine's a hatchback too!' she said in a little-girl whiny voice. 'OK, mine'd probably fit into your boot. But I pay for the petrol. Hell, that was a dreadful foul!'

Half-time, and Braysfield Baptists were trailing two nil. Kate handed out cut oranges and advice. She returned to the touchline smelling strongly of juice and even colder than she'd realised.

Paul, who'd kept a remarkably discreet distance, presumably decided it was time to muscle in. 'Are you going to strip off and put yourself on as a sub?' he asked.

She would not bite. 'It'd be warmer than hanging round here. I'm going to have to get some Damart thermals if I'm going to do this every weekend. Come on, Marcus! It's just the same as on the carpark! Shoot! Ye-e-es!' She jumped up and down, hugging anyone handy – in this case Alec, who hugged her cheerfully back. 'Another! Go on, you can do it!'

Braysfield surged back towards the opposition's goal. A professional referee might have blown for off-side but the ref – an opposition parent – was either blind or determined to show his impartiality. One of their backs scrambled the ball into touch.

'Remember what I said about corners!' she yelled. 'Stay cool! That's it!'

Sam lofted the ball towards the goal-mouth. Marcus, looking startled at finding himself such an easy chance, nonetheless touched it into the goal. There was an eruption of Braysfield parents.

'Hey, d'you suppose that's a scout?' Derek grabbed her arm and pointed. A thickly jacketed figure lurking under sunglasses was picking his way towards them. Alongside was another, stockier figure. No sunglasses. But she'd never seen him smile before.

'Jesus, d'you see who I see?' Colin asked.

Kate nodded. It was a good job Cope was with him or she might have run to Graham.

'Hey, Gaffer – did you see that goal?' she said to them both.

'If you don't shut up and turn round, you'll miss the next,' Cope observed, spitting. 'Go on, kid. In the fucking net, man!'

Alec coughed: 'This is a church team,' he said.

'Don't care if it's a team of bloody angels – get it in the fucking net!'

But the opposition hustled it clear. She could have wept. Only a game, Kate. It degenerated into a lot of rather pointless midfield passing.

She realised Graham was beside her. 'You sure you should be out, Gaffer?' she asked. Public question for a public occasion.

'Course he should be bloody out. I told his wife he'd got to have some fresh air. Hey up, what's going on now? What's the matter with that kid?'

'Paul – Marcus's spray. Quick! No, you're not allowed on the pitch. Give it here.' Kate sprinted to the knot gathered round the gasping boy. 'OK, love. Couple of deep breaths. Good lad. Now,' she smiled at the referee, 'can I have him on the sidelines for a couple of minutes and then he comes back on? Or would you need us to send on a sub straightaway?'

'Time you read your rule book, sister. OK, you're playing with just ten till he comes back on?'

Marcus's parents were waiting on the touchline: 'That's it for today, then, old son. Home we go!'

'Dad! No, Dad. I've got to stay.'

'Can't have you getting cold, lad. And you can see your mother's perished with all this standing round.'

'Dad –'

'That was a nice goal, son.' Cope had joined them. 'But you'd better get back on that pitch or you'll get bloody pneumonia. Go on, shift your arse.'

Marcus did as he was told. Cope stomped off. Kate and Marcus's parents gaped.

'If only we could have won,' Kate said, waving off the last of the parents' cars. 'It would have meant so much to them all.'

'And to you,' Colin said quietly. 'But to turn round – how many defeats in a row?'

'Fourteen or fifteen,' Paul said.

'OK, to turn round a run of defeats that long to a score-draw isn't bad. Only a couple of weeks' coaching. Imagine what a whole season's work will achieve.'

Kate imagined. Committed to all those evenings, all those mornings. Still, she had a lot to be pleased with.

'Fancy Cope coming along,' she said.

Colin finished her thought, out loud, but for her ears only. 'And fancy him bringing Graham. Nowt so queer as folk, Kate. I'd never have imagined him even visiting Graham, let alone persuading him to come out to something like this. Perhaps he didn't take a lot of persuading. Mind you, Mrs H might have done.'

Kate thought back to the good-looking, neat woman. 'Wonder what made her like that?'

Colin shrugged. 'What's made Cope the way he is? Look, I'd best be off – someone's trying to catch your eye, in case you hadn't noticed. See you at your place tomorrow?'

'Better make it the Manse. About one. We'll get something on the motorway, shall we?'

'Or better still, before we get on it. Plenty of pubs off the Alcester Road. Lots of them'll do a Sunday lunch fairly cheap. See you, our kid.'

The one trying to catch her eye was Derek. He looked at his watch ostentatiously.

'Time we were moving,' he said. 'Especially if you want to change.'

She looked more closely: under his sheepskin coat, he was certainly smarter than she was. She'd have given anything to call off: all she wanted was a hot bath. 'I haven't got all that many warm clothes,' she began.

'No problem,' he said.

Would he peel off his coat and wrap it round her?

'After all, we shall be indoors all afternoon.'

★

'So there I was in a hospitality box, amongst all the nobs,' Kate told Cassie that evening. 'Buffet lunch, wine, coffee, chocs. Even a brandy or liqueur with the coffee. And then you move from the back of the box to the front, and watch it all happen in comfort. There's even a TV screen so if you're too busy talking business to see a goal then you see it again in slow motion.'

'Did you enjoy it?' Cassie asked. 'And while you're deciding, you could freshen up my gin.'

Kate shook a couple more ice cubes from the flask, sliced in some lemon, and was lavish with the gin. No point in being lavish with the tonic – Cassie was drinking it almost neat tonight. On the other hand, she herself was so tired she was drinking almost undiluted tonic. She walked back to the bed, and sat down. 'Enjoy it? Yes, of course I did. I'm not so sure about the company – Derek and Alec's contacts were a bit pompous for me.'

'You mean rich. You young people and your inverted snobbery. There's nothing wrong in working hard for your money and then enjoying it. You mark my words, these Labour people will be putting up taxes, for all their promises.'

Kate chose not to hear. 'But it was funny seeing the game at one remove from reality. All these people outside roaring and yelling – and inside we could hardly hear them.' Yes, she'd missed that. Whenever she'd been to matches in the past, there'd always been that huge roar; even if you were still outside it was thrilling. Paul had got the same sort of excitement when that orchestra had tuned up. 'And it wasn't as exciting as this morning. We deserved to win, we really did. If I can only build up their stamina . . . They were just run off their legs by the last ten minutes – did ever so well to keep the opposition out.'

Cassie yawned, openly.

'And such a lot of people turned up. All the parents. And some of my people from work.'

'Was that handsome young man there? Paul?'

'Yes.' But she didn't want to talk about him. She wanted to talk about Cope bringing Graham. No. About Graham being there. About Graham's departure, with his unobtrusive touch on her arm. About Graham's wife and the telephone subterfuges Graham had asked for. About the phone ringing as soon as their call was over. But then she found she didn't want to talk about Graham at all. 'I had a coffee with Zenia Mackenzie last night,' she said.

'Who?'

'Zenia Mackenzie – your next-door neighbour.'

'That Jamaican!'

Kate ignored the disdain. 'That's right. She sends her regards. She's been very kind to me since I moved in. But I think she's worrying about that lad of hers. Royston.'

'Royston; Zenia. Where do these people get their names from?'

'Zenia got hers because her parents wanted to call her after the flower. She's just bought herself a new outfit – she looks really lovely. Which reminds me, I'm off to get my clothes tomorrow. From London. I'm whizzing down with a friend of mine.'

'Paul?'

'Colin. My colleague.'

'But he's the one that's queer.'

'Gay.' Was it too late to teach Cassie a bit of political correctness? Perhaps she should have picked her up on her attitude to African-Caribbeans. Was it too late? Or was it simply too late in the evening?

Chapter Twenty-Two

She and Colin had only had time on Sunday evening – nearer Monday morning, to be precise – to dash into her house and dump her clothes on any cleanish flat surface they could find upstairs. She'd had no idea she possessed so many. She rather wished her tenant hadn't removed about half the coat-hangers, but, as the woman had pointed out, furnished accommodation might be thought to include such vital items. Two trips were called for when she had time – one to a charity shop with black sacks full of superfluous clothes, another to Woolworth's for a fistful of hangers. In the event, however, Colin rendered that unnecessary: he came in on the Monday morning with two carriers full of wire.

'Vile things. I'm sure they have a life of their own. Look at them – weaving in and out of each other before your very eyes.' He shuddered.

Kate made them both coffee. Sally and Reg appeared, then Selby.

'Set 'em up, then, Power,' Cope yelled. 'And then we'll have a few minutes' private prayer in the Incident Room.'

Kate made tea and coffee impartially, resolving to be at the back of the queue in future. Tea-lady she was not. The huge tins of coffee and tea bags were getting perilously low, but she had a nasty feeling that if she asked who ran the tea-swindle she'd find the prompt answer was her. Though she didn't begrudge a minute of the time she'd spent collecting money since she'd arrived, she didn't want to be typecast. If necessary, she'd stick to water, or invite herself to share the delights of Graham's supplies.

There was no sign of him in the Incident Room.

'Right, ladies and gents: let's see what we've got. Power, anything on the schools?'

'Not a lot of blue-eyed golden-haired boys in the area,' she said. 'But I wonder if we're not taking too narrow a view of male beauty. What if our friend fancies pretty black kids, but just hasn't snatched one yet?'

'I'm not an expert in male beauty, Power.'

She laughed. 'Nor am I when it comes to ten-year-olds, Sir!' It was out before she could stop it. The first time she'd ever quipped back to Cope. How would he take it?

'Come off it, Power: last time I saw you you were surrounded by the little bastards. And a lot of bigger ones, too.' It was his usual jeering tone, but he didn't seem to have taken offence. 'But the experience seems to have been too much for the Gaffer. He's had to take a sickie or two. Must be the sight of your boobs in that tracksuit, eh, Power? Or that snazzy jacket you were wearing, Roper. Nice bit of cloth, that.'

'You mean he's bad?' Reg prompted.

'According to his wife, yes. My guess it's because she blacked the other eye for him. Any road, we've got to manage without him a bit longer. That all right by you, Reg?'

'Shame. He's a good copper, young Graham.'

'He can rely on you to write him a testimonial, then. I'm sure he'll be vastly relieved. Right – as I recall we were talking about a particularly nasty crime. Anything else, gents?'

'Nothing to report from the surveillance, Sir. No suspicious behaviour from anyone. Thing is, Sir,' the young man – Brian Fenton – continued, 'going to school seems quite a social thing, if you see what I mean. Families come and go together. Very few kids come on their own. Almost all are collected. Maybe we should be looking at schools where the mums come by car and drop their kids off. More time for them to moon round the playground and be picked out.'

Kate nodded. 'So more middle-class areas?'

Cope nodded. 'We've already circulated all the schools. But we haven't the manpower – sorry, Kate! – to keep on eye on every bloody school in Brum.'

Kate shook her head sympathetically, her face sober. Inside she was grinning like a chimpanzee, however – fancy the old bastard using her first name after all this time. Probably just a one-off. She braced herself for the next onslaught; he wouldn't want her to get the idea he'd gone soft, would he?

Reg coughed: 'With all due respect to the ladies present, aren't we being a bit narrow in our investigations? It's not unknown for women to participate in child abuse.'

'Fenton?'

'No reports of anyone of either sex hanging round, Sir.'

'So now you're satisfied the Force has been getting on with its work while you were jaunting round the globe?'

Reg nodded.

And perhaps now was the moment for normal service to be resumed to Kate. The meeting over, he called her back. 'Power?' But he was straight, business-like. 'Got a job for you. Sally Richards has been liaising with Family Protection. She'll be packing the job in soon. Mightn't do any harm if we had a bit of continuity.'

Exactly what Graham had thought.

'Next time she talks to them, you'd better be there.'

'Sir!'

Christmas had come early this year.

Except there was no Graham. If he'd been well enough to go to the match on Saturday, why wasn't he well enough to work, two days later? On impulse, not allowing herself to think about it, she sat at her desk and dialled his mobile number. She was invited to leave a message. She didn't. His home number? She'd risk it. Any outgoing police call had its number withheld from the caller, so there was no need to dial 141. But she must be ready to dab a finger down to stop the call should the wrong voice answer. The number was ringing. She held on, biting her lip.

And was asked to leave a message on a machine.

But he'd find a way of contacting her; he'd want to reassure her that all was well. He'd mentioned an anwerphone. Well, she'd get one this lunch-time and fix it this evening if it was the last thing she did.

'It's a long process,' Gail, the social worker, was explaining. 'They don't just grab a kid and violate him. That's too quick. They want the thrill of the chase, too. So they'll single out a child – one who comes alone or plays alone: some kids are natural loners. Maybe the one who gets bullied. So they have a kind, sympathetic adult to turn to. And then, as they gain the boy's trust, the stakes are raised. A visit to the paedophile's house. Oh, not his own, of course. The kid finds a roomful of toys. But the rumour is there are better rooms with better toys. And if he co-operates, he'll get to see it. Maybe "co-operating" means just having his photo taken. But it'll mean more and more as the toys get better, believe me.' She curled her lip in distaste. 'And don't get the idea you're looking for a Mr Nasty. On the contrary, you're looking for a Mr Nice-Guy, a trusted pillar of society. Every mother's favourite son. The nicest boss.'

'Well, it can't be Cope, can it?' Sally whispered.

Or could it? Kate locked herself in the lavatory to think. It wasn't unknown for policemen at all levels to be involved in crime against children – well, all sorts of crime, come to think of it. She'd have gone on oath for most of her colleagues' honesty and decency. But not all. And it was in that grey area that Cope came. She knew enough about child abuse to know it wasn't just about sex. It was about domination. And if there was one person in this squad who enjoyed abusing his rank to bully others, it was Cope. She thought back. The day Danny had been killed, Cope was almost in tears. He'd omitted the vital physiological information in his report to the Devon police. He'd even come to the match on Saturday: lots of small boys to inspect then. And what if he'd brought Graham along simply to annoy Mrs Harvey, so that Graham would be kept away from work and thus from the investigation? The idea was far-fetched. Parts were lunatic. But. It was the but that wouldn't go away. Wouldn't. Other memories floated in: the time he'd rejected out of hand the idea of checking for the safe house: if he thought she was on to anything, of course he'd try to stop her.

And who could she chew this over with? Colin?

He was the obvious person. But one item of her catalogue against Cope applied to him. He'd turned up at the match, too. But that was because he was a friend, wanted to support her. He'd been with her to the schools, too, hadn't he – plenty of chances then for him to size up kids. Hell!

Graham? Hell and hell and hell!

At least she now had an answerphone and some cellophane-wrapped ready-made curtains, plus some lengths of curtain rail, rawl-plugs and curtain hooks. She shoved them into her Fiesta: no point in advertising to Cope the domesticity of her lunch break – and the fact it had stretched a bit to accommodate all her activities.

She spent a depressing afternoon checking every known woman child-abuser. No help at all. Most were plainly certifiable, like the one who bathed her child in bleach to lighten its skin or the one who fed her teenage daughter iodine to stop menstrual bleeding. There was a nasty clutch who aided and abetted their men, often, it seemed, under some sort of sexual coercion. But none of them was anywhere near this patch, nor would be for some little time. A first-timer? Which got everyone back to square one.

Reg walked down to the carpark with her, laughing at the contents of her car.

'Only one thing missing, me love. Your electric drill, of course. And some long screws to go through the rawl-plugs into the wall. Now, where d'you live? Well, Shirley's only just down the road. I'll be round about eight. Fix them in half an hour. OK, love?'

'Reg, you are an angel.'

★

Reg had finished the upstairs ones, when the doorbell rang. Paul.

'Hi! Just thought I'd see how you were getting on.'

'Getting on well. A friend of mine from work's helping me replace all auntie's metal curtain rails with nice smooth plastic ones. Reg!' she called up the stairs. 'Tea break!'

Paul was always a little awkward when introduced to other men, so she wasn't surprised when he hesitated at the sight of Reg. But Reg – the light over the stair spotlit his face – looked positively taken aback to see Paul. The two stared at each other, if for no more than a second. It was enough for her to say, 'Do you two know each other? Paul Taylor, Reg Tanner,' she added, in parentheses.

'I reckon I do know you from somewhere,' Reg was first to speak.

'I do a lot with the Boys' Brigade,' Paul volunteered. 'Maybe something to do with that?'

'Ah, that'd be it. My kids were dead keen on the Brigade. Used to drag me all over the country, what with their bands and their outdoor activities and that.'

'And now we've got Kate involved, too.' Paul's smile was affectionate. 'You should see her running our under-fourteen team. Got them a score draw – first time they'd got a ball in a net for two seasons!'

Reg looked at her: 'Well done – ah! That'd be what Cope was carrying on about this morning. I know I'm getting on, Kate me love, but I didn't like his remarks about your – well, you know. Sexual harassment, that's what I'd call that.'

'Haven't you got rules in the police against that sort of thing?' Paul asked. 'We have in education.'

' 'Course we have. And there's a team of senior women officers at the end of a phone to help counsel women who have that sort of thing inflicted on them. You should get on to them, me love.' Reg nodded his point home. 'You mustn't let people get away with behaviour like that.'

She filled the kettle from the outside tap. It wouldn't help to point out that Cope had been far nastier to Reg himself than to Kate – no, at least as nasty. She compromised.

'It seems to me that Cope bullies everyone, regardless. One of these days he'll go too far, maybe.'

She locked the door behind her, and switched on the kettle. 'Tea or coffee? Powdered milk, I'm afraid.'

'Any herbal tea?' Paul asked.

As if in this dump there might be. She gave an exaggerated shrug and peered around, hand shading her eyes. But then she remembered, and laughed, apologetically.

'There's some de-caffeinated tea-bags somewhere. And I think Cassie kept real camomile flowers.'

He settled for coffee, the fully-caffeinated variety, taking it black. 'What's this about curtain rails, Reg?'

'I've done the upstairs. Wouldn't mind a hand with the landing, if you've got time. A bit awkward – nowhere safe to wedge the ladder. And you're a good bit taller than me, lad.'

Kate was afraid the ladders would scuff her newly painted walls, and busied herself with rags to pad the ends. At last the men got busy. They worked in comparative silence, broken only by a suppressed curse if one dropped a screw.

'There! Now, what about your curtains?'

Kate gasped, pressing her hands to her mouth in embarrassment. 'You'll never guess – I never bought any for the landing. Just the bedrooms. Never mind. This window's not overlooked.'

Paul smiled kindly: 'I'll come round to hang then whenever you get them. Provided,' he added, his voice becoming mock-serious, 'neither of you dares to get anywhere near my wet paint with that dusty drill.'

'Paint?' Kate echoed.

They trooped down to her dining room.

'Tara!' Paul shouted. 'Undercoat!'

And indeed, there was undercoat. He'd painted the whole of the frame.

'Paul – that's so kind of you. I never expected –'

'Well,' he said, blushing, 'that's what friends are for.'

Chapter Twenty-Three

Reg was making their coffee this morning. 'Milk and sugar, Kate? Oh, and there's some post for you. On your desk.'

There had been no phone message from Graham: perhaps this was a note from him. Though why he should send it here, where people would recognise his hand-writing, she'd no idea. Perhaps he wasn't sure of the Manse address, and he'd be reasonably certain that she was still based there, rather than at her home. Yes, that would be it.

It wasn't a letter from Graham, that was certain. It was a small packet, well sealed in a jiffy-bag.

'So have you known this Paul long?' Reg asked, coming to sit on the corner of her desk.

'Just since I came to Brum. It's all his fault I've got so involved with the BB.'

'Love, is it?'

'Reg, you men are just as romantic as we women are supposed to be!'

'More,' said Colin. 'We like a nice cry at a wedding. Hell, doesn't that phone ever stop ringing? Your turn, Kate.'

She reached for it, tucking the handset on to her shoulder and peeling back the Sellotape on the packet. 'Selby! It's for you!'

He peeled himself slowly from the computer.

Inside the jiffy-bag was a small tin. 'Come on! Caller's waiting!' She prised open the can.

Maggots. Maggots.

She dropped the tin, screaming like Jenny in a nightmare. The maggots bounced out. The scream shook her whole body. She couldn't stop. Couldn't stop crying. Couldn't stop until a hand slapped her face. Even then the shuddering didn't stop.

They were still there, on her desk. Pushing from whoever was holding her, she dashed to the loo. She made it; stayed huddled on the cubicle floor.

She'd no idea how long she stayed there. Probably not long. Sally was there, and a uniformed woman inspector she'd seen around but didn't know to talk to.

How she got to this woman's office she didn't know.

'Can you talk about it?' The inspector clasped Kate's hands round a mug of very sweet tea. 'Go on, another sip. You lost all your breakfast.'

'I'm so sorry – I –'

'No need to apologise. It was a vile thing to have happen to you. Any idea who could have done it?'

Kate shook her head. 'I've not really had time to make enemies while I've been up here. I mean, I must have made plenty when I was in the Met – people I got sent down, they'd have a grudge.'

'Sometimes people don't have to have rational reasons to bear a grudge.' The inspector looked her straight in the eye. She was about thirty-three. A bit of a high-flyer, then. And pretty, indeed glamorous, too. She wore the uniform like a fashion item. 'Some people might think this was a joke – a bit of horse-play?'

Had Graham mentioned Cope and Selby? Kate dismissed the idea almost as it formed. That didn't mean other people hadn't – especially other women.

Kate shook her head. 'There's always a bit of bullying, isn't there,' she said, conscious of the evasion. 'But nothing like that, I promise you. And God knows I over-reacted. My partner was killed a few months ago. His wife insisted on having him buried, not cremated. Since then I've got this – this phobia.'

'We can get you support with that,' the Inspector said. 'You'll need it if you're going to carry on in this job. And the problem is, I'll bet you're due for a rash of maggot stories from your less sensitive colleagues.'

Kate nodded. 'Yes. Selby and Cope will have a field day. All the long-dead corpses they discovered when they were on the beat. I know.'

'So you'll go and get support?'

'Try and stop me.'

'I think you should take the rest of the day off, you know. Meanwhile I'll make sure your office and desk have the going over of their lives – there'll be no evidence of this morning's events.'

Kate shook her head. The thoughts came appallingly slowly. 'That's just it. Evidence. Finger-prints and saliva under the stamp. The post-mark. I want to find who did that.'

The inspector – if only Kate knew her name: she must have told Kate when she helped gather her up from the loo floor – looked at her intently.

Kate gathered together the wisps and shreds of her brain. 'Do you ever do crosswords? You see, I'm working on this paedophilia case at the moment. Been asking questions, outside and here in the nick. Maybe asked the right questions, only I didn't know it.'

'I'm sorry – I don't follow.'

Kate tried harder. 'Ever heard the expression, *Opening up a can of worms?*'

By the time she'd eaten a second breakfast and checked in for an appointment with the shrink, Kate knew she wasn't going to go home. OK, it would have made sense to mooch round doing domestic tasks, but she wanted to make sure that tin, that jiffy-bag, didn't get mysteriously lost. She wanted to nail the bugger that had sent it. Revenge was a wonderful remedy for shock, she decided.

Colin was alone in the office when she got back. He gathered her up into his arms. 'You poor kid. That was all to do with Robin, was it? Hell, someone likes kicking in the most painful place. Now, shall I run you home?'

She shook her head. 'Not yet. I want to get the wrapping off to Forensics.'

'Too late, Power,' said a voice from the door. You're not the only one as can act fast, you know. It's already on its way.'

'Sir!' She pulled away from Colin.

'That's all right,' Cope said affably, coming into the room. 'You're entitled to a bit of canoodling after something like this. But I tell you, Power, that was a bloody stupid thing to do, and I'll have you on a disciplinary if you do anything like it again.'

'Sir?'

'Opening a package like that, of course. Could have been a fucking bomb, woman. Then where would you have been? Bloody kingdom come, that's where. Now, I want you out of this office for the rest of the day. Get that?'

'But Sir —'

'But Sir nothing. I want to make sure there's no more of them little bleeders around, you silly girl. Now, shift. You can come back here when you've taken her home, Colin. Right?'

Home? It was all very well, but she didn't exactly have one. She did have a car, however, and that was what she'd do. It would be easier by day-light anyway. She'd take her car and her *A–Z* and run rings round the 50 bus route. The opportunity she'd been waiting for, come to think of it. But Colin was talking.

'— was Helen Carter who saw to you?'

'Sorry? Who? When?'

'This morning, Kate. When you were throwing up in the bog. Was it Helen Carter who saw to you?'

'Wish I knew. I never caught her name. And I'd like to thank her — she was very kind.'

'Kind and — ?'

'Very pretty, beautifully turned out. Looked more like a model than a policewoman.'

'That'd be Helen. Face that launched a thousand squad cars. Christ, Kate, one look at her and I wish I were a lesbian.'

She'd have to eat again before she drove anywhere, that was certain. She was still unpleasantly wobbly. An early lunch, then. And then get on the road.

She'd not noticed before, but it was another pleasant day. If she bought a sandwich she could always eat it in the park – maybe even look at the more interesting-looking park the Moseley end of Kings Heath. First she looked in on her house. No post, except a couple of bills. Time to get the payments for the utilities on monthly direct debit. She could do that while she was here. And hang the rest of the upstairs curtains. And see if the paint was dry enough to fit the dining-room curtain rail.

No! She had to check out that house. Today.

In the end, she compromised. She made a little timetable on the back of the gas bill. 12.00–1.30 – lunch; 1.30–4.00, hunting for the house; 4.00–5.00, domestic chores, including buying a vacuum cleaner and dusters. Right. Start with sorting the bills, then off to Sainsbury's for some portable lunch.

She found a sheltered bench, from which she could see nothing but grass. She heard her joints relaxing, they did it so crunchily, one vertebra after another. My God, she'd been under that sort of pressure, had she? A squirrel, flowing along an ash tree branch, agreed, chittering at her as she threw it some crumbs of cherry cake. The sooner she got herself to therapy the better. Except she suspected it would mean confronting everything, including maggots, head on. She'd have to talk about Robin. How she still saw him, still smelt his aftershave: Colin sometimes used the same one. How she saw the car heading for them, saw him hurling her out of the way. Saw his shattered body. Saw the maggots.

At least there'd be support. She leaned back. Another vertebra cracked. So when was the last time she'd run, not with the kids, but for her own pleasure? Before she got involved with the BB, that was when. Maybe a lifetime ago, perhaps a couple of weeks. She'd have to remedy that. An unfit officer was a hazard to herself and others in the team. Look at her this morning: what if she'd been in the middle of checking out a scene of crime?

No, no more of this. She screwed up the wrappers, swigged the last drop of water, and headed for her car.

Her slow progress and constant three-point-turning didn't seem to attract anyone's attention. She found neat modern culs-de-sac, newly-privatised council ones. Thirties, fifties, sixties, seventies culs-de-sac. By four she was ready to give up – should have done so if she meant to stick to her schedule. But there were two more. Milton Avenue and Leavensbrook Close. Flipping a mental coin, she turned back to Leavensbrook.

And found it!

Yes, an expensive late eighties development, all manicured grass and newly-painted wood, with a startling crop of window-boxes, tubs and pseudo-wheelbarrows full of winter pansies. Any cars were up-market – hers Audis and BMWs, waiting to be joined by his. There was a rash of Austrian blinds at the bedroom windows – hadn't someone said they reminded him of old ladies who'd gone to the lav and got their petticoats caught in their knickers? She grinned at the thought. Nice to grin again. She sighed. Her back cracked its relief as she sat back. A job well done.

Now all she had to do was find the house in question.

At least this was something she was good at. She went systematically from house to house with an easy line on looking for one Cassie Wright. She even had a convincing-looking slightly scrumpled envelope with a hand-written note on it. Her envelope, her hand-writing. Most of the houses were still empty. Those with cars in front were occupied by a nice set of pleasant, helpful housewives, all, to judge by the smells emanating from the kitchens, using up-market cookbooks to provide something for hubby's tea. Not partners, but husbands, in this sort of cul-de-sac.

Making a note of the houses which looked as if they were awaiting their owners' return, she went back to the car. Did she risk a quick peer through letter-boxes? Of course. Four had those bristly draught-excluder fringes round them. Two had both draught-excluders and flaps of something heavy tacked across them. She made a further note, and looked around her.

No, from this position it wasn't possible to guess which house her unwitting informant lived in. She'd settle down in the car and wait for the commuters' return.

It was her bladder that let her down in the end. She could hardly go and squat behind a neatly-shaved bush to relieve herself, and she couldn't recall seeing anything as vulgar as a public loo in an area like this, so she'd have to go home. But she could come back later.

Alf and his crew were just packing up when she got home. She fled upstairs before engaging in any conversation, however, and by the time she'd got back down it was only Alf who was left. Since he had a bill for the fence to slip her, it wasn't surprising he'd hung back. She walked out into the desert the poor garden had become to inspect his handwork. Whether he'd used one or not, she suspected she could have laid a spirit-level on the fence and found the bubble slap in the middle of the lines. When she fished out her chequebook, he looked awkward. He'd rather have cash, wouldn't he? But she could scarcely endorse the Black Economy. She wrote out the cheque quickly, adding another fifty. He looked at it askance. 'A little extra for bed-shifting,' she said. 'If you need cash to buy the security light and fittings, let me know.'

'Could do with it in the next couple of days,' he said. 'Autumn coming in, work's getting slack.'

She nodded. She'd seen what happened to families when the seasonal work ran out.

'You wouldn't tackle gutters, would you?'

She was just leaving for her surveillance stint when the phone rang. Maz. Could she manage a little ad hoc baby-sitting this evening? From about eight?

She could hardly refuse, could she?

'I'll be there as close to eight as I can,' she said cautiously, 'but I've got to finish something for work, first.'

'You're as bad as Paul,' Maz laughed. 'You two could have a little competition about who works longer hours.'

'I'd back your Giles, myself,' Kate said. 'See you later.'

The phone rang again, straight away. It went dead as soon as she answered. It couldn't, could it, have been Graham caught *in flagrante*, as it were, by his wife? She waited another five minutes to see if the caller would try again. At last, setting the answerphone, she set off to Leavensbrook Close.

She'd reckoned without the rush-hour traffic. Cursing herself for sticking to the main roads, she turned into rat-runs. They were just as solid.

By the time she got to it, the close was neatly packed with cars. If she had a drive, let alone a garage, she thought bitterly, she wouldn't clutter the road. She thought of the morning and mid-afternoon chaos outside her house. What if she had her front garden flattened to provide an off-road parking-space? Paul would love to do that for her. The trouble was, she thought dourly, as she inched into a space, that Joe Public would either ignore her need to get in or out – or, more likely, park there when she wasn't in it. Meanwhile, she told herself grimly, just on the off-chance she'd better look at the cars, too, just on the off-chance she might recognise one. Like Cope's Mondeo, maybe.

This time her inquiries took longer, but were no more fruitful. Presumably because their womenfolk were busy making last minute adjustments to the *haute cuisine* that was to constitute their supper, a lot of men answered the front doors she knocked. Sighing, she turned back to the car. Next time she'd provide herself with an excuse to ask for the lady of the house – that'd be the terminology round here; next time she'd crack it.

Chapter Twenty-Four

Kate made it to the Manse with three minutes to spare, to be greeted by an anxious Giles and a heady smell of cooking fruit.

'We've got tons of pears,' he said, as he shrugged on his coat. 'We're stewing them in red wine.'

'An Elizabeth David recipe?' she asked, straight-faced.

Fortunately there was something more solid simmering on the hob: a curry, authentic to judge by the smell.

'Naan in the freezer or cook yourself some rice,' said Maz, grabbing her coat from the kitchen table. 'Kids in bed soon as you can organise it. Paul's promised to pop round later to keep you company.'

By whose invitation, Kate wondered silently.

She'd washed up and was in Tim's bedroom, being allowed to run George V round the track, when she felt, rather than heard, someone approaching from behind. Not Tim. He was fiddling with the HST's coupling. Not one of the girls – one was in bed, the other singing in the shower. If she did what she wanted, she'd flip whoever it was over her back on to the railway layout – a pity the locos weren't several sizes larger. Instead, she simply dodged sideways at what she judged to be the right moment, leaving Paul in an ungainly sprawl across the track, to Tim's loud annoyance.

'It's taken us ages to fit this lot together, and you go and knock the lot off. Honestly, you could have damaged it badly, you know.'

'Sorry, Tim. I seem to have tripped on something. How's my favourite nephew, anyway?' Paul moved round the table to kiss Tim and ruffle his hair. Tim acquiesced, but showed no signs of welcoming his uncle's affection. Any day now he'd be embarrassed by it, and within a couple of years would completely avoid any such display.

Kate watched, smiling wryly: kids weren't cuddly long enough.

Paul caught her eye. 'You realise you're doing my job?' His tone wasn't as light and mocking as she'd expected.

'Job?'

'Baby-sitting.'

Tim pushed past him: 'That's because we're not babies any more. Kate's – Kate's *kid-watching*,' he declared. 'Could you change those points, Kate? They're sticking.'

'You're too old to sit on my knee and have a story read?' Locking his fingers across Tim's chest, Paul pulled him back towards him.

Tim pulled away. 'I should have thought that was obvious,' he said loftily.

Paul grimaced. 'See how the mighty are fallen,' he said. 'There was I, for years the patcher of knees, provider of pocket money, fielder at cricket, and generally useful uncle, and now I'm redundant. Well,' he added, his face becoming lugubrious, 'maybe the pocket money's redundant too.'

Tim was too busy with Duck to reply.

The three children finally in bed and lights officially out, Kate wandered downstairs. What she wanted was her bed, but clearly etiquette demanded that she talk at least for a while to Paul. She found him in the kitchen – a bonus, since she could take a chair opposite him without appearing to be picky about where she sat.

'You all right?' he asked almost at once.

'Fine,' she said. Yes, it was true, she did feel fine. Her outburst this morning seemed to have purged her, and what she was sure would prove a successful afternoon's work was already beginning to heal.

'You're sure?' He peered anxiously at her face. 'You look very pale. Are you sure you won't have a drink?'

'I certainly wouldn't say no to a drink. But I'm perfectly OK. Maybe a bit tired,' she admitted. Yes, now she came to think of it, she was knackered.

'Tired?' he prompted, reaching glasses and gin. 'Had a bad day at work?'

'Very good, actually.' Yes, all things considered it had been excellent. 'Perhaps I just haven't got over the weekend yet. All that football – I'm surprised the kids could kick a ball on Sunday! And then I dashed down to collect my clothes. Time I really settled into my house. Made it my home. Cheers!' she toasted him. 'And thanks for all your help.'

'No problem. You seem to work very hard.'

'No harder than a lot of professionals. No harder than you, probably.' Though it did occur to her that recently he'd been devoting a great deal of time to her painting, rather than his work at college. 'And there are the good days when things come together. My colleague Colin, now. He was looking quite washed out recently, but he gets the right verdict the other day and suddenly he's leaping round like a spring lamb. Bet you're the same when one of your kids finally gets the hang of something or gets decent grades in the exams.'

He smiled. 'They've got such problems, these kids. So deprived . . . What on earth's that?'

Kate was on her feet and running. 'One of Jenny's nightmares.'

Paul had the tact to stay downstairs: he was still sitting at the kitchen table with the gin bottle in front of him when Kate came back. It was clear he'd freshened his drink. She pushed her glass across for similar treatment, but waved at him to slosh in much more tonic.

'Poor little mite,' she said. 'I had to wake her up properly this time. And find a dry nightie.'

'She wet the bed? At her age?' Paul looked horrified.

'Sweat. As if she has a fever. Tim woke up too – he took her one of his favourite teddies.' It was the one he'd previously lent Kate. 'He's such a delight, that child. I wonder what he'll grow up to be.'

'Do you want children, Kate?'

'It isn't a matter of wanting or not. It's the circumstances. I expect Maz has told you. My partner was killed this summer. We were happy to have his children. Maybe I'd have wanted my own, my *biological* ones. Maybe not. But I'm not ready for another relationship yet, and I wouldn't consider having a child of my own, just for the sake of it.'

Paul nodded, his head down.

Kate waited: it would have been altogether more adult to tell him some of this earlier, rather than simply rebuff him. Should she apologise, or would that make matters worse?

'Christ!' he said, making her jump. 'They make me mad, these single mothers. Totally irresponsible.' He took a long swig of gin. But he didn't elaborate.

Kate wasn't sure she wanted him to. The silence deepened, became increasingly awkward to break. One of them had to make the effort. Just for once she didn't want it to have to be her.

'So you didn't have a bad day at work? Did you catch a lot of criminals, then?'

Good for him. She smiled, shaking her head. 'Don't often get to do that. It's like doing a jigsaw without the picture on the box. And half the pieces are missing. But today I think I found an important bit.'

He pulled himself more upright. 'Tell me all about it, then!'

It would have been nice to tell someone. But she shook her head. 'Not until I've found the other pieces. And asked my boss if it's for this particular jigsaw.'

'Hush-hush is it?'

'Not especially. It's just habit, Paul, not to say anything. And policy too, I suppose. I dare say there are things at your college you don't talk about outside.'

'Hmm. And one of them's marking.' He grinned. 'Piles of

which await my attention even as we speak. OK, Kate – I'll have to love you and leave you. No, stay where you are: I'll let myself out.'

But she got up, following him into the hall.

'I'll just go and kiss the kids good-night,' he said, heading for the stairs.

'Hang on! Look,' she added awkwardly, 'don't you think it'd be better to let them settle? Lynn's really funny about people in her room these days, and I'm afraid she'll yell at you and wake up Tim again. And – well, you heard Jenny. I'd hate to have her disturbed again. Sorry. Teaching my grandmother,' she added apologetically.

His face tightened, but at last he turned. 'OK. Makes sense. See they have these, won't you?' He laid three fivers on the hall table. 'Night, then.'

The house blessedly quiet, she was torn by two imperatives: sleep, which she ached for, and talking today's events through with Graham. He'd told her to find the safe house. OK, she hadn't any proof of anything, only the strongest of hunches, but she needed his help – his permission! – to move things on. She dialled his home number first. The answerphone. And his mobile's answering service too. She could have wept with frustration.

Perhaps throwing the handset down hadn't damaged it. She picked it up cautiously and listened: yes, still a dialling tone. She replaced it carefully.

This time she had the sense to phone Colin at home, to ask him to tell Cope in person that she was doing some checking on the Danny case and would be in late. Very late. She'd wait at the 50 bus-stop in the hope of seeing one of the women. Both.

Neither. Chilled and irritated she got on a bus at last and seethed all the way into town.

No coffee. No tea. No one's job, of course. Colin was working through something with Reg, Sally was dialling a succession of numbers, tutting with irritation as apparently none was answered. The others were quietly going about their business. Even Selby, who was already on his computer, eyes fixed on the screen, his mouse darting quickly backwards and forwards. He'd certainly come on a bundle since this course. She strolled across to congratulate him.

And stopped.

'Red queen on black king,' she said quietly. 'And black six on red seven. Christ in heaven, Selby!' She could hear her voice rising. 'A word. Outside. Now.'

When he ignored her she reached across and took the mouse. She closed the solitaire window.

'You bitch! I was just about to get it out!' He got truculently to his feet.

'I said outside. Now.'

'What the fuck d'you want?'

Keeping her voice low, she continued, 'I want to talk to you. About that. In private. Unless, of course, you want the whole room to hear? The whole squad to know?'

She whisked him down to an interview room.

'Sit,' she said.

He obeyed.

She remained standing. 'I'd like to know what work you've actually done since that computer course.'

He stood, pushing away from the table. 'I don't have to tell you anything.'

She leaned against the wall, her shoulder on a greasy spot where countless other shoulders had leaned. 'No, you don't. You'd rather tell Cope and Harvey. Fine. No problem.'

'It's not — I get my share done.' Addressing the door, he shoved his hands in his pockets.

'Share? When the rest of us are working our arses off? Whenever I've seen you recently, either in the office or in the incident room, you've been glued to the computer, shifting and clicking that mouse. What gen have you got off the screen? What reports have you written?'

'Just shut the fuck up! I've done my bleeding share.'

'When? Where? Oh, yes. On the streets, maybe, when

you've been sent out. But not even in meetings – you've been messing with that mouse whenever I've seen you,' she repeated. She was blisteringly angry. 'Out there is a bloke who's messing up not just kids' bodies, but their minds, their whole lives. And all you're doing is playing bloody patience. And that's just what I haven't got, not at the moment, Selby.' She ran her eyes over him. Six foot and fifteen stone taking up space. 'Get back up there and get stuck into your work.'

'What about Cope? Harvey?' Selby sounded genuinely frightened.

'If you shift the backlog you must have built up – in your own time, mind, Selby! – and that computer stays off, I'll keep quiet. OK? But if I ever catch you at it again, you'll be in Cope's room before you can say ace of spades.'

He looked at her with a degree of hatred and resentment she'd only met before in cons and slammed out of the room. She followed, more slowly.

She stood staring at herself in the mirror over the washbasin. The chance of a lifetime to have a little sweet revenge on a nasty sexist bully and she'd thrown it up. God only knew whether she was right to do so. Half of her would still have like to spill every last bean to Cope. But you didn't do that, did you, didn't grass up colleagues, not even those who'd pretended to rape you as part of your welcome to the squad. No. Not straight away.

She'd warned him, almost officially. Next time it would be her responsibility to report it to Harvey. Cope in his absence. And she would. She'd have to.

God, was it only half past nine?

Cope was waiting in the office when she got back. 'I want to get everyone into the incident room. That schoolboy's given us a good description of the man following him.'

Good description it might be. In fact, it was so good Reg fished out his copy of the morning's *Post*. 'That's your man!' he said. 'Aston Villa have just signed him for half a million. You're sure this kid's got all his marbles?'

'So we look for blokes *like* this character,' Cope said heavily. 'Bloody hell, Reg, it's the only lead we've got. Kate, the kid reckons there's no one in the mug shots. Go and double check, would you? And – where the fuck are you off too, Turner?'

Colin had bolted from the room. There were unmistakable sounds to suggest why. Kate was ready to follow.

'No, none of your ministering angel stuff.' Cope thrust a phone at her. 'Just get on to the caretakers, will you? Tell them one of our tried and trusted men has just spewed his guts up in the corridor and someone's going to have to shift it before I for one stir from here. I always come out in sympathy,' he added ruefully as she dialled.

Eventually Reg was allowed to go after him. 'No, he won't be going anywhere for a bit, Gaffer,' he said. 'Something in last night's balti, I should think.'

'Shit!'

Reg laughed. 'Not the best word, in the circumstances, Gaffer!'

'OK. Power. You're the nearest thing he's got to a partner. If he needs to get home, you'd better take him. Then have a go at ID-ing that young bloke. The rest of us – well, we all know what we've got to do.'

By the end of the morning, half the squad were ill, and there was a strong rumour about the canteen.

She knew what response she'd have given if she'd asked Cope for a team of colleagues to check out the cul-de-sac, so she didn't even bother asking. That was something she'd do tonight. She got stuck into the job he'd given her. She came up with a couple of men who looked not unlike the handsome footballer the kid claimed had followed him, but one was in Long Lartin and the other up in Durham, both for the duration. A cynical part of her brain wanted to believe that the boy had rather wished a footballing hero were following him, but she couldn't entirely accept that. It was too convenient for one thing. It made more sense to step up the surveillance on his school, and to follow him discreetly on his paper round. Not involved in either of those, she had a chance to turn to some of Colin's paperwork, and had the satisfaction – if the irritation – of picking up the very bit of information she needed for her car-theft file. She wrapped the whole thing up and took it to Cope.

'I think this is ready when you are, Sir.'

He stuck out a fist for it. 'Anything immediate?'

'I reckon we're ready to pick him up when you give the say-so.'

He nodded. 'That'll be my tonight's homework, then. Planning it. Jesus, Kate, how can I run this lot when I've got two-thirds of the men off?'

'Let's just say, "don't eat in the canteen", Sir! Seriously, any news of DCI Harvey, Sir? I was a bit surprised he wasn't in, since he managed to get to the match.' She'd practised this, outloud in the loo. Professional interest only – that was the message of both voice and posture.

'Could do with him, couldn't we? Hang on – what are you doing here? Thought you were supposed to be off sick?'

'I've got an appointment with the shrink coming through, Sir. It's all to do with my partner's death.' She examined her voice: no, no quavers. 'Anyway, I'd rather work through it. There seems to be quite a lot to do.'

'Hmph. Well, we could use you, provided you don't get the screaming hab-dabs again. Christ, woman, what with your maggots and the canteen, we shall need danger money to work here.'

Still no news about Graham. She was just about to make her escape when Reg called her.

'Fancy a medicinal half? You look a bit washed out, you know. Maybe you're not over that maggot business.'

Hell! Not that she didn't owe him a half – several pints, in fact. But she wanted to get moving.

'Love one. But we'll have to put it on the back burner,' she said, remembering saying the same thing to Graham. 'I'm checking out something – for Graham Harvey,' she added, unconvincing even to her own ears. 'Tell you what – I'll stand you a sarnie tomorrow. OK?'

'Must be important if it makes you miss a beer,' Reg said. She couldn't work out whether he was joking or not.

'Just a long shot.' She shrugged. 'And these days, if the Gaffer says jump, you just ask, how high?'

'Or if he wants a Fosbury flop! OK, my wench, we'll have that sarnie tomorrow. See you!'

Feeling vaguely guilty, she set off. The traffic was so bad, however, she might just as well have had that drink. Half an hour in a pub beat half an hour in a traffic jam any day. But she'd had this feeling before, when she thought she was on to something – she wanted to be alone. She laughed: *Me and Greta Garbo both.*

Chapter Twenty-Five

Equipped with a clipboard and a bright smile, Kate would have passed muster as a market researcher. The only problem would be if anyone wanted to see her ID. From her Met days she'd kept a quite spurious card guaranteeing her to be something or other official in the market research field. The bottom line was, of course, her police ID.

She asked a few friendly questions – about dustbin collection, as it happened – at several houses. She always managed to bring the conversation round to the neighbours – she'd gesture convincingly with her Biro. But there were no useful anecdotes, no whispered half-accusations. Despite the drawn curtains at their windows, two houses remained firmly incommunicado. Only one – number six – had a furry draught-excluder covering the letterbox flap; the other – number twenty two – both a draught excluder and a piece of heavy felt. Imagine being a poor postie, trying to get your fingers through that lot.

She'd done that before, too – pretended even to herself she was thinking about something else when all she wanted to do was leap up and down in triumph. She checked. Yes, the drive was used – there were a couple of oil spots. There was also a double garage, at right angles to the rest of the house but with a connecting passage – what looked like a utility room – to the house itself. The garage was angled so comings and goings would be private. And a Leylandii hedge was doing its bit, too. The windows were so heavily curtained that it was impossible to tell whether anyone was inside or not – not so much as a crack of light escaped.

Number twenty-two. She wrote it down, just in case. In case of what? A sudden and complete attack of amnesia?

Head and heart dancing, she made herself walk slowly down the drive.

She'd give herself another half hour. She'd sit in the car and listen to the radio and pray that someone would come. It was beyond hoping for that anyone would go to twenty-two. It was just possible that someone might go to the last house. The woman on the bus. Please! Anyone, but let it be the woman on the bus.

She waited an hour. OK, so there was a good programme about diet in the Third World and another about a woman who'd discovered she was a lesbian after twenty years of marriage and two children. She offered it up briefly as an explanation of Mrs Harvey's behaviour but wasn't convinced. Odd that she didn't even know the woman's Christian name: 'my wife' or 'Mrs Harvey' were the norm. Weird.

She was getting very cold, and was in desperate need of a loo. Right. Give up. That'd be the logical thing.

Five more minutes. She'd give it five more minutes. Well, ten. An arts programme, now, with people being pretentious about a violent film. Funny how people could be so casual about what actually hurt a good deal. Catharsis be blowed: bet that crit-ic'd be in casualty if he so much as shut his finger in the door.

A car. There'd been plenty of car movement – none to do with number twenty-two, of course – but this was the car she wanted. Yes, she'd be a Golf GTI woman, that expensive woman on the bus. And yes, she'd park at number six, and fish out the sort of bag that she'd take to aerobics. Yes!

She gave her a couple of minutes to go in. She could trace her movements through the house. Switch off the burglar alarm. A light in what must be the downstairs cloakroom. *Hurry up* – I need a pee, too! And at last that light went off and the living-room lights brightened.

Kate recognised her as soon as she opened her front door and couldn't stop herself smiling as broadly as if they'd been friends for years. The woman was taken aback, but smiled too.

Kate had decided that she wouldn't lie to her. She seemed the sort of person who would like to do her public duty.

'Good evening,' she began – she nearly called her Pam. 'I'm a police officer and I believe you may be able to help me.' She allowed the dimples to show on her smile – no, this wasn't going to be a threatening talk.

It was a very pleasant one, complete with first-class coffee and expensive biscuits, after a visit to a well-appointed loo. The living room was a bit heavily fringed and floral for Kate's taste, but it was beautifully lit by some very elegant floor-level lamps: another idea Kate would have liked to borrow but for the smallness of her house.

Pam Corby was emphatic. She still harboured suspicions of the house. 'Fancy your overhearing me! I must be more careful what I say in future! I suppose I mustn't ask what case you're investigating?'

''Fraid not. In any case, it isn't a proper case as such. Not yet. Just my nosiness. You made it so intriguing the way you described it to your friend.'

'Hazel. Yes, well, if you never see anyone and know someone's there . . . I reckon they've got a new trick now. They drive this van straight into the garage. Goodness knows what they're unloading. Oh, d'you think it's drugs, Ms Power? Or one of those immigration rackets?'

'Immigration racket?'

'Bringing these coloureds in.'

'Have you ever seen any Black or Asian people around?'

'No. But then, I've never seen anyone around. Now, my friend Joyce from Colesbrook Road – it backs on to here, Ms Power. Some of the houses are a bit too close for my liking. I like my privacy. The last house we had, the gardens were fifty yards long, so there was no need for net curtains. Like being in the country, almost. Do you know Harborne at all?'

'Not yet. I've only just moved to Birmingham. It's nicer here than where I'm living. But you're overlooked by these Colesbrook Road houses, are you?'

'Some of us. Not at this end. But the house we're talking about is. A bit. And Joyce swears she's seen – Look, why don't I take you round to Joyce's? Then you can see through her windows. Make up your own mind.'

Yes! 'D'you suppose we should phone first? Make sure it's convenient?'

Pam slapped her head. 'Tuesday's her class too. She goes to creative writing, I do keep fit. She'll be in any moment. I'll leave a message on her machine – ask her to phone me back the second she gets here. Now, will you have another coffee while you wait? No? Would you mind if I put *News at Ten* on? I like to keep up to date. Can't read on the bus, you see – makes me ill.'

'Please – go ahead.'

They pretended to watch in silence. But Kate at least was listening for the phone.

'There's not much to see at this time of night,' Joyce explained, peering round her thickly lined curtains. 'As you can see.'

Kate peered. Nothing. Suspiciously nothing. Not a glimmer from a light.

'I do wish you could tell us what's going on,' Joyce said, as she led the way downstairs. Her house was much smaller than Pam's: probably the floor area was less than Kate's, although the available space was much more compact. The kitchen was much smaller, Kate noted with a hint of self-congratulation, as if she'd chosen the house rather than had it thrust upon her. But it was the sort of units she'd chosen, and the women settled down with a glass of white wine for a conversation about kitchens. Pam was a widow: her husband had bought an extremely profitable insurance policy before he died in a hit-and-run accident. At least she had no difficulties maintaining her house, though she said she rattled round it. Joyce was bitter after a divorce, having come down in the property world. The wine went round again. This time Kate covered her glass.

'Driving,' she said.

'You look quite tired,' Pam said. 'Have you been on duty all day?'

Kate nodded. 'To be fair, this is something I want to do for myself. Following a hunch. But if anything comes of my hunch, your bus conversation could be crucial to our investigations. And I'll tell you what they're into the moment I can.' She drained her glass and set it regretfully on the new working surface.

Although she'd helped herself to some of the Manse cocoa, she was too busy fizzing with success to sleep. If she were honest, however, she had to admit that all she'd done was locate a house that was causing suspicion. Honest detective work, she told herself. But what good would it do? There was a matter of tying it in with a crime. Any crime, not necessarily the paedophile business.

The women had been nice. They'd talked of her going out to a show with them, or sharing a meal. And though they were so much older than she, she'd take them up on the offer as soon as this business was over.

Cope rapped his knuckles against her forehead. 'Is there anyone at home? Half the path. labs in Brum swamped with E.coli specimens from the squad and you want me to set up surveillance for a house that a set of nosy women thinks is being used for some unspecified crime? Are you off your head? God, some of them maggots must have got your brain. Piss off, now. I've got work to do.'

What else had she expected? She left his office, closing the door with meticulous precision. The office seemed empty, however, and she slammed her hands on the desk. 'Fuck it!'

'Hang on, my wench, that's not the sort of language I expect from you. What's up?'

'Sorry, Reg. Didn't realise you were there. Just –'

But Cope was in the doorway. 'God knows how we're going to allocate work loads today. Selby's in: he's in the Incident Room working away. Seems he's not very happy with something you said, Power. You need to be a bit more tactful the way you talk to people, you know. Can't go putting people's backs up all the time. Colin reckons he'll be in tomorrow. Sally's in hospital.'

'Hospital?'

'Hospital's what I said. Now, Reg, what I'd like you to do is this . . .'

Lunch-time. Kate would have been happy to work through, but Reg appeared at the office door. 'Come on, my wench: they'll have run out of booze. No, we're going to a little bar a bit out of the way. It's one thing working with policemen all day, it's another sharing you beer with a load of flat-feet pretending to be something else.'

They found a small bar full of lawyers instead. The champagne seemed to be flowing. 'Hey up, there's a table over there. Shove your way through, Kate. I'll get – what d'you want?'

'Half of bitter, please!' she called as she pushed through some very expensive suits.

'Chose the wrong job, didn't we, my wench?' Reg dropped a packet of crisps on the table. 'I ordered a couple of ploughman's platters – OK?'

'Great.' She pushed a tenner across. 'My shout. Only fair.'

'Fair enough. Hey, I got my son's wedding photos here. Last set arrived today. Fancy a shufti?'

'Try and stop me. I'm a sucker for weddings.' Not that she was. But Reg didn't want to hear that.

'Let's start at the beginning, shall we? That's the plane we went out in.'

It was to be a frame by careful frame examination – none of your quick shuffles through for Reg. He'd got a new camera, he said. Did everything bar playing 'God Save the Queen'. Kate took each one and looked at it carefully, trying to find some perceptive comment to make about each. At last, her powers of invention failing her, she pointed to the figures in the bottom of each print.

'Oh yes, the time and date of each one. Saves no end of time when you put them in the album,' he said.

The procession continued.

The ploughman's platters arrived. The photographs continued unabated. The last photos were dated early September, two days before she'd come to Birmingham. Kate was just about to ask why he'd taken none for the last three weeks of his visit when a loud lawyer stepped backwards, knocking their table. Kate swooped, lifting the prints before they were engulfed in a tide of beer.

By the time apologies had been made and accepted – rather grudgingly on Reg's side – it was time to go.

'Hey, you were going to tell me all about this row you had with Cope,' Reg said as they shrugged into their jackets.

'Not worth the breath it would take,' Kate temporised. 'You know what he's like.'

'Ah. But you mustn't let it get to you, see.'

They set off, Kate setting a brisk pace.

'Hang on, love. Your legs must be longer than mine. Younger, any road.'

As they climbed the stairs, Reg's breathing notably heavier than Kate's, he turned to her. 'You never told me about this job for young Graham. Anything special?'

'Just a long shot. To do with this –'

'That you, Power?' It was Cope, yelling from the office door. 'Get a move on, woman, there's someone hanging on the phone for you.'

Kate sped.

But it was only Maureen, from Kings Heath police station. 'We may have made a bit of progress on your rape case,' she said. 'Since you lot in the city centre never do a stroke, why don't you drop round here for a balti and a bit of a natter? You could meet my new fiancé,' she said.

Fiancé. It was almost a term from another era. People moved in, didn't they? Got married if kids came along. But there was something touching about Maureen's tone, as if meeting the man concerned was an honour.

Kate smiled. 'Great,' she said. 'What time? Only I've got my football training till about eight-thirty.'

More small boys seemed to have appeared from the woodwork: news of comparative success had travelled fast. Alec and Derek were there, stretching and bending with the best of them. They backed out when it came to shooting practice, on the grounds that it was the boys who really needed to polish that particular set of skills. But they stayed with Kate.

'Not that our presence is necessary any more. Your references shone from the page, Kate.'

'We could have read them in the dark, they were so glowing,' Alec added. 'But I shall continue coming anyway – oh, don't get me wrong! The exercise is so good. And at my age that's a consideration.' He seemed about to say something else, but dropped to one knee to fiddle with his trainer laces.

Derek coughed. He was clearly embarrassed – had no doubt relied on his father to do the necessary. 'Kate – there's something I – we – wanted to mention to you. You being in the police, you'll be used to the seedier side of life. Or we wouldn't have raised it.'

'That's right.' Alec straightened. 'We'd have mentioned it to Paul or Giles. But the lads seem to get on well with you, and you might be – I don't know, it might be easier for them to talk to you than to one of their officers.'

'I'll certainly do whatever I can,' Kate prompted him.

'It's – this is really embarrassing.'

All three laughed. Kate waited.

'It's just that there seem to be some – well, I don't know whether they're photos or postcards going round. You know,' Alec screwed his face up quite unexpectedly and added, 'feelthy pictures,' in a supposedly Middle-Eastern accent.

'What sort?'

'I haven't seen them. But there was some giggling after Church Parade the other day. And a lot of furtive shoving into pockets. Reminded me of when I was ten, with *Titbits* or *Picture Post*, or something. Probably just a bit of silliness.'

Derek shook his head. 'Photos, I'm afraid. Of boys. Naked, mostly. Some . . . with, with men . . .'

Kate hoped she looked calm and capable. But inside her head all sorts of alarm bells were ringing. 'Perhaps we should talk about it indoors.' Then she remembered. 'Look, I've got a dinner appointment – work! – so I'll have to call a halt to practice – with that carpark light broken they can hardly see anyway. Could one of you hang on out here until the last boy's been collected? And then I can talk with whoever prefers . . .'

The men exchanged glances. Alec said, 'I'll hang on, shall I? While you talk, son?'

She shut the door of the little room they used as an office and flicked the catch. She perched on the corner of the desk. He leaned against the filing cabinet.

'It is something serious, isn't it?'

He fidgeted with a torn drawer label. 'Yes and no. I mean nothing ever happened. I mean, it was before Giles' time – the last minister was a crusty old bastard none of us would have dared approach. Not like Giles: I'm sure the kids could talk to him.'

She waited.

'It was when I was a boy. There was a rash of this dirty photo business. Photos, not cards. Mostly harmless. Just naked boys. But if you pretended to giggle over them, you got shown some more. I think there was a sort of progression. I know some of those I saw eventually were – well, pretty obscene. With men. You know. I must have looked pretty furtive – Dad wormed it out of me in the end.'

It could be serious. It was one of the ways paedophiles started to groom little boys, according to Gail, the social worker. 'Have you any idea who was circulating them?'

He shook his head. 'One of the older boys, according to rumour. Maybe even an officer.'

'An *officer*?'

He nodded. 'It all stopped quite suddenly. Perhaps someone warned whoever it was.'

'Or perhaps he left?'

'I don't know. I'm not even sure who the officers were then.'

'Do you remember precisely what year this was, Derek?' Damn it, she sounded just like a policewoman. Another part of her brain was racing – could this be why young Royston wasn't happy at this chapel? Why his family had started to go to the one on the High Street? 'This could be important.'

He shook his head. 'I was a kid.'

'Roughly?'

'I must have been about twelve or thirteen. I can't remember.'

'Would there be records of the Brigade going back then – what, ten years?'

'Should be. I suppose. You'll have to ask Giles: as Minister, he's in overall control, remember.'

She nodded.

'What'll you do?' Derek asked. 'You see, there was another rumour. That whoever it was did more than pass round photos. One camp. With one of the lads . . . Ah, that'll be Dad.' He turned to slip the catch.

'There! That's the last one off our hands. All the parents collected them in person.'

'It's getting as bad as the school run. You can't move in my road at school starting and finishing time. When are the poor little buggers ever going to learn to walk?' She pulled a face. 'When we've cleaned this child molester off the streets, I suppose.'

Alec looked at her: 'You don't suppose he and this business are connected?'

She shook her head. 'I don't know. But I promise you this, I shall treat what you've told me as seriously as if they are.'

★

Maureen's fiancé was a handsome man in his early forties, a CID Superintendent, as it turned out. Maureen introduced him with evident pride: although they'd worked in the same station for months, they'd met socially on an OU Psychology course.

'There was this woman saying how civilised Philip was. As if police officers weren't! I didn't dare say I was a sergeant. Anyway, I thought he was civilised too.'

'And Maureen is, despite being a sergeant,' Philip added.

The developments in the rape case included another attempted rape and another small stab wound, not unlike Kate's. This time the victim was an African-Caribbean who had a family prepared to support her whatever had happened. Whether as a consequence or not, she was much more forthcoming, and had furiously alleged her attackers were African-Caribbean too. She was equally furious that none of them were on police files.

'She swears she'll know them again,' Philip added. 'And has promised to yell blue murder if she sees them.'

'Trouble is, I wouldn't put it past her to have a go at them,' Maureen said. 'I did warn her. "Don't even think of acting on your own," I said.'

Kate grimaced. 'That's exactly what I've been doing,' she said. And found herself pouring out the story of her travels round Kings Heath and its environs and the official reaction. 'No names, no pack-drill,' she added, pouring lager all round.

'No need for names. There's a certain CID inspector whose charm and wit are renowned throughout the whole West Midlands,' Maureen said.

'But when it comes down to it, he's a good copper,' Philip amended.

'Usually. But this same anonymous inspector only sent me down to Devon. Well, it's a nice place, Devon. Except the case he said I was providing information on was nothing like ours. And the information was curiously incomplete.'

'Talk to him about it,' Philip said. 'Maybe someone told him to amend it.'

'Bloody hell! You'd have me talk to the next fifty bus when it's at full tilt down the High Street, would you?'

'Since full tilt down the High Street is usually one mile an hour, you might be all right. But I take your point. Trouble is, if no one says anything, nothing gets done. Have you thought about talking to your DCI? Or a senior woman colleague?'

' 'Course I have. But there's a fine line between talking things over and grassing someone up.'

They nodded.

'Trouble is, he's now absolutely vetoed any sort of surveillance of this house, and even if the DCI weren't off sick, I don't see how I could go over his head.'

'If it's on our patch, Philip could do something. Couldn't you?'

He grimaced. 'I was hoping you wouldn't say that. But we're not laid low with food poisoning. And our CID like to keep abreast of what's happening round here. Tell you what, Kate, have some more naan, no more talking shop, and I'll think about it. I can't say fairer than that.'

Kate smiled. 'Indeed you can't. No, no more naan, thanks. And now, just to improve life, I've got this problem with the Boys' Brigade. I suppose you've never heard any rumours about Braysfield Road Baptists, have you?'

Graham. She had to talk to Graham. She couldn't let Philip do anything without Graham's approval. All he'd authorised was finding the house. Setting up a surveillance operation after Cope had specifically vetoed it was quite another matter. And then there was the business at the chapel. She had to phone, and this time, whatever the consequences, she had to leave a message.

Deciding was easy, of course. Doing it another matter. It was a good job she'd got into the habit of rehearsing difficult conversations in a loo beforehand. And a good job the Manse loo was away from the bedrooms. All the same, she wasn't entirely satisfied with the cool, business-like tone of her voice as she left messages on both his home and his mobile numbers.

She'd have liked to start talking to Giles, but he and Maz were already in bed when she'd got back. She half thought about tapping on their door to see if they were awake. But it was late, and they got little enough time together. The morning would have to do.

Chapter Twenty-Six

As Kate opened the Manse front door to leave for work, Giles was standing on the step, patting his jacket pockets to check for keys. He was so grey and drained that Kate's urgent questions died on her lips. She touched his arm. 'Giles?'

'Death-bed,' he said briefly. 'A child.'

'I'm so sorry.' She must wait, then. But then she thought of Danny and Darren – even of Tim, arguing with Maz about porridge – and changed her mind. 'Look, I know this isn't a good time to ask you this. But I'm going to anyway, because it involves other children.' She stepped back into the house with him. 'Alec and Derek say you're the one who'll have the records of the BB. Right?'

He nodded. 'I suppose – yes, they're in the files, some-where. Why?'

'I need to know who was in and who was running the BB about ten to twelve years ago.'

He shrugged off his jacket. 'I'll dig them out for you. But if you want quick answers, ask Paul – he's got a wonderful memory.'

'But he wouldn't have been here then, surely.'

'Oh, yes. He and Maz had been in this congregation years before I came on the scene. Brummies born and bred.'

'But –'

'We met and married years before I entered the ministry, remember. Up in Sunderland. Maz always wanted to come

229

back to Birmingham. It was just a miracle that I was asked to take on the ministry here.'

'And you did it wonderfully, love.' Maz emerged from the kitchen, putting her arm round his waist.

Robin used to like Kate to do that. He'd grasp the hand and pull it tight.

Giles dotted a kiss on Maz's forehead. 'I was just saying, if Kate wants BB information, Paul's her man. But I'll dig out the files, Kate. For this evening. Is that coffee I smell?'

'You couldn't possibly do it now?'

His face tightened. Maz spoke for him. 'He'll do it as soon as he can, Kate – isn't that good enough?'

Kate took a breath. 'It may be so important I'll come home from work to pick them up as soon as you've found them. You've got my number. I know I'm off the Richter scale for insensitivity, but please understand children's lives could be at risk.'

'Why don't you simply ask Paul, if it's so urgent?'

Maz's question was reasonable. So why was it so impossible to answer?

'I don't want to involve anyone except you two. It's as confidential as that.'

'Come off it: you don't expect Paul not to know about it? The BB's his life.'

'Maz, believe me, I'm not one for dramatic secrets. But at this moment, it's imperative that this is kept quiet. I didn't want to spell it out, but I'm going to have to. Someone has alleged that there may have been sexual – shall we call it malpractice? – in the Brigade some years ago. It may be a vicious rumour, in which case clearly no one should know about it. It may be the truth, in which case the first thing the perpetrator should know about it is my boss fingering his collar.'

Maz still glared, her mouth tight with anger. Giles covered his face.

'Well before your time, Giles,' Kate reminded him. 'You can't hold yourself responsible for things that happened then.'

'No,' he said. 'But what if they were to recur?'

Kate pounced: 'What makes you ask that?'

He shook his head. 'Sorry. I've been up since two. No, I suppose I was just panicking – it's what everyone in charge of young people dreads, isn't it?'

Kate's mobile phone chirruped. 'Excuse me. Yes?'

'Don't know where you are, Power.' Cope's voice sounded strained. 'But you'd better get your arse in fast. I seem to have picked up that bug. You're in charge, woman – answerable to Superintendent Gordon. OK?'

Answerable to the Invisible Man, more like.

'Sir!' She took a breath. 'I think I've found something important in the paedophile case, Sir. Can I press on?'

'Do what you fucking want – oh, shit –'

Kate turned back to them. 'I've got to go. I'm sorry to be so – so pressing. But believe me – those files could be a matter of life and death.'

Giles nodded: 'D'you want to wait? As soon as I've had a coffee . . .'

'Can't you see he's all in? A few more hours won't make any difference, surely to goodness! Let him sleep a couple of hours before he turns the loft upside down!'

At least if she went in by bus she could sit and think, and God knew that she'd not move much more quickly in a car. And buses had the advantage of bus lanes.

She tried to pull together her ideas by jotting them down, but the bus bucked so much her writing would be illegible. And the man sitting next to her was peering at her hieroglyphics – it would be just her luck if he could read what she couldn't. So she sat and stared ahead.

The question that most taxed her was why she didn't want Paul involved. She'd no reason to believe he'd blab – but his tendency to excessive helpfulness could be a problem. Remember how he wanted to run the football training. And now he was busy sorting out her house. No, Paul would have to interfere – he couldn't help it. And like the posters used to say, careless talk costs lives.

The person she most needed to talk to was Graham, of course. A sympathetic ear, ready with constructive suggestions. She couldn't weep that Cope was stricken with the bug. Funny that it should be so much later than the others – it seemed to eliminate the canteen. And she must find out about Sally – hospital suggested complications. She felt cold. Not gynaecological complications, please. Colin – she hoped he'd be back. And then there was the matter of Selby and his Patience.

'Graham!' Her face must have shown her surprise and relief.

'My office, please, DS Power. Now.'

She stared. His mouth was moving but the words didn't make sense.

'Now.' He turned on his heel and strode off.

She had no option but to follow. She'd never heard him use that tone, not even the first time he summoned her: that had been simple authority – this sounded like cold anger. Colin, back at his desk but still pale, raised exaggerated eyebrows. Selby clicked and dragged his mouse. She'd have to sort that out. She registered that Reg was looking serious, that there was no Sally.

The walk to his office seemed very long. The door was closed when she arrived. She tapped. Waited.

'Come!'

She stood to attention in front of him, a naughty fourth-former. He was seated at his desk, and leaned forward, as if to spring across the desk at her. Then he stood, confronting her. 'How dare you? How dare you?'

There was nothing to say, was there? Not until she knew how she'd offended.

'I come back off sick leave to find this!' He flicked an answerphone tape across the desk. 'Keeping me informed, are you? Wanting my advice? Well, my advice is to keep our squad's work within our squad and not go running to someone else to sort out our problems. Have you any idea how this will look to – to other people? What does it say about the way I organise things that I can't re-deploy people if necessary? At very least you should have asked Cope.'

'I did. The flea's still in my ear.' Perhaps a weak joke would remind him that they had a friendship growing.

It didn't.

'And little Ms Power can't take no for an answer. Or, more likely, not no, but just wait until we can sort it. For goodness' sake, you're like a child of four wanting its ice cream now.'

She said nothing. She registered facts: he was white, the bruises ugly browns and yellows. The inflamed eye now looked simply bloodshot. She was shaking: there was distress, but also anger at the injustice of her treatment. Graham, of all people, behaving like a jealous schoolgirl. Why on earth wasn't he simply welcoming what she'd done? It was no more than she'd done before – as a sergeant, she had the authority to ask other areas, other forces, indeed, for support.

He turned to the window, shoving his hands in his pockets. Then he withdrew them, folding his arms tightly across his chest.

There was no point in demeaning herself by offering what he'd see as excuses. And he was in the wrong, she was sure of it. Was it some sort of delayed shock? A row with his wife? Perhaps it hadn't been the most tactful thing in the world to leave messages on his home answerphone. She waited a few moments, and left, closing the door very quietly.

However she tried to school her expression her face didn't feel right. In any case, as long as she was waiting for the call from Giles, she couldn't settle.

Reg looked across at her. 'Ah, he has his moods, does the Gaffer. Just keep your head down and say nothing: he'll be OK in a day or two.'

Her head was certainly down when Graham appeared, wanting to talk to Colin.

She pounced when the phone rang. Giles must have had time to sort out the files by now. But it was a personal call for Reg. He snapped down the phone at the caller and slammed down the hand-set.

She got up. It was one thing to be hurt dreadfully by someone's temper – it was horribly like Robin's when his wife had been on the phone – but another to let it get in the way of the job. If Giles's sleepless night was no excuse for not searching for the files, how could she chicken out and not tell Graham about them? If he yelled, she'd just have to yell more loudly. She hung round in the corridor outside the office, waiting to intercept him.

He stopped short when he saw her. His mouth tightened.

'Brayfield Road Baptist Church Boys' Brigade may have had child abuse incidents about ten years ago,' she said flatly.

'What!'

She couldn't tell whether his explosion was anger at her persistence or interest. He stared coldly for a moment, and then gestured with his head. His office. He closed the door behind them.

'And it seems someone's busily circulating dirty pictures now,' she continued. 'Which was how it started first time round. Photos, then rumours about one of the others interfering with kids at camp. My next-door-neighbour's lad left the chapel round about that time – something happened he won't talk about.'

He walked to his desk, sitting heavily. He gestured her to a chair. She chose the hard one.

'This is stuff you've uncovered through your football coaching, is it?'

'An adult told me – don't worry, I haven't muddied any waters by trying to talk to the children.'

He nodded. A grim smile softened the rigid line of his mouth. 'At least that's one thing you haven't put your foot in. These things have to be handled with extreme care. One false move from us and we blow the case before it even gets to court.'

'I was going to contact Gail this morning, Sir.'

He nodded. 'What else have you done?'

'I've asked Giles – you remember –'

'Yes, the minister you're staying with. Yes?'

'I've asked him to dig out the records for that period. In fact, I've asked him to phone me as soon as he's found them. I said I'd go and collect them.'

'Anyone else involved?'

'Maz, his wife. They wanted me to talk to Paul –'

'You haven't?' he broke in. No, Paul wasn't his favourite person.

She shook her head. 'He'd muscle in, wouldn't he? Has to be in the thick of things, Paul. Fingers in every available pie –'

'– and a few others. Good. Will they be discreet – Giles and Maz?'

She hesitated. 'I hope so. I laid on the need for confidentiality quite thick. But Maz and Paul are very close: she was offended that I wanted him kept out of it. I felt very bad – she and Giles have been so good to me.'

Graham nodded. He got up again, heading for the kettle. The water bottle was empty, the cups dirty. 'Which will you tackle?' he asked, managing a faint smile.

They were standing side by side waiting for the kettle to boil. 'At least Reg Tanner and I seem to have escaped the bug – we ate out on Monday lunch-time. He showed me all his wedding photos.'

Graham nodded: 'Sound bloke, Reg. Been a sergeant far too long. I gather Sally's had a miscarriage, poor kid. She's unlikely to be back before her notice runs out. There's a new lass coming up soon. Keep an eye on her, will you, Kate? Any hint of any rough stuff – I want to know. Whoever's involved. OK?'

She nodded. 'Of course.'

'Anything else I should know?'

Selby? She didn't want to snitch until she'd had one more go at him.

'There is, isn't there? Look, Kate, I'm running this show –'

'I know. But I've started to deal with the – the issue. I'd like to see it through if I can. But if I can't –'

'OK.' He dabbed his hand on the kettle. 'This is taking a long time to boil. Don't say it's packed up.'

She picked up the trailing cable. 'I think it helps if you put this end in a socket – Sir!'

★

Selby was going through files with a pencil when she returned; perhaps she'd been mistaken about his mouse activities earlier. She was glad she'd said nothing to Graham. She still couldn't work out the reason for his over-reaction, his fury. It seemed so personal. Perhaps Colin could enlighten her. Not yet, though – she'd got to get an envelope started for poor Sally. She'd ask Reg if he'd mind organising it – he was the sort of kindly uncle figure to screw the maximum out of reluctant fists. OK, he'd probably be quite maudlin in his approach – but a bit of sentimentality in the matter of lost babies wasn't inappropriate.

By eleven Giles still hadn't phoned.

'If he doesn't get his finger out, we'll turn up with a search warrant,' Graham said, half sitting on her desk. 'Can't have him sitting on vital evidence.'

'He's a friend,' Kate said.

'OK. Well, you go round and offer to help. Collect the lot, if he hasn't time to sort it out. We'll sort it here.'

She nodded. 'Now?'

'Try ten minutes ago.'

It made sense to go back home first, to collect her car, just in case she did have to take the whole caboodle into the city centre. Now she came to think of it, she'd no idea how much was involved – a single file or a whole cabinet-full.

She looked in despair at the cars parked solidly along her street: it would take her five minutes to get out of her space. Not that the car was in front of her house. She'd no idea who that privilege was reserved for. Damn, there was a scar on her front bumper she hadn't noticed before. She did a slow circuit – yes, now she came to look at it, there was a scar on each corner. None hers, she was sure of that. People parking by touch.

She might as well go and check on her post and answerphone now she was here. The door wasn't dead-locked – Alf must be working.

'You look as if you could do with a cup of tea!' he

greeted her. 'Quite washed out, you look. Here – have a biscuit.'

She took one. 'How's things?'

'Well, fine and dandy, once we get that surface. I been doing your security light. Just screwing down the floorboards now.'

'Find any diamonds?' She explained.

He looked awkward.

'Alf?'

'Did find summat,' he said. 'Not diamonds, though. Not – not very nice, really. I was going to put it on my next bonfire.'

'What sort of thing?'

'Don't like to show it to a lady. Not nice at all.'

'I'm not a lady, Alf. I'm a policewoman. We get to see lots of nasty things.'

He shook his head. 'Fair turned my stomach.' He burrowed in the back pocket of his overalls. 'If you're sure?'

'Sure.'

He slammed a photograph on his saw-horse. 'There. See what I mean?'

Chapter Twenty-Seven

Alf watched while she evicted a seed catalogue from its polythene envelope, and slipped the photograph in its place.

'You won't be throwing that book away?' he asked indignantly. 'Not with the state the garden's in!'

She shook her head. 'Fancy a coffee? I reckon I could use one.' She tapped the photograph as an excuse. Perhaps it wasn't an excuse.

They stared at the frozen images of the man and the boy. At last Alf turned it face down. 'That coffee,' he said.

He swilled mugs under the outside tap and poured from his flask.

'I guess the front room's the most civilised,' she said. It was the second time this morning she was having difficulty making her mouth work.

He raised an eyebrow, but followed.

'That Paul's done a decent job,' he said, running a critical thumb down the window frame. 'Mind you, he ought to have done, the amount of time he's taken. Must have used a brush with two bristles.'

'He's been here a lot, then?'

'Afternoons, mostly. Some dinner times. Thought he'd got a job to go to.'

Kate nodded. 'Works slowly, you said?'

'Glad he's not one of my lads. He'd take a month of Sundays to finish a job. Mind you, he says he'll be back to do your ceiling. Arse-ended way of doing things.'

'Right.' She couldn't think of anything she wanted to say aloud. Her head, on the other hand, was ringing with things she didn't want to hear.

'You all right? Fancy a biscuit?' He produced some from the bib of his overalls.

She sank on to a flat-pack 'Thanks.'

'Don't want to let that sort of thing get to you. Saw a lot worse in the Army. Mind you, that was pictures of men and *women*.'

She nodded.

'Makes you wonder what goes on in these people's minds.'

She nodded. What went on in the mind of someone who'd give up lunch-time and afternoons to paint a front window frame slowly; to sort out a front but not a back garden.

'What sort of time would he come to do his painting?' she asked.

'Funny. No one in their right mind'd come then. Parent-time. You know, this morning, it took me twenty minutes to get into your road, let alone park. Just as bad in the afternoon. The mothers start arriving before three: want to chafe the fat, I suppose. And he comes then. God knows where he parks. It's like the bloody dodgems. Someone smashed into my ute the other day. Well, did her more damage than me.'

'Mine's got a few scars.'

'Nice little motor like that? That's a shame. Look, the wife's brother knows a bit about cars – might be able to tidy it up a bit.'

'Would you ask him? It's nothing serious –'

'Don't want to let it rust. I'll have a word.'

'So you'll have to talk to Paul after all,' Maz said. 'Giles turned over the whole of the loft – got absolutely filthy. My goodness, it's time we threw some of it away – the ceiling'll be coming down if we're not careful. Then he remembered: Paul had this idea of writing a history of the Brayfield Baptists BB. Golly: what do they call that? Alliteration?'

Kate's smile was perfunctory. Or was it just that her face still wasn't working?

'Fancy some lunch?'

'No, thanks. I'd better be getting back. We've got this bug at work – half the squad's off sick.'

'Tell you what, I'll get on the phone to Paul – get him to drop it round to you. That'd save you some time.'

'No – honestly, it's all right. I can pop into his college and see him there.'

'If you can find him! Seriously, you mustn't interrupt his classes. It's almost as bad as interrupting a service! And he never answers his college phone – he says he's tied up with students all the time. I might as well have a direct line to his answerphone. I've got to talk to him about this weekend – he's coming over to look after the kids while Giles and I have a sinful break. I won this prize, did I tell you? In Manchester, of all places! I'll tell him then.'

'Does he need to? I shall still be here, after all.'

'No arguments. You look washed out enough as it is without looking for extra work.'

'I'm sorry, Gaffer. I've really let you down.'

'I don't see why you're making such a song and dance about it, Kate. So what if she phones him? All you've got is a busy-body knowing a bit more than we'd like him to know. I'd much rather he didn't go shoving his oar in. But I have been known to put the fear of God into people.' He smiled. She suspected this was his way of apologising.

She shook her head. 'There's much more, Graham. It was Paul who scrabbled round under the floorboards to fish out Cassie's diamonds lying flat. I thought I heard something fall then. In fact, he even checked his organiser to see if he'd lost anything. Alf found this under the same floorboards when he put in the wiring for my security light.' She laid the photograph on his desk. 'And before you say any one of Alf's lads could have left it there, you ought to know something else. Paul's turned his attention from my front garden to my front window. And the times he finds it most convenient to appear at my house are lunch break and the end of afternoon school.'

He nodded. 'Go on.'

She shook her head. 'I'd rather you worked it out. Maz is my friend.'

'We're not talking about Maz, here. We're talking about Paul. Come on, spit it out.'

'If we're looking for a paedophile, Graham – I think Paul might just fit our bill.'

He'd taken charge of her, making her coffee and feeding her sandwiches from the neat little lunch-box his wife had packed.

'We'll go and get something else in a few minutes. Not from the canteen. But you're like a ghost, Kate – I don't want you passing out all over me.'

'I don't know what's the matter with me these days.'

'Seen the shrink yet? It's all right. I've a full report on that item in your post. Cope had prioritised it. Not that any of us expect to get much from it. God knows we've got little enough so far.'

'Not even a box of files.'

'Not even a box of files. But I'll get Selby and Roper round there – a pleasant little reception committee. Unless you want to be involved?'

'I've started so I'll finish, like the man said. All he needs to know is that we're conducting a possibly routine enquiry into something that happened ten years ago. I'd like to take Colin along with me, if I may.' She ran through the scenario in her head. It didn't seem unmanageable. And then she remembered what Maz had been saying. She put her sandwich down, half got to her feet.

'Kate?' His hand on her arm, he gently pushed her back into the chair.

'It's now one-thirty on Friday,' she said. 'And Paul's looking after the three Manse children all weekend.'

Chapter Twenty-Eight

Graham looked at her hard. 'Are you afraid he'll try to interfere with any of them?'

Kate got to her feet, ringing her hands. 'No. Yes. I don't know. He loves them, there's no doubt of that. The classic favourite uncle.'

'Is that what they think?'

'They love him. But he does touch them, try to get close to them. And they don't like it. Maybe it's just because he doesn't fully realise they're too old for cuddles. Or maybe there's something a hell of a lot more sinister. The younger daughter has nightmares. She wakes screaming,' she added flatly.

He raised his eyebrows. 'I don't like the sound of that. You'll be there as usual, this weekend, won't you, Kate?'

'But I sleep at night!'

'And no doubt he'll go home at night.'

'And I can't be with them all the time!'

'Hey, calm down. Let's try to work this out. Is there a match this weekend?'

'Against Halesowen. I'll invite him and the kids. Whether they'll want to come —'

'Miss seeing your first home win? Of course they'll be there.'

'But what about the rest of the time?'

'Safety in numbers, I'd have thought. So what we have to worry about is if he splits them up.'

'Which can only be at night, surely?'

'Possibly. I don't like this. Leave me to think it through. I think my brain got addled when I knocked my head. You and Colin go and get the files. When you get back we'll scan them fast as we can. We've got to get the Family Protection people talking to the boys in the Brigade – find the source of this –' he flipped the photograph with his index finger – 'assuming, of course, that they have the same source. Which I think, for the moment, we must. I take it the current files are available?'

'Giles'll have those. You've got his number?'

He nodded.

'And there's Royston, my next-door-neighbour's son. He left the BB for some reason his mother couldn't – or wouldn't – tell me. In fact, whatever it was, the whole family stopped going to the Baptist church. Might be worth someone talking to him, too.'

'Right.' He made a note. 'Off you go then. I don't need to tell you to be careful.' He smiled, but dropped his head and was already writing when she closed the door of his office.

Colin hauled on the hand-brake and stared at the college carpark barrier: 'How do we get in here then? Told you we should have come in something more official than this.' He patted the steering-wheel of the unmarked Rover. 'We could have dumped it on double-yellow lines.'

'Don't worry. Here's someone now. Except he could be a job's-worth.'

The ID worked, however, and they were soon nosing into a slot. There were quite a lot of free spaces.

'Looks like your educated élite don't work Friday afternoons,' Colin said.

'Ah – this is the management section. Looks as if the plebs are still toiling away. Let's hope Paul's one of them.'

They locked up, walking briskly towards the entrance. Students singly and in groups drifted around. Many of the girls were swathed from head to toe in black. Kate thought of her rape victim. The men were nothing like so self-effacing, jostling and shoving.

A middle-aged receptionist ruled the foyer. She smiled, checked their IDs, asked them to sit and offered them coffee. They shook their heads, and sat, staring at their hands.

'You're not happy about this, are you? Best let me do the talking, maybe,' Colin said.

'Might look a bit unnatural. After all, I know him quite well. Ah!'

The receptionist was returning. They got to their feet, smiling.

'Bad news, I'm afraid. Mr Taylor left for a dental appointment ten minutes ago. He's unlikely to be back.'

'We'd like his address, then, please,' Colin said. 'This is a very urgent matter – a matter of life and death,' he added, persuasively.

The receptionist bridled. 'I'm not at liberty to disclose such information. I'll have to refer you to Personnel.'

Who were at lunch.

'Come on, Kate – you must have some idea where he lives! You've been out with the man!' Colin flared his fingers in frustration.

'Isn't it odd? The question of going to his place never arose. No problem, anyway. I'll phone Maz. I'll have to grovel and say I should have taken her advice in the first place.'

'So much the better – people usually like to be in the right.'

'Why, I was talking to him only half an hour ago. Yes, I said you were going to pop into college to see him. I didn't say what for, though, since you'd told me this was confidential.'

'Thanks. I'll have to catch him when he comes back from the dentist.'

There was the tiniest pause. It sounded as if the dentist had been a hastily invented excuse.

'Oh, right. Of course. Anyway, you'll be able to make him a cup of tea when he gets back, won't you? Here's the address.'

★

They parked behind a crop of black plastic sacks awaiting the maw of the dustcart. They'd overtaken it a few hundred yards back: the sacks wouldn't have to wait long.

'He's done remarkably well for himself,' Colin observed, looking at the cottage behind the high wall. 'This is practically the country. These teachers must get a good screw if he can afford to live here.'

'I think that could be better rephrased,' Kate said, smiling sourly. 'But they're not all that well-paid. We were talking about it once. So how come he lives in a posh little place like this?'

'Lottery win?'

She shrugged. 'Colin – if he's been on all these camps with the BB, he could have used his video camera and sold the results. He tried to film the kids the first time we trained. It was a nice evening and they were all stripped down to shorts.'

'And you thought he wanted to do it for his holiday records. Kate, you were a bit slow, weren't you?'

She nodded. 'Or maybe a bit fast now in jumping to conclusions. I don't know. Let's go and see if he's recovered from his dental treatment. He's back, all right. That's his car.'

The engine was still warm – just.

They exchanged glances.

'Colin – I'm going to do the talking, on my own. And you're going to check those sacks aren't full of files. Sorry.'

'OK. Unless you'd prefer to do it the other way round, seeing as you know him.'

She looked at the cottage, bland in its rather dull garden. There was a depressed air about it – flowers that should have been dead-headed, the grass over-long. To be fair, he'd been too busy painting her window to do much for himself.

'When it comes down to it, who knows anyone?' she asked. 'OK. She flipped an invisible coin. 'Look, it's heads. I'll do Paul.'

She set off up the path.

Paul answered her ring promptly. If he was surprised to see her he didn't show it. She hoped Maz hadn't phoned to warn him that he should officially have been at the dentist's.

She hadn't wanted Maz involved at all – Paul had obviously been a cherished, perhaps spoiled, baby far too long.

'Kate?'

'Paul. Obviously I'm not here just to thank you for all your painting. It's work, too. Shall we – ?' She gestured.

He stepped back, but with some reluctance. Just puzzlement, perhaps. 'Work?' He stopped just inside the front door. There was no hall – they were in his living room.

'*My* work. There's some rumour about Brayfield BB – things going wrong ten to fifteen years ago. Nothing serious, so far as I know. But we need to have the files to check who was in charge then. Giles says you've probably got them.'

'My God! Have I still got them? Oh, I was young and crazy once, Kate – had this idea of writing a history of the chapel. And then I realised that history's more than listing facts in chronological order – that's if you want anyone to read it! I suppose I must still have the files somewhere.' He looked around the room doubtfully.

So did Kate. However good he was with a shovel or a paintbrush, Paul was hardly house proud. There were newspapers in a couple of piles at least two feet high – months of dust-harbouring paper. They'd have toppled if anyone had added so much as another freebie. There were other piles, too – books, notes, letters. The bookshelves were crammed, with books stacked in all directions.

'I suppose they might be in my study. Follow me.' He led the way upstairs which opened off the corner of the room. 'What sort of problem are we talking about? Someone been diddling the finances?' he asked derisively.

She'd been waiting for the question – was rather surprised it had come so late. 'That sort of thing,' she said, off-hand. 'Probably nothing at all. But once my boss gets hold of something he's not going to let it go without checking first.' She stopped, trying not to gasp with horror. Paul had opened his study door to reveal the sort of chaos that she was living with – cardboard boxes in hazardous stacks. There was a space on the desk for his computer, a neat-looking lap-top complete with modem, but he'd have to shift what looked like stacks of teaching notes if he wanted to use the printer.

'I always meant to sort this out,' he said cheerfully. 'Looks as if I'm going to have to – if you really want that stuff? Right! Now, where might it be?' He stood in the middle of it all, shaking his head.

Kate peered at the side of some of the nearest boxes: oranges from Morocco, South African grapes, Geest bananas. No more recent, more apposite labels. Each was full of envelope files, only the spines of which were visible. He hadn't written the contents on them. Many had split and were bulging. Not many clues there, either.

'I've always meant to develop a system,' he said. 'Maz was going to come and help me. She's never got round to it – too busy. And now – well, where would you start?'

What she really would have done was get a skip and throw the whole lot into it, on the principle that if he hadn't looked at it since he moved, it could scarcely be vital to his wellbeing.

'There's more in the loft, too. Now, it might be in there, come to think of it.' He backed out of the room. She followed. 'The loft door's in my bedroom – I hope you won't be embarrassed. Hang on while I shove some of this stuff in the linen basket. Heavens, it's time I put a load through the washer.'

It was. The room was thick with the smell of male. And male socks.

'Why don't you go and do it now? I can have a quick look at the boxes in your study. Well, one box!' She stood in the doorway watching him gather up pants and T-shirts, standing aside as he headed with a stinking armful for the stairs. Would he be offended if she opened a window?

Preferring the mustiness of the study, she started on the nearest box. Shakespeare's sonnets; Marlowe's *Edward II*. Not promising. His university notes, perhaps. She'd started on the next when she heard him come back upstairs. Monet's gardens; Pre-Raphaelite sexuality. She'd never known they had any, all those glum, goitred creatures.

'Will you hold the steps?' he called. 'Only they're a bit wobbly,' he added as she went back into the bedroom. He was already half-way up, pushing at the small hatch in the ceiling. 'It's a bit of a tight fit, this.'

It was. But he heaved and kicked his way upwards, finally disappearing. His face quickly reappeared. 'Could you pass me that torch?' He pointed to what was intended as a dressing table but was hidden under a detritus of coffee mugs and dust. Standing on the steps, she reached up.

Had she made a ghastly mistake? He was so innocent, so helpful, she was sure she must have done. And there was poor Colin fossicking in all those bags. Talk about egg on your face. His and hers, both – if in different ways.

'There's some more up here,' Paul called. 'D'you want to have a flick through while I hold the torch?'

She popped her head through the hatch. 'Have you got boards down or is it just joists?' Like the floor of her back bedroom, the one through which the wires ran to her security light . . . No, she didn't want to be in that loft with him, come to think of it.

'A few boards. Mostly joists.'

'And you'd trust me not to put my foot through your ceiling? *I* wouldn't!' she laughed. 'Why don't you pass them down here, and we can check them in more comfort?'

'They're pretty heavy, mind. Take care – you don't want to rick your back. Got it?'

They managed to bring down five altogether. None was labelled, and all were filthy. He came down, feet flailing for a safe hold. She grabbed his right ankle and steered him to a tread.

'My goodness,' he said staring at the mess.

She supposed it was touching, his refusal to swear. In his place she'd have unleashed a string of expletives.

'It's going to take a bit of time to check that lot,' he said. 'And I'm supposed to be looking after the kids this weekend. I suppose I could bring them here . . .'

Not on his life. She kept her face impassive. 'I shall still be at the Manse this weekend,' she said.

'How urgent is it? To find whatever it is you want?'

She shrugged. 'I'm not sure: the Gaffer didn't say. Tell you what,' she said, more brightly than she felt, 'if it is desperate, why don't I get one of my colleagues to come and sort through it? Or they could take it all away if you'd prefer? You never know, it might even come back indexed and labelled.'

'What if they don't find anything? Do you think they'll charge me with wasting police time?' he laughed.

She grinned back. 'For someone, it gives a whole new meaning to the term dirty weekend, doesn't it?'

Chapter Twenty-Nine

Colin, sprawled in the passenger seat of the Rover, was reading the *Guardian*. He folded it quickly round something as Kate staggered up with the first of the cardboard boxes. The folders in this one were stacked on end, making it even more awkward to carry. Paul followed more slowly, but since he was demonstrating his masculinity by carrying two at once, Kate could hardly blame him, nor when he had to put on a final spurt to reach the car without dropping them.

'Look what Paul's found for us,' Kate said brightly. 'And there's another thirteen or fourteen to go. Better fold down the back seat.'

All three of them were exhausted and filthy by the time they had packed them away.

Kate wrote an official receipt. 'I nearly forgot,' she said. 'How did you get on at the dentist?'

Paul grinned cheerfully and laid a finger on his lips. 'There was this dreadful planning meeting at work. I just decided I couldn't face it. I'm busy job hunting at the moment. Don't tell Maz – she'd hate it if she knew I might have to leave Brum. Look, I'm going in to have a shower.' But he didn't move.

'See you at the Manse. I just need a couple of days to get my house clean,' she said to Colin. 'One of my neighbours may come up with a team if I come up with the money. You may know her son, Paul. Royston Mackenzie. He used to be in our BB.'

He shook his head.

'Black kid,' she prompted. 'Good looking apart from his scowl. Anyway, he and his family have gone C of E now. Don't know which church. Very happy there, I gather.'

Paul shook his head. 'No. Not if he didn't stay long. Or I may have been off at University. I'm sorry his family left Brayfield Road, though. Will you be at the playing fields tomorrow? With the team?'

'Try and stop me. And I'll expect a full turn-out from the Manse, since you'll be in charge. Even Lynn. She whinges for Europe, Colin. Hormones, I reckon. Will you be coming?'

Colin gestured at the laden car. 'I reckon Graham's going to volunteer me into looking through this lot. Bit of a job, isn't it, Paul, taking on kids like that for a whole weekend? How on earth d'you keep them quiet? I may have some chloroform somewhere!'

Paul stared. At last, he smiled stiffly: 'I may take you up on that. OK, Kate. See you later, then.'

'See you!' Kate flipped the keys to Colin, opening the passenger door. 'I'll help out with the kids, if you like. I'm getting quite an expert on steam engines.'

This time Paul didn't attempt to smile. He hardly did more than flap a hand as Colin drove away.

'I'd say he didn't think much of our jokes,' Colin said. 'Not that they were all that funny. Hardly more than quips, I suppose.'

'Hmm.'

'You all right, our kid? You were a long time in there – I was about to come and join in the party.'

'No party to join.'

'Are you telling me you were happy being closeted with him?'

She shook her head. 'Not unhappy. Except when I thought he wanted me to go up into the loft. I could have panicked.'

'You could have kicked your way through the ceiling quickly enough.'

'Quite. Just – unreasoning panic. Anyway, we've got what we came for. God knows how long it'll take root through that lot, though.'

He glanced over his shoulder at the boxes. 'All weekend, at least. Two people. The bugger of it is, we'll have to list everything. Document it. Seems a bit of a pisser to be doing it for him, idle bugger.'

'I'm not sure he's idle. Just too busy doing other things. And then the whole job's so overwhelming you don't know where to start. I wouldn't myself.'

'What a good job you won't have to, then.'

'What's the betting I won't be? OK, Graham'll let me off tomorrow just so I can keep an eye on the kids. And Sunday – well, he knows I'm tied up in the mornings. But if he can work out some form of surveillance, he might well rope me in.'

'He might. But then, he might not. Not unless he's exceptionally nosy. Or perhaps I mean, exceptionally sadistic.' His pause was meaningful. No doubt about it. 'After all,' he continued eventually, 'there's no need to sort out anything. The files you're after are under my paper. There you are. By your right foot. At least I presume it's them. Funny that he'd popped them in a black sack and left them for the bin men. Everything anyone could want to know about the BB ten years ago. Boys. Officers. Who went to camp. Everything.'

'Once upon a time I knew this bloke in the South African police,' Graham said. 'These two suspects had just moved house, and the police had been ordered to search for incriminating papers. Could be anywhere. Even in a teapot. And the suspects weren't allowed to touch anything, of course. So they sat back and watched while the police unpacked every last bit of their stuff. Clothes, china, books, records.'

'And did they put them away?' Kate asked.

Graham laughed. 'It was towards the end of the regime, and my mate had a fairly strong sense of which way the wind was blowing. So he made his colleagues dust everything and stack the shelves neatly and hang up the clothes properly. Didn't find anything, of course. Future cabinet ministers don't leave incriminating material for country cops to find.' He smiled, pouring boiling water into three mugs. 'Anyway, I'm very pleased with you both. It was quick thinking on both your parts.'

'Kate's, Graham – no, no more milk, thanks.'

'Colin had the easy part,' Kate said, her voice ironic. 'Sorting through dirty nappies and second-hand condoms –'

'I can assure you there were no nappies in Paul's sack. Newspapers and cans – hasn't the man ever heard of recycling?'

'What sort of cans?' Kate asked quickly.

'No, no kids' stuff. Imported lager.'

Graham passed Kate her chocolate. 'Quite unimpeachable. Like these files'll be. You realise we'll still have to go through them. But not until we've checked through what you retrieved, Colin. Come on: let's get moving.'

If the official leaving-time had come and gone, no one was getting vocal about it. They were in the Incident Room, all filthy together. But the group working on the documents Colin had retrieved were the most intent.

'Right,' Graham said, 'Now we know who the BB officers were, I want to get weaving on checking them all: convictions before or since, where they are now – everything. Reg: that's for you. Selby – are you with us, Selby? Or are you lost in virtual reality? – you'll do the same with the older boys – there's the list. See if there are boys who graduated into being officers here or anywhere else. No – I don't expect you to do it yourselves – get local CIDs to help. Now, here's what I want the rest of you to do . . .' He worked his way systematically through what was left of the squad. Then he caught Colin's eye. And Kate's.

He let them into his room, then closed the door.

'Kate: I'm going to bend a rule or two this weekend. I want you to make sure the Manse is empty this evening. I've asked for and got permission to use surveillance equipment to protect the children –'

'What do Maz and Giles say?'

'Nothing. Because I shan't decide it's necessary until they're safely on their way to wherever it is. OK? I can't have Maz messing this up. Either she wouldn't believe a word and she'd fly off the handle, or she would believe it all and she'd refuse to go.'

'And in either scenario she might tell Paul,' Colin added. 'I can see you're not happy, Kate, but he's right. Even if he goes home, he can always let himself back in again. You can't guard the kids all the time. Even if you sat outside Tim's room all night the chances are you'd fall asleep.'

'And it's not just prevention we're after, I suppose. It's discreet prevention. And apprehension if he should try anything.'

Graham nodded. 'Believe me, he won't even scratch his backside without us knowing. I'll talk to Kings Heath about rostering. Now, you two have done well. Time you were – Hang on.' He picked up the phone.

It was all too obvious that the call wasn't about work. He turned from them; simultaneously they started to talk quietly about how Kate could occupy all three children that evening.

'And if you don't go now,' Colin said, opening the door, 'there won't be an evening.'

He was right, of course. But she didn't want to go without Graham's agreement – he might have some last minute instructions. She hovered. At last, still listening to the phone, he turned to them both, gave them a thumbs-up and waved them away.

During the whole of the journey home – not as long as usual, because the rush-hour was over – Kate was clenching her fists against the fear that she would find the Manse completely empty and she would have to raise the alarm. The scenarios became more convoluted with each red traffic light. But she wasn't alone. She had to keep reminding herself she wasn't alone. She was backed by a large – if invisible – team. Kings Heath carrying out surveillance. The boffins ready to plant all sorts of extraordinary electronic equipment. Her colleagues from central Birmingham – yes, she felt safer now Graham was back in charge. So stop gripping the wheel as if you were on a white-knuckle ride!

When she got to the Manse Maz and Giles were just getting into their car. Feeling a heel, she parked and ran over: 'Not a very long weekend,' she said.

'Meeting overran,' Maz said. 'You know how they do. Anyway, we're off!' She cupped her ear. 'I can hear that jacuzzi calling from here. Drive on, Macduff!'

The cluster on the steps did not include Lynn.

'She's off at a friend's,' Tim said airily. 'Sleeping over.'

'You mean she won't be back to watch the game tomorrow? But I was relying on you all! You'll be there, Paul? And Jenny? Tim?'

'I was thinking of taking them out for the day,' Paul said, scooping them back into the house.

'Hell! Tell you what, you couldn't postpone it till Sunday? We really are hoping for a decent result. Young Marcus is coming on by leaps and bounds. You can't all let us down!'

'Does it really make a difference?' Tim asked. 'Do you think it's time we switched the central heating on? Dad said we could.'

'It really does make a difference. Like putting the heating on!'

'I want to go,' said Jenny. 'And I'll bring Wol too. He's wise. He'll help.'

'You're too big for toys,' Tim said over his shoulder. 'I'm going to switch on the heating.'

'D'you think there's any point? I was going to take you all out for burgers,' Kate said.

'BSE and rainforests,' Tim said, stopping short. 'But there's a lovely pizza place in Harborne. We'd have to book.'

'I was going to cook one of my specials,' Paul said. 'Steak –'

'Won't that have BSE?' Kate asked, conscious of her lack of logic.

'I go to this organic butcher.'

'Pizza! Pizza! Don't want to go mad!' Tim yelled, putting hands to his head for horns and charging around. Jenny joined in.

'So we have steak tomorrow. With chips and onions,' Kate said.

'And I'll make some of my own ice cream.'

'I suppose you two will want wine,' Tim said.

'What do you and Jenny have if we do?'

'We have wine too! Wine too!' Jenny declared. 'With fizz.'

'Soda water,' Tim explained.

'Wine and water it shall be,' Kate said.

'Sounds like a wedding in Cana,' Paul agreed.

Kate had persuaded the children into bed by promising a small but valuable prize to whichever was undressed, washed and in bed first. Without assistance from either grown-up, she had added, as if it were an afterthought, not something she'd been taxing her brain over for the best part of the evening. She and Paul had declared a dead heat – two small but valuable prizes coming up! – and together kissed the children goodnight. There was no sign anywhere that Kate's colleagues might have been busy. But she would bet her teeth they had.

Paul had poured a couple of glasses of wine and retired to the living room when she came down from the bathroom. He was squatting by the CD player, going through the small collection beside it.

'English string music OK for you?' He flourished a double album. 'There's not much choice. They only had the player last Christmas. We all chipped in – all the family, that is. Maz loves music, but she hardly gets a chance to hear any – what with the kids and the cost. I mean, some of the Symphony Hall prices are absurd.'

Kate nodded. She wasn't sure of his mood. She hoped it wasn't romantic. She prowled round looking at books till he sat down. Then she came to rest facing him. She gestured with the wine glass: 'Cheers!'

He responded, almost absently, then slumped back in his chair. 'You were really good with those kids,' he said.

'It was a lovely evening all round,' she said. 'They obviously think the world of you, Paul.'

'I love them more than I can say. They are all the world to me. I wish they were mine.' He drank slowly. 'I just haven't met the right woman, I suppose. One I could care for and who could return my feelings. It's always been unrequited love, one way or the other. I mean – you know how attractive I find you, but you're still grieving for – for –'

'For Robin,' she agreed quietly. She nodded as if she understood what he was saying. It sounded so right, so honest and truthful. If it hadn't been for the business of the folders, she might have believed him. Perhaps she still should. She drank too.

'I'd die for them, you know. Literally die. And yet they're growing up and they won't want me any more.'

'They will. In a different way. But just as much. It must be hard, growing up in a Manse – all these people popping in and out. Your parents public property. God's property, come to think of it. All the congregation expecting you to be somehow "gooder" than your friends and contemporaries. Imagine being caught puffing your first spliff!'

' "Spliff"?' He sat upright. 'Surely you never smoked cannabis, Kate?'

'At Uni I did – didn't you?'

'Never!'

No, he was too busy being good, no doubt. And maybe buggering little boys. 'See what I mean? A bit of honest, decent law-breaking in your teens can have a lot to commend it. And it might become an absolute necessity if your dad's a clergyman. Which is where you'd come in. The non-judgmental shoulder to cry on when it all goes pear-shaped.'

'I could never encourage them to do anything like that.'

'Not encourage. Just understand.'

He frowned into his drink.

So how could a man with such morals do what she thought he was doing? She too frowned into her wine. The music played on.

Chapter Thirty

'Please, Uncle Paul, please, *please*, PLEASE!' Jenny held on to his hand, swinging it from side to side. 'Please say yes! A sleep-over!'

Jenny had met her best friend, her very best friend, at the playing fields, where, on a fine mild morning, Brayfield Road were trailing three-one.

'I'm cooking your very favourite dinner tonight,' Paul objected. 'Why don't you stay till six o'clock and then come home? Yes, Marcus! Yes!'

The joys of surrogate parenthood, Kate thought with dour amusement. Robin's kids had been just the same. Robin had always been hurt that they didn't want to spend whole weekends with him and Kate; Kate had always tried to remind him that kids had social lives too. They'd had rows about it. 'Yes, Marcus! Shoot!'

Three-two! That was better.

'None of your friends here today,' Paul observed.

'They'll still be up to their elbows in your files,' she said, carefree as if he hadn't tried to get rid of the important ones. She could see them toiling away, and felt momentarily guilty. But her job was just as important as theirs – more! – and a good deal more delicate. And now a good deal more difficult. With the family splitting up, it would be really tricky if Paul had the nous to play on Tim's vanity and suggest they go off and do manly things together.

No. However evil he might be, Paul would never harm

Tim. Not his own flesh and blood. Not someone he loved as much as he loved Tim. Unbidden – and she found herself shuddering – came the memory of Cope crying the night Darren had been killed.

She hadn't mentioned her fears – scarcely even suspicions – to anyone. Not even Graham. There was the business of the incomplete file to explore. *Could* Cope be bent? Could he?

There was a flurry in Halesowen's goal-mouth. She'd no idea what had led up to it. But Marcus was in there somewhere! And on the ground!

'Foul!' A pity Cope wasn't here with his stentorian yells. But the ref had got the message, and blew for a penalty. And Marcus, dusting himself down, was preparing to take it. It didn't make sense. He'd be shaken. It would be better for someone else to take it. She didn't know which would be worse, absolute silence or the chorus of 'Come on, Marcus!' from the touchline.

Cool as a pro, Marcus re-adjusted the ball to his liking, ran, and kicked. And as accurately!

Yes!

It was too much to hope for another. There were only five more minutes to go, and Brayfield always flagged with fatigue at the end. But it was as if someone had switched them on to overdrive – they brought the ball back effortlessly into the opposition's penalty area, and won a corner. They'd been through this scenario with her at practice. Marcus was to stay in the middle, Martin to take the kick. So what the hell were they playing at now? What was tubby little Leo up to?

Kicking like an angel, that's what!

But it was too high, too high! She'd give him clever stuff when she saw him. But there was Marcus, jumping like a young gazelle, and heading it home, sweet as if they'd rehearsed it a hundred times.

Three minutes, and still Brayfield were swarming round the opposition goal. You couldn't pray for something like another goal, could you? Could you? If she couldn't, Kate could still will them through. Another. Another. Please. She was running to get closer. And then she realised they all were, all the parents and brothers and hangers-on. All that will-power concentrated on those young feet.

It worked. Young Marcus again, with a touch like silk.

She was hugging Tim and Jenny and even Paul. Certainly young Marcus the minute he came off the field. And suddenly she found she was hugging Graham. Graham!

'Just popped round for the last couple of minutes. And what do I get? Two smashing goals. Well done, lad.' He'd pulled away from her and was patting Marcus on the back.

They all surged back to the pitiful apology for a pavilion, Graham and Kate in the midst of the yelling, sweaty kids. Paul too.

'Tell me,' he called across the bobbing heads, 'have you found what you were looking for, Graham?'

'Needle in a haystack time,' Graham smiled affably. 'But we usually find what we're looking for. Sooner or later.' His smile and voice were sociable but surely no one could have missed the implicit threat. 'Are you and Kate going to celebrate?'

'With Tim,' Kate said quickly. 'Jenny here's going to her best friend. But you will be back for six, won't you, love?' She smiled across her head to the best friend's mother. 'Paul and I are cooking a special dinner.'

'We're going to have fizzy wine,' Jenny added.

'And what are you all doing this afternoon?'

Kate almost saw the idea coming into her head. 'Let's go on a train!' she said. 'On a real steam train. How about that, Tim? My treat. Though I shan't have time to make my special ice cream.'

'We can get some from Sainsbury's,' he said, irrefutably.

She was aware of Graham listening in silence to all that was being said. She'd have his approval, she was sure of that. What she wanted was two minutes' conversation with him. That was all. Two.

'I'll go in there and keep some sort of order,' Paul announced, heading into the pavilion.

Over Tim's head, Graham looked at her, his face exuding angry amusement. She pulled a similar face back. 'Everything's set up,' he said. 'Took a lot of talking: money, cost centres, ethics – I've been through the lot with the management.

Gordon took an enormous amount of persuading. You don't half owe me, Kate!'

'Yes, Gaffer!' She returned his smile. 'How's the rest of the business?'

'Kings Heath surveillance has thrown up a very nasty development – hell!'

Paul was coming out.

'Forgot his camera,' Graham muttered.

'The conditions in there are shocking,' Paul announced. 'I've told the lads not to bother with showers – just get themselves home as quickly as they can.' He looked across to the fleet of cars waiting. 'Looks as if most of them will be chauffeured.'

'What innocent pleasures these bloody perverts have destroyed!' Marcus's father agreed loudly, joining the group. 'No one walks any –'

'Hi, Mr Fulton – wow, your son!' Kate interrupted.

'Doug.' He shook hands with her. 'Yes, bit of all right, that, wasn't it? Thanks to your coaching. Funny thing is, he isn't getting so much asthma these days. Anyway, as I was saying, in my day walking to school was the norm. My parents used to walk everywhere – a ten-mile round trip was nothing. Well, you only have to read Hardy or Lawrence to see how times have changed.'

'My road wasn't built for all the parents' cars,' Kate agreed. 'Parking's a nightmare, isn't it, Paul?'

'Specially at going-home time,' he agreed. 'Or first thing in the morning, I'd guess. My special hate is the parents who just stop in the middle of the road and open their car door for the kids to jump out. Don't they realise that there's more real danger from cars than from any of these so-called perverts? Cars kill!'

'So do perverts,' Fulton pointed out. 'And if they don't, the damage can be immense, physically and mentally. God knows, I'm not the best of parents to young Marcus, but I can't imagine – Jesus!' He broke off, shuddering. 'And they're all over the place,' he continued. 'Aren't I right, Kate? In the police force, in social services, in the judiciary – everywhere. Look at that business in Belgium! I hope you lot are better at hunting down the monsters than they were.'

Graham said, 'We always do our best. But you're right: you may even find some in – what line are you in, Mr Fulton?'

'Business consultancy.'

Not bad for an erstwhile English teacher, sacked because of his relationship with a pupil. And was he protesting too much – a man, after all, with a taste for younger women? Come off it, Kate. A taste for one young woman, to the best of your knowledge.

'How are you going to celebrate Marcus's triumph?' Kate asked.

'With the last thing he wants, I'm afraid. A baby brother or sister. Melanie was just starting to twinge when I left.'

'Why doesn't he come with us to the Severn Valley Railway?' Paul said. 'We could pick him up – only a few yards out of our way. And he could stay over at the Manse with Tim.'

How reasonable it all sounded. Kate caught Graham's eye.

'What a splendid idea,' he said, with a smile that confirmed the presence of some very expensive equipment at the Manse.

They had the perfect afternoon for their trip – yes, they'd go the whole length of the line. They started from Kidderminster, two, or in this context three, small boys and Kate. Marcus had not been keen on consorting with someone as young as Tim, but, on the basis that it was that or the rest of the day at his grandmother's, had conceded it might just be all right. In the event, he was lapping it up. The train was already in the station, a huge Great Western loco pulling it. Hagley Hall. The driving wheels must have been nearly six feet in diameter, the tapered boiler equally massive. Kate felt disorientated – the pretty prettiness of the stations, with hanging baskets still glowing with late season colour, seemed at odds with the noise, no, the sheer size and power of the locomotive. But that was elegant too, in its own way. At last she sat back and prepared to enjoy herself. She began to: the engine's silly shrill Toy-Town whistle for a start. 'Not the sort of whistle Gordon would approve of,' she said to Tim.

He grinned, but rather self-consciously. One didn't mention children's books in front of older boys like Marcus, of course.

Then there was another noise. Deep, regular.

'What on earth's that?' she asked. 'That woofing?'

'They call it barking,' Paul explained. 'It's typical of the Great Western engines. It's caused when the cylinders exhaust the steam.'

He must be using some technical term; but she couldn't suppress a quick vision of thin, emaciated trickles of steam staggering around. This would clearly be woman's talk, however, not the sort of thing to introduce into this male company.

There was a model railway at one of the stations, operated by coins. The boys couldn't resist it. Neither could she. And then she remembered other uses of small locos.

Tucked away in one of the engine sheds was a pannier tank.

'Look,' Tim yelled. 'Duck!'

Paul took photographs at each station, and the boys, armed with pocket-money from Doug Fulton – a very successful business consultant to judge by the way he bank-rolled his son – and Giles and Maz, had bought wagons for their model railways.

'A friend of mine has a huge layout,' Paul said. 'It runs on several different levels, with tunnels and bridges and whatnot. He's landscaped it all, too. It's really quite realistic. And he's got some good stock, too.'

He left the information dangling in the air.

Kate knew it for a bait as soon as she heard it. She wanted to hit herself: she should have foreseen it. If the boys responded, she'd better feign an interest she didn't feel – her own motive for playing trains was to play with Tim, after all.

They bit: 'Uncle Paul, you don't suppose he'd let us see it, do you? To get a few ideas?'

'Has he gone in for farms and things?' Kate asked.

'It's the locos we're interested in,' said Marcus, loftily.

'I'll have a word with him when I see him. Which isn't all that often. But it's not for playing with, like you knock your stock around, Tim. It's serious.'

A train set not meant for playing with. That defeated Kate. But her mind was working nineteen to the dozen. Yes: she'd bet her pension that the man with the train set used an ultra-quiet house in Leavensbrook Close. What else would make a tiny whirring noise that stopped suddenly when someone rang the bell? And what would the noise suddenly cut off be, but a boy protesting when his game was ended?

It was too late to think about cooking. They'd phoned Jenny's friend's mother from Kidderminster – yes, Jenny would be delighted to stay over. So they went straight to a balti restaurant. The genial waiter, who might have been the brother of the jolly man who served Kate with monster chicken tikka naans, gently steered the boys away from the hottest options, and then encouraged them to try kulfi for their sweet. The only thing that Kate lacked was a drink. The restaurant was unlicensed, and Paul was so reluctant to dive into Safeway for a pack of lager Kate felt she couldn't press the case. In any case, wasn't she supposed to be above the need for alcohol now? And the restaurant had good bottled water: she should be grateful for that. What she wanted, and wasn't going to get, was a chance to phone Graham. It occurred to her at last that Paul might be sticking to her at least as hard as she was sticking to him.

They knew the boys would natter before they went to sleep, but Kate and Paul insisted that lights would be out at ten, and that absolute silence was required by ten-thirty. Kate had a suspicion that their parents might have preferred the cut-off point to be at least half an hour earlier. And in fact, when they went up to switch the lights out, they found both boys fast asleep. Paul leaned over them with enormous tenderness, kissing Tim so lightly he didn't wake.

Paedophilia, Kate recalled sadly, originally meant the love of children.

She wanted to phone Graham about that train set idea. She made an excuse to go to her bedroom, but even as she dialled one ear was alert for sounds in the corridor outside. Remembering the routine, she tapped one four one before his number, and prepared to end the call quickly. But it was he who answered.

'Glad you called,' he said. 'How was the railway?'

'It's given me an idea.' She explained briefly.

'My God. You could just be right, couldn't you? Funny, a couple of interesting things have been thrown up by our surveillance. Fill you in tomorrow.' His voice dropped and he spoke very rapidly. Mrs Harvey was no doubt getting out of the bath sooner than he'd expected. Or whatever. 'Now, your neighbour, Mrs Mackintosh wants to talk to you – something she wouldn't talk about to anyone else. Can I give her your number? It's something that came up when they were trying to find if Royston had been abused.'

'Had he?'

'I'd reckon. We'll talk about it tomorrow. But Mrs M has something else on her mind. And she wants to talk to you.'

'It'll have to be by phone, won't it? And, it'd be better face to face, if it's what I think it's about.'

'Which is?'

'Do you remember I interrupted a rape?'

'Pretty well your first day here. And were stabbed, as I recall.'

'Hardly enough damage to call it a stab. Mrs Mackenzie – Zenia – dressed it for me. And the latest rape victim had a similar tiny stab. I've got a terrible feeling it might have been made by the same weapon.'

'Stanley knife? Something like that?'

'Yes. The sort of thing any household would have. Christ,

Graham, it's bad enough for me putting pressure on Maz – I literally wouldn't have survived without her, you know.' She would risk it. 'I was getting a drink problem. If she hadn't have taken me I'd – but she did. But Zenia – God knows what it's like to worry about shopping your own son. Only son.'

'Do you want to take the call?'

'I can't let another woman down. Oh, Graham, have you any idea how long it is since I went to see Aunt Cassie?'

'Tell you what, I'll pop in myself for five minutes tomorrow morning. On my way into work. I'll tell her it's all my fault you've been working so hard. Cope's back in the land of the living so he can take charge for a bit.' And the phone went dead.

All they'd been talking about was a couple of serious crimes! Couldn't the woman understand that police officers' work didn't end at five o'clock, and that some officers just happened to be women? She sat on the bed staring at the silent phone.

She snatched it so quickly it hardly rang.

'Kate Power.'

'Kate – it's Zenia. Can't I see you? I got such problems, man.'

'I'm actually on a job now, Zenia. But Graham said you needed to talk to me. I know the phone's not very –'

'Better than nothing. It's advice I'm wanting.' Her accent was much stronger over the phone. 'That social worker – she was very good, very good indeed. I never thought anyone'd get through to my Royston. Well, you've seen him. Anyway, he's promised to see her again, talk to her if he remembers any more. I think he remembers, all right. Just not ready to say it yet. But I come on him in the kitchen, in his dad's tool kit. And he's got this knife. And I'm afraid he's going to do himself harm. When he sees me, he puts it away again – some excuse about wanting to sharpen some pencils for school.'

'Excuse?'

'It's his face. It's not the truth, Kate.' Zenia's voice shook. 'Anyway, he went out. This'd be seven-seven-thirty. And I wondered where my boy might be going where he'd need a knife. And I remembered that cut, Kate.' She was sobbing, now. 'And I remembered that black girl that was raped – the papers say she was stabbed. And that knife! It's stained, Kate! What shall I do?'

What indeed?

'Is he at home now?'

'On a Saturday night? You got to be joking. I've hidden the knife, Kate. Locked it away.'

'Let's not jump to conclusions, Zenia. Why don't you just wait till tomorrow, and talk to him? Even if he were involved in those rapes, it doesn't mean he used the knife.'

'Better to stab someone or rape them?' Zenia's voice rose alarmingly.

'Maybe neither. Talk to him, love. And if he has done anything, whatever it is, it's better if he turns himself in. You can go with him, you and Joseph. But it's much better if he does it himself. Honestly.' She waited for a moment which seemed to become a minute. 'I wish I could be with you but I can't, Zenia. This case I'm on – it's a matter of life and death. And I shall be stuck on it all day tomorrow, or I'd be round, I promise you.'

'It's that business with the church, isn't it? Oh my God, Kate – what harm we do each other.'

Chapter Thirty-One

Kate played through the whole service on automatic pilot: she neither knew nor cared whether the choir was with her or following half a bar behind. Zenia hadn't phoned again, nor had Graham. She still had no idea what the interesting leads might be that surveillance had thrown up. This was without doubt the worst assignment she'd ever had – cut off from all the action and with no support. She reasoned with herself: it was far less tricky than working undercover. She had to trust her colleagues. Hadn't they planted listening devices so she could sleep?

Tim and Marcus overslept, and she'd had to call three times before they'd appeared for their sausages and bacon – also organic, according to a tetchy Paul. He'd taken a couple of phone calls while she was frying eggs, neither of which he assured her was for her. Whoever they were from, they hadn't improved his health or temper.

The boys had agreed with some reluctance to go to church, on the grounds that it wasn't Giles who would be taking the service. It was part of Marcus's contract with the Boys' Brigade that he should turn up regularly, and Kate told Tim not to be parochial, a word he enjoyed when he'd looked it up. Paul didn't back Kate, but there was a general assumption that he'd be going. Marcus and Kate took tracksuits to change into.

At this point Kate realised the flaw in her plans. Tim wasn't in the BB, was he, nor was he sufficiently keen on football to join in training as a treat of sorts. And she'd made it abundantly clear to Paul that she preferred his room to his company at training sessions. Hoist with her own petard. As soon as she was able she slipped upstairs to phone Graham's number – at work, this time. It rang and rang. Next she tried the extension on Colin's desk. It might have to be Graham's mobile, after all. But then it was answered, by Reg Tanner. She passed a message on as tersely as she could – they were all waiting downstairs.

'Leave it to me, sweetheart. You can't maintain surveillance and the suspect needs to be tailed. Right? Right!'

They were just leaving when the Manse phone rang. Doug Fulton, asking for his son.

'I'll be able to go to soccer practice, won't I? I mean, I haven't got to see them straightaway?'

A muffled murmur.

'Yes. But I've got to train, haven't I? . . . We're supposed to be having dinner here, Dad. Steak and ice-cream.'

This time the murmur was less muffled.

'A real pub? Steak there? OK.'

'Well?' Kate prompted, when he seemed about to walk out of the door. 'Well? Have you got a brother or a sister?'

He turned. 'I think it's a girl. Or it might be a boy.'

'Ever had your neck wrung, Marcus? What's its name?'

He pushed out his lower lip. 'Ah. Emma.'

'And is your mum all right?'

'I suppose so. Look, aren't we going to be late?'

So all the way through the hymns and the readings and the sermon she was waiting for it: Paul's casual announcement that he was taking Tim to see his anonymous friend's train set. And she couldn't think of a single reason why he shouldn't. Not one. She knew if she said she wanted to go too he'd find an excuse – would insist that before lunch was the only option. Knew it. And played a really violent closing meditation.

Paul and Tim had already left by the time she had finished.

Considering the team had done so well the day before, she worked them very hard. She had words with Leo about taking corners without having practised.

'But I did, Miss. Practice. At school. I do it all the time. We're top of the league.'

Kate pulled a face. 'Sorry. I'll be telling Cantona off next when he drops by for the odd match. Well done. Right, everyone. No time for resting on our laurels. Let's try that all over again only faster!'

Kate never did know what order the thoughts came in. Paul and Tim. Her car: was it at the Manse or outside her house? Her house. And probably boxed in. It would take time to shuffle it out. The railway set. Reg Tanner. A lift to her house. Paul and Reg Tanner. And she was the adult in charge of all these kids with no one to deputise while she went off. Paul and Reg and Tim.

Working the kids hard wouldn't bring escape time any quicker. Go easy on them. Remember Marcus' asthma. Go easy.

For all that, she had the balls locked away and the kids ready for collection a good five minutes before time. Thank goodness for prompt parents. And damn the dilatory ones. Damn them all to hell. She paced, trying not to glare at the three lads remaining. Two, now. And then one. Marcus. At least she felt entitled to hurtle to the car as he did.

'Doug: can you do me the most enormous favour? Give me a lift to my house?'

He nodded, opened the door. 'Problems?' He pulled away, and drove commendably quickly. Only a few yards, when all was said and done. A few yards. Hardly time to congratulate him. And then the wretched man started to talk about her sponsoring the child at her dedication.

'A sort of Baptist godparent,' he added. 'You'd be a role model.'

They were opposite her house. He wanted an answer.

'It's a great honour. But I'm not –'

'Please – you've done so much –'

'It's not that. We'll talk about it later – right? What I want you to do now is see me out of this space. Or I shall shunt that cretin into the middle of next week.' And she was out of the car, trailing tights and suit and handbag, all of which she dumped on her passenger seat.

Even with Doug it took six or seven slow backwards and forwards moves. And then she was on her way.

No sign of Paul's car, of course. Nor of the surveillance team – would they be in the house at the back or in that tatty builder's van? Quite a lot of unmarked vans around, come to think of it. So she wasn't alone. And a marked car: Graham! What was he doing here?

Slinging her car on to the kerb, she ran across.

'Talk about timing. I've decided it's time we went in, Kate. Despite Gordon's reservations. There was what surveillance threw up, then you and the train sets. Then – then Paul and Tim arrived five minutes ago.'

'Only five minutes? Where have they been for the last hour?'

'We'll find out.'

'Who's here?'

'Everyone. Plus Kings Heath in force.'

'Tanner?'

'Gone off sick. Got the bug at last, it seems.'

'You believe him? Graham – he knows Paul!'

'Does he, by Christ! OK.' Voices crackled over his radio. He nodded, just as if they could see him. 'Right. You stay in the rear, Kate. Take over the kid as soon as we get him out. OK?'

He was already out of the car. And she didn't need to ask whether it was an order. It was. She'd missed the briefing, all the careful arrangements. This was the price she paid. Just so a few kids could score a few more goals.

The team were moving in. She brought up the rear, taut with anxiety, despondent, angry. She was halfway up the immaculate path when the little door that no doubt concealed the dustbin in these refined parts was flung open from the inside. The bastards must have fixed an escape route. Yelling for back-up, she hurtled towards it. And to Tim and Paul who were coming out. And then there was a shout, and Tim and Paul turned – in slow motion, they all, Kate included, turned towards a big Mercedes van. It was coming up the drive, straight towards them, bull-bars at body height. Coming towards her and Tim. Aiming at them.

Robin throwing her clear. The bust going wrong. She remembered seeing the driver's face as he drove at them, sheer horror at what he couldn't stop doing because his van was out of control. But this driver, he was in control. He was smiling. Nice, friendly smile. Reg Tanner's smile. And he was going to kill all three of them. No. Just her and Tim.

No time to do more than try to shield Tim. Although it was all in slow motion. No time. And then a huge blow in her back, and she was lying on top of Tim, and there was a scream she would never forget.

Chapter Thirty-Two

The Autumn sun was unexpectedly warm, reflected from the red-and-blue brickwork and the murky waters of the canals.

'Cuts, we call them in this neck of the woods,' Graham said, keeping his pace slow to match Kate's. 'You've no idea how much pleasure it gives me to see this part of Brum being done up. I'm never sure about Symphony Hall and I really dislike the Indoor Arena, but look at this.' He gestured at the newly restored bridges, at the old school, now a pub where they were to eat, at the round-house that had once held not engines but horses.

'I'd no idea Birmingham had parts like this,' she said, suddenly shy. 'I mean, things were changing when I was up working undercover, and I like the pedestrianisation and everything. But this is magic.' She risked a smile.

'And flat. Are you sure that leg of yours is OK?'

'Getting better every day. All that physio. I shed the stick tomorrow – and maybe the eye-patch and the parrot! – and the strapping at the weekend. Good as new by next week.'

'I doubt that. You'll always have a weakness there – it's the second time you've injured it in six months.'

'Lots of quads exercises – I shall have thighs like Gazza's.'

'We can look forward to miniskirts this winter, then, can we?' He looked away. 'How's Tim?'

'Hard to say with such an equable child. Maz, now – she's still deeply shocked. It's a good job I could move out. She doesn't know whether to be grateful to me for saving Tim or hate and resent me for what happened to Paul.'

'What happened to Paul was a good deal better for the family than massive media exposure and a muck-raking trial. It was better for Paul himself than years in a high security gaol being kept away from the other inmates for fear of reprisals. And then being shunted from pillar to post afterwards by Joe Moral Public.'

'I don't think she really believes he did anything wrong.'

'But then, she hasn't seen all the stuff we got off his computer, has she? Or all the little delights of that house. I kid you not, I was so sick I wondered if I'd picked up that bloody bug. And yet the people in the Porn Squad deal with even worse stuff without turning a hair.'

'Apparently. How much has Reg said?' she asked abruptly.

'Not much, yet. A canny bloke, Reg. I had him down as Mr Nice Guy, you know. The model officer, full of old-fashioned virtues. Who comes home from Australia a couple of weeks early and buggers a kid with a toy engine and throws him in the path of a lorry so he can't talk. It was a funny thing for you to talk about in the ambulance, Kate, someone else's wedding photos. I thought you must have banged your head or something. But we got him.'

'You would have done anyway. Pretty conclusive evidence, driving a bloody great van at an innocent kid. And a colleague.' She stopped, staring at the water. 'Graham — why did Paul do it?' She heard the sounds of the impact again. Smelt the blood, the urine, the faeces. It had been a nasty, messy death all right. And she didn't think she regretted a minute of his agony.

'Throw himself at you both? Who can tell? To save Tim, certainly. That stuff he'd written about him — you'll see it when you're back on duty — certainly convinced me that he loved him. And you. I think if a man like that could love a woman he loved you.' His voice was tight.

'Love? I wouldn't want the love of a man like that.' She lowered her voice — there were others on the towpath, after all. 'Buggering little boys! Prepared to deliver up his own flesh and blood for others to bugger! Spare me the tears, Graham. The man was a shit. OK, it was great of him to paint my window, but think what he was really doing when he was there. Eyeing up new victims.' She stopped short.

'But the pressure was being put on him by others, Kate. Bring in more boys. And he wouldn't foul the Boys' Brigade nest, so he was after kids from that school. In the end, someone put sufficient pressure on him to introduce Tim, at very least. The room with the train set was the start of their system. Co-operate, and you'll see the next room. Whether he'd have let Tim progress I don't know. But he was under enormous pressure. From Superintendent Gordon. The man who sent me on my courses, Kate, to get me out of the way when I was needed here.'

'I thought you were being set up for promotion.'

'I thought I was.'

So that was why he was so angry when she'd taken work away from his squad – he was afraid it would damage his reputation and mess up his prospects.

'Do you suppose he got at Cope somehow – to make him rewrite his report for the Devon and Cornwall people? I looked a right idiot, I can tell you. If the woman down there hadn't yelled at me for wasting her time, I might never have known.'

'Got yelled at some more, did you?'

So they both remembered his outburst.

She grinned forgiveness at him. 'It seems to be my lot in life. What seems odd is Cope doing what he's told. The man's a bully but he's straight. Isn't he?'

'If I didn't think so he wouldn't be in my squad. He's an old-fashioned policeman, isn't he? Believes in the hierarchy. Which got him where he is. But no further. He's not like you whizz-kids. Maybe Gordon promised him something: who knows? Promotion at this stage would improve his pension. It'll come out eventually. He may even tell you, if you choose your moment to ask him. He likes you. Likes your guts.'

'Got strange ways of showing it.'

'He did all that was proper over those maggots of yours.'

'So he ought. Like me or not, he'd have had to do that. What did they find, anyway?'

'What you'd expect: sweet F.A. The tin was clean, the stamp was stuck on with water, not saliva, the Sellotape hadn't caught any hairs or any fabric. Everything done under laboratory conditions, in fact.'

'An inside job done by a bloke in a white paper suit?'

'Could be. Could have been Reg, or another of Gordon's minions.'

That night Paul had been especially solicitous about her health and her day's work. 'Paul knew. He kept trying to find out if anything had gone wrong. He knew even if he didn't do it. And – yes, he knew I hated maggots. He kept on talking about them one night. I ended up being sick. And I think he'd tried to find out if I had any other weaknesses.' She pointed back to the International Convention Centre. 'He took me there. To Symphony Hall. And booked the very highest seats.'

'Did you get vertigo?'

She shook her head. 'Not a smidgen. Maggots, yes; heights, not at all. Funny.'

He set them in motion once again, his hand ready to take Kate's elbow if she wobbled.

'So will we be able to nail Gordon?' she asked.

'It'll take some doing, but believe me, we haven't been sitting twiddling our thumbs while you've been off.'

'He'll have all the fancy lawyers going, won't he, and if that doesn't work he'll roll up his trouser leg and shake hands with someone.'

A chill breeze swirled the water.

'This must be so difficult for you, Kate. After all you went through – this summer.' He paused, awkwardly. 'With Robin. But – but I hope you'll feel – that you won't want –'

She shook her head. 'I won't be hot-footing it off to some other force, Graham. I want to make a go of it here.' There was so much unfinished business, wasn't there? 'After all, I've only just got the house straight. And I have it on the very best authority that my working surface will arrive on Friday. Imagine it, having a kitchen!'

He laughed briefly. 'Good girl!' Then, in a different voice, he asked, 'Has Mrs Mackenzie been to see you?'

'A couple of times. And she even drove me to see Cassie once. You should have seen the old girl's face.'

'You gave her the right advice. At least Royston didn't actually rape either girl. And it wasn't he who used the knife in the second attack. Bad ways. What put you on to him?'

'Such a little thing. He was so furtive when I turned up in his mother's kitchen. So horrified. And he tried to hide something, double quick. And the assailants weren't white, I was fairly sure of that. And his mother was plainly worried. Never enough to make a case though.'

'Good job he turned himself in, then. He's redeemable, please God.'

'Amen. They've managed to find a new organist, by the way. A music student at the university.'

'An organ scholar?' he grinned.

'Oh, they take specialisation too far, these days!' And then she became serious. 'I don't know about the football team, though. I may have to stick with them. Derek and Alec came to see me, too. They were very cut up – someone they knew and trusted.'

'There is no one on God's earth more devious than a paedophile, Kate. No vetting could have shown up his proclivities. Any more than they'd have shown up Reg's. Until someone's committed an offence.' He broke off, shaking his head. 'Unless you've got a crystal ball.'

'Even Cassie was taken in,' she reflected. And then she squared her shoulders. 'I must try and see more of Cassie. And the rest of my friends,' she added, smiling at him.

If it was an invitation, he chose to ignore it. At last, coughing awkwardly, he said, 'We are friends, aren't we? Friends? You see –' But he tailed off, gesturing.

His gesture spoke of his marriage, his religion and his feelings for her. And whatever she wanted to say – and she wasn't sure – she leaned on her stick, and said to the waters of the cut, 'Friends.'